Perley Derby

The Hutchinson Family

The descendants of Barnard Hutchinson, of Cowlam, England

Perley Derby

The Hutchinson Family
The descendants of Barnard Hutchinson, of Cowlam, England

ISBN/EAN: 9783337182533

Printed in Europe, USA, Canada, Australia, Japan

Cover: Foto ©Raphael Reischuk / pixelio.de

More available books at **www.hansebooks.com**

THE

HUTCHINSON FAMILY:

OR THE

DESCENDANTS

OF

BARNARD HUTCHINSON,

OF

COWLAM, ENGLAND.

COMPILED BY PERLEY DERBY.

SALEM.
ESSEX INSTITUTE PRESS.
1870.

EXPLANATION.

Figures enclosed in a parenthesis at the head or end of a name, thus, (1) Richard, or (2) Joseph, son of Richard (1), denote the number of the individual, in their numerical order, and the small figures at the end of each name, thus, JOSEPH^2, denote the generation to which they belong.

Names printed in large capitals, without date of birth, indicate that it is a subject of particular notice, and will be found without reference to the Index, among the list under the generation attached to the end of the name, — as 4 JOSEPH^2, or JOSEPH, No. 4, Gen. 2, and will be found treated of under that Generation.

(2)

PREFACE.

THE compilation of this work was commenced in Nov., 1857, and finished as far as circumstances would then admit, in Dec., 1858, covering a space of thirteen months of unceasing labor, being employed under the patronage of Hiram Hutchinson, Esq., of New York. The work was intended at that time for publication, but on its completion, for some particular reason at the time on the part of the projector, it was thought best to withhold it from publication, thereby disappointing a large number who were eagerly anticipating its appearance in print. The matter thus rested till the fall of 1867, when, being warmly urged by several influential gentlemen, the compiler again resumed the work, adding many more families, and much new and interesting matter, giving the whole work almost an entire new character, which will more than compensate for the delay. To many who have lived to a very advanced age, most of whom have since passed away, the author is greatly indebted for much valuable assistance, which in a delay of a year or two, would have been irrecoverably lost. Others there are who have been indefatigable in lending their aid, some of whom anticipated the author's wants in procuring data and records of several families among their relatives, thus greatly facilitating his labors. Great care has been exercised in rendering all the details as correct as possible; and where information has been supplied by others, it has been carefully examined, and such only made use of as the author had good reason to believe correct.

Since the completion of the American Genealogy, Mr. Alcander Hutchinson, now a resident of France, after a long and careful investigation, assisted by J. L. Chester, Esq., of London, has prepared and published, in the Genealogical Register of Boston, July number, 1868, the English Pedigree, or descendants of Barnard Hutchinson, living in 1282. It is a most valuable and interesting production, and undoubtedly perfect in all its details; and the author has incurred the responsibility of its partial introduction in this work, being entirely indebted to him for every particular, thus bringing the history under two heads, English and American.

The old story is rife among many (applicable also to any other family name) that "three brothers" composed the original American stock from whom this line of Hutchinsons descended; and it is asserted that one settled in New Hampshire, another in Massachusetts, and the third in Connecticut. However true it may be of others, it is certain that Richard is the only representative of this particular branch of the Hutchinsons in this country.

The following description of the family arms is given by Mr. Hutchinson, in his English history.

"GERIT CRUCEM FORTITER."

"Per pale gules and azure, semée of cross-crosslets *or*, a lion rampant argent. Crest, out of a ducal coronet *or*, a cockatrice with wings endorsed azure, beaked, combed and, wattled gules."   P. D.

SALEM, Oct., 1868.

The Hutchinson Family:

OR, THE DESCENDANTS OF BARNARD HUTCHINSON OF COWLAM, ENGLAND.

HISTORY OF THE ENGLISH BRANCH.

FIRST GEN. (1) BARNARD HUTCHINSON, of Cowlam, County of York, living in the year 1282, in the reign of King Edward I, appears to be the first reliable representative and progenitor of the Hutchinsons in England. But little is known of his personal history, and for an extended account of him, and the most prominent of his English posterity, the reader is referred to the July No., 1868, of Drake's Genealogical Register, as referred to in the Preface. Mr. Hutchinson md. a dau. of John Boyville, Esq., and had three children:
2. JOHN. 3. ROBERT. 4. MARY.

SECOND GEN. (2) JOHN, son of BARNARD (1), md. Edith, dau. of Wm. Wouldbie. Four children:—
5. JAMES. 6. BARBARA. 7. JULIA. 8. MARGARET.

THIRD GEN. (5) JAMES, son of JOHN (2), md. Ursula, dau. of Mr. Gregory, of Nafferton. Five children:—
9. WILLIAM. 10. JOHN. 11. BARBARA. 12. a dau. 13. ELEANOR.

FOURTH GEN. (9) WILLIAM, son of JAMES (5), md. Anna, dau. of Wm. Bennet, Esq., of Theckley. Four children:—
14. ANTHONY. 15. OLIVER. 16. MARY. 17. ALICE.

FIFTH GEN. (14) ANTHONY, son of WILLIAM (9), md. 1st, Judith, dau. of Thos. Crosland; md. 2d, Isabel, dau. of Robert Harvie. Eight children:—
18. WILLIAM. 19. THOMAS. 20. JOHN. 21. RICHARD. 22. LEONARD. 23. EDMOND. 24. FRANCIS. 25. ANDREW.

SIXTH GEN. (19) THOMAS, son of ANTHONY (14), supposed to have md. the dau. of Mr. Drake, of Kinoulton, County of Nottingham. He was living Oct. 9, 1550. Three children:—
26. WILLIAM, died 1550. 27. JOHN. 28. LAWRENCE.

(5)

SEVENTH GEN. (28) LAWRENCE, son of THOMAS (19), of Owlthorpe; Will proved Oct. 9, 1577; md. Isabel ———, who was living 1577. Five children:—

29. ROBERT. 30. THOMAS. 31. AGNES. 32. RICHARD. 33. WILLIAM.

EIGHTH GEN. (30) THOMAS, son of LAWRENCE (28), resided at Newark; d. 1598. Three children:—
34. WILLIAM. 35. THOMAS. 36. JOAN.

NINTH GEN. (35) THOMAS, son of THOMAS (30); buried at Arnold, Aug. 17, 1618; md. Alice ———. Seven children:—
37. JOHN, buried Sept. 2, 1627. 38. ISABEL. 39. HUMPHREY. 40. ELIZABETH. 41. ROBERT, bapt. Sept. 6, 1601. 42. RICHARD. 43. THOMAS, bapt. June 16, 1605.

THE HUTCHINSONS OF NEW ENGLAND.

FIRST GENERATION.

(1) RICHARD[1], son of THOMAS (35), of Arnold, Eng., was born in 1602. The date of his birth is ascertained from a deposition on file in the office of the Essex County Court, Salem, Mass., where in a case of Cromwell *vs.* Ruck, 1660, he states his age as being 58 years. He emigrated to America in 1634, with his wife Alice, and four children, and settled in Salem Village, now Danvers, in the vicinity of Whipple and Hathorne's hill. There is some evidence, however, gleaned from the town records of Salem, that he may have primarily settled in the town proper, from the fact that in July 25, 1639, one Philemon Dickerson was granted four poles of land "neere Richard Hutchinson's house, to make tan pitts and to dress goates skinnes and hides." As tanning was not known to have been carried on in Salem Village at so early a period, much time has been spent in discovering this locality, but without avail; as after this, his name seems to have disappeared from the records of Salem. In 1636, Mr. Hutchinson received a grant of 60 acres of land from the town, and Apr. 3, following, 20 acres more. In the same year he was appointed on a committee to survey Jeffrey's Creek (now Manchester), and Mackerell Cove. April 17, 1637, it was voted "that in case Ric'd Huchenson shall sett up plowing within 2 years he may haue 20 acres more to bee added to his pportion." This appears to be in consequence of the great scarcity of ploughs, there being but thirty-seven in all the settlements. In 1648, at Salem Village, he bought of Elias Stileman,

his farm of 150 acres, for £15. The records do not show him to have been officially engaged in many matters of public trust, but he was undoubtedly a man of indomitable perseverance, great vigor of mind and physical endurance, a strict disciplinarian in religious affairs, a thorough agriculturist, and as he had amassed a large landed estate, he had, before the close of his life, divided much of his property among his children. He and his wife were members of the first ch., Salem, as early as 1636, on whose records he is first mentioned in connection with the baptism of his dau. Abigail.

He md. 1st, Dec. 7, 1627, Alice, dau. of Joseph Bosworth, of Holgrave; md. 2d, Oct., 1668, Susanna, wid. of Samuel Archard, who d. Nov. 26, 1674; md. 3d, Sarah, wid. of James Standish. On the decease of the latter, Mr. Hutchinson was appointed administrator, At this third marriage he must have been at least 79 years of age, and certainly 66 on his second. His Will was signed Jan. 19, 1679, and proved Sept. 28, 1682. His widow survived him, and shortly after married for her third husband, Thomas Roots, of Manchester, whose Will was proved Nov. 27, 1683. She was living as late as March 1683-4. Eight ch. by Alice:—

2. ALICE, bapt. Eng., Sept. 27, 1628, buried the same year. 3. ELIZABETH, bapt. Eng., Aug. 30, 1629, d. June 24, 1688; md. Nathaniel, son of Lt. John and Priscilla Putnam, b. 1621, d. July 23, 1700. Yeoman. Seven ch:—SAMUEL, b. Feb. 18, 1653; NATHANIEL, b. Apr. 24, 1655; JOHN, b. Mar. 26, 1657, d. 1722; JOSEPH, b. Oct. 29, 1659, d. 1723; ELIZABETH, b. Aug. 11, 1662, d. Mar. 6, 1697; BENJAMIN, b. Dec. 24, 1644, d. 1744; MARY, b. Sept. 15, 1668.

4. MARY, bapt. Eng., Dec. 28, 1630; md. May 26, 1657, Thomas, son of Thomas and Tamosin Hale, of Newbury, b. 1633, d. Oct. 22, 1688. Yeoman. Eight ch:—THOMAS, b. Feb. 11, 1659, d. Jan. 8, 1746; MARY, b. July 15, 1660; ABIGAIL, b. April 8, 1662; HANNAH, b. Nov. 28, 1663; LYDIA, b. April 17, 1666; ELIZABETH, b. Oct. 16, 1668; JOSEPH, b. Feb. 20, 1671; SAMUEL, b. June 6, 1674, d. 1723. 5. REBECCA, b. Eng., 1632; md. May, 1658, James Hadlock (yeoman) of Salem Vill. Three ch:—HANNAH, b. July 1657; SARAH, b. Sept., 1659; MARY, b. Mar. 2, 1662.

6. JOSEPH². 7. ABIGAIL, bapt. 1st ch., Salem, Dec. 25, 1636; md. Anthony Ashby of Bradford, Mass. Lived at Salem Vill. Yeoman. Two ch:—Sarah, b. Dec. 16, 1672; a dau. b. Dec. 20, 1674. 8. HANNAH, bapt. 1st ch., Jan. 20, 1639; md. Apr. 12, 1662, Daniel, son of Thomas and Hannah Boardman, of Ipswich. Yeoman. Five ch:— Thomas, b. July 15, 1666, d. 1751; Hannah, b. Feb. 18, 1670-1; Wait-John, b. Aug. 23, 1676; David and Jonathan, twins, b. June 21, 1682; the latter d. 1720.

9. JOHN.²

[For the Will of Richard, see Appendix A.]

SECOND GENERATION.

(6) JOSEPH², son of RICHARD (1), b. No. Muskham, Eng., 1633. His deposition in Court is given at the same time, and is borne upon the same instrument, as that of his father, in 1660, where he gives his age as 27. He lived on the homestead, and acquired nearly all his property by deed of gift from his father. May 10, 1666, he received a "dwelling house, barne and land already broken up, which he hath now in his possession, * * * with all his meddowes & two acres & a halfe of meddow more or less within my son Nathanyell Putnam's field, the meddow comonly caled Peases meddow with the meddow which he hath at the meddow comonly caled Bishops meddow containing by estimation five acres * * * & at ye river comonly caled ye great river [Ipswich river] containing two acres and half," with another piece "lying at the S. end of that medow, which formerly belonged to Capt. Price," containing 4 acres. In addition to the above, describing the bounds, he received two parcels more, one containing 200 acres, and the other 100 acres, besides "all the apple trees that are in my old orchard which lyes to the S. W. from my now dwelling house and two apple trees that are in the orchard behind the house." His homestead was situated and joined the site of the first meeting house in Salem Vill., the said site being an acre of his own land, he contributed to the proprietors to build upon. Recent investigations have led to the conclusion that his dwelling house was not far removed from this spot, standing in a field where traces of an old cellar are yet visible.

In 1700, or thereabouts, the above church was taken down and erected upon another spot near by, and the site reverted to him again. The dimensions of the old meeting house were 34 feet in length, 28 feet and 16 feet between joints. "It is believed," says Upham, "that he removed the frame to the other side of the road, and converted it into a barn, and used as such, where it remained till within the memory of aged people now living."

Mr. Hutchinson lived through the ever memorable period of the Witchcraft delusion of 1692. Strong in his mind, and sensible as he was on every other subject, yet he was not proof against the current of thought which pervaded some of the noblest intellects of that age. He was one of a number who entered a complaint against Tituba, an Indian woman living in the family of Rev. Samuel Parris, Sarah, the wife of Wm. Good, and Sarah, wife of Alex'r Osborn.

In his father's Will, it is expressed that the care of Sarah, his mother-in-law, be devolved on him. But shortly after his decease, she desired "to take her abode among her relations," which was just prior to her marriage with Mr. Roots. In doing this some difficulty occurred in the settlement of her affairs, between herself and Joseph, which appears in the following warrant taken from the Essex Co. Ct. Rec. "Joseph Hutchinson to appear at Court at Ipswich to answer to Complaint of Sarah Roots alias Hutchinson and Nathaniel Putnam for with holding a debt of due for charge & Expense In suport & maintenance of said Sarah dureing the time of their Administration on the estate of Richard Hutchinson deceased. Mar. 12, 1683-4."

The following is her deposition. "Mar. 1684. Whereas I have signed to a wrighting which was made by my son in law Joseph Hutchinson which I understood was only a discharge for the goods that I carried away from my husband hutchinson, his house, which said wrighting to my best remembrance I never heard red, but was then Ready to confide in my son in lawes honesty for he told me I must give him a discharge for what I then carried away which I thought was reason and therefore signed to the said righting as a receit for which I then received and no other waies. Sworne 22th of March 1683-4. Before Barth'w Gedney, Asst."

The testimony of Joseph Holten and others, show that the conversation between Jos. Hutchinson and his mother-in-law, was conducted on the most friendly terms, and the separation was perfectly amicable. The following bill of costs produced against Nath'l Putnam is a curiosity in its style.

"Joseph Hutchinson's Bill of Cost against Nathaniel putnam.

3 somensis taking out and sarving	0	4	6
3 witnesis one day	9	6	0
my going to get them sworn	0	2	0
One day for getting a copy of my fathers Will and the record	0	2	6
three dais atandons	0	6	0
This bill of cost allowed by Court." . .	1	1	0

In 1658 he was chosen constable and tax gatherer, and his name appears on the jury list for 1679 ; he was frequently chosen administrator and overseer, and often was witness to wills, deeds and inventories. There is no will or administration of his estate on record, he having during his life time, distributed his large property among his children. To his son Robert he gave his mansion house, barn,-stock of cattle, and all his movable estate not given to his other children by deed of gift, viz. :—A lot of 25 acres where his house stands, 4½ acres where the old meeting house stood, 12 acres on Thorndike hill, and a lot on Ipswich river, bearing date June 3, 1708. To son Joseph, 50 acres where he now dwells, 4 acres on W. side of Ipswich river, and his rights in Cromwell's and Price's meadows, being 7 acres, and a right in a piece of meadow on Ipswich river, dated July 1, 1703; to his son John, 50 acres in 1694; to son Samuel, in 1707, 30 acres ; to his son

Ambrose, 20 acres, dated June 3, 1708; and in 1707, to son Richard, 30 acres near Beaver dam; and to his son Benjamin, 30 acres. There is no other evidence respecting the date of his decease, but that recorded in Reg. of Deeds, of a deposition made June 26, 1716, by John Houlton, who takes oath at an Inferior Ct. of Pleas, that he saw Joseph Hutchinson, Sen'r., late of Salem, dec'd, sign a deed conveying 2 acres of land to Thomas Haines; and as he was living Jan. 30, 1715-16, he certainly died between these two dates, aged about 83 years.

He md. 1st, probably a daughter of John Gedney. In the administration of the estate of Joseph's daughter, Bethiah, mention is made of a legacy of £13, 11s, 7d, given her by her grandfather Gedney. The latter had a son Bartholomew, who had a dau. Bethiah; and as these names frequently occur in different families afterwards, the supposition is quite plausible. Md. 2d, Feb. 28, 1677-8, Lydia, dau. of Anthony and Elizabeth Buxton. She was wid. of Joseph Small, her second husband, md. Dec. 26, 1672; and at his dec. was appointed adm'x, May, 1676; Joseph Hutchinson and Jona. Walcott, appraisers. She was bapt. Apr. 27, 1689, and was living in June, 1708. Five ch :—

10. ABIGAIL, and 11. BETHIAH, bapt. Sept. 26, 1666, latter d. Nov., 1690. 12. JOSEPH³. 13. JOHN³. 14. BENJAMIN³. Six ch. by Lydia.

15. ABIGAIL, b. Jan. 14, 1678-9; md. Joseph Allen, bapt. 1st ch., Oct. 1672; Will app. May 13, 1740. Ten ch:—ABIGAIL, b. June 1, 1696; JOSEPH, b. Feb. 11, 1697-8; BENJAMIN, b. Apr. 26, 1699; JOHN, bapt. June 1, 1701; JOHN, bapt. Sept. 19, 1703; ABIGAIL, bapt. Aug. 12, 1705; ZEBULON, bapt. Sept. 15, 1706. ROBERT. BETHIAH. ELIZABETH, bapt. Oct. 3, 1714.

16. RICHARD³. 17. SAMUEL, b. Oct. 9, 1682, living 1710. 18. AMBROSE³. 19. LYDIA, b. Sept. 13, 1685; md. George, son of Samuel and Mary Nourse, b. July 29, 1682, d. 1759. Lived in Lynn; yeoman. Four ch :—ELIZABETH, bapt. Sept. 24, 1710. MARY, bapt. Aug. 2, 1713. GEORGE, bapt. Oct. 16, 1715, d. 1799. ABIGAIL. 20. ROBERT.³

(9) JOHN², son of RICHARD (1), b. Salem Vill., May, 1643, d. Aug. 2, 1676. Estate valued at £273, 5s, 6d. He settled on a portion of his father's farm, and at his decease he was in possession of about 650 acres of land. He and his brother Joseph, prior to Mch., 1672, had erected a saw mill on Beaver Dam. A road being laid out from their father's house to said Dam, a complaint was preferred against them for obstructing the way, but there is no further record to show how the affair terminated. He md. July, 1672, Sarah, dau. of John and Rebecca Putnam, b. Sept. 4, 1654. One ch :—

21. SARAH, who md. Dea. Joseph Whipple, b. Nov. 1, 1666, d. Sept. 19, 1740. Seven ch:—SARAH, b. Feb. 26, 1691-2. LYDIA, b. Feb. 2, 1693-4. JOHN, b. Oct. 23, 1695. MARY, bapt. Oct. 22, 1699. MARY and JOSEPH, b. Feb. 2, 1701-2; MATTHEW, b. Aug. 25, 1704.

THIRD GENERATION.

(12) JOSEPH, son of JOSEPH² (6), bapt. 1st ch., Salem, Sept. 26, 1666; Will rec'd to Probate, June 3, 1751. He was rec'd as a mem. of the ch. at Salem Vill., Feb. 4. 1700, and afterwards chosen, Oct. 31, 1732, a delegate to the church in Wenham, to assist in the ordination of Rev. John Warren. He settled on a portion of the old homestead farm, owned by his father, consisting of fifty acres of upland, which he afterwards rec'd by deed of gift, bearing date July 1, 1703. Inv. of his est. taken July 20, 1751, £393, 6s. He md. 1st., Elizabeth ———, b. 1664, "d. Dec. 21, 1700, aged 36 years;" md. 2d, Jan. 30, 1700-1, Rebecca Knight, of Topsfield. Nine ch. by Elizabeth.

22. JOSEPH⁴. 33. RUTH, b. Feb. 26, 1690-1, living in 1766; md. Feb. 19, 1712-13, Josiah, son of John and Hannah Putnam, b. Oct. 29, 1686; Will proved Sept. 2, 1766. *Both rec'd into ch. Dec. 10, 1727. Yeoman. Seven ch:—ASA, b. July 31, 1714, d. ——— 1775. ENOS, b. Oct. 6, 1716; Will prob. Oct. 2, 1780. JOSIAH, b. Mar. 3, 1718-19, living 1766. PETER, bapt. Apr. 5, 1724, d. 1773. ELIZABETH, bapt. July 4, 1725, living 1766. ELISHA, bapt. Mch. 24, 1727-8, d. Feb. 16, 1817. RUTH, bapt. June 4, 1732, living 1766.

24. BETHIAH⁴, b. Dec. 24, 1693, d. Dec. 9, 1726; md. June 9, 1715, Benjamin, son of Benjamin and Sarah Putnam, b. Jan. 8, 1692; Will prob. Oct. 15, 1744. Yeoman. Two ch:—Benjamin b. Oct. 12, 1718; Eunice, b. May 21, 1722. 25. EBENEZER⁴. 26. ELIZABETH, b. Feb. 22, 1695, d. Feb. 18, 1702. 27. A son, b. Feb. 22, 1695. 28. ELISHA, b. Mch. 14, 1697, d. Mch. 1, 1702. 29. JASPER, b. Jan. 31, 1698, d. Feb. 16, 1701. 30. ELISHA⁴. One ch. by Rebecca.

31. ELIZABETH, bapt. Apr. 19, 1702; Will signed Oct. 14, 1778, approved Jan. 1, 1779; md. May 5, 1724, Benjamin, son of John and Elizabeth (Holton) Buxton, of Salem Vill., b. Mch. 11, 1694-5; Will approved Dec. 3. 1770. Yeoman. No issue.

(13) JOHN³, son of JOSEPH² (6), bapt. 1st ch., Salem, Sept. 26, 1666; estate appraised Apr. 1, 1746, son William, adm. Inv. £61, 12s, 9d. He was a farmer and lived on the homestead. He owned a large and valuable farm in Sutton, containing 179 acres, which he sold, Dec. 26, 1723, to Isaac Richards, of Salem, for £150; also another farm of 129 acres, which he sold two days after to Cornelius Putnam, of Salem, for £150. He was rec'd into ch. Sept. 19, 1703. Constable and tax gatherer for the year 1706; md. 1st, May 7, 1694, Mary Gould; md.

2d, Mch. 4, 1710, Hannah, dau. of Nehemiah and Ann (Dixey) Howard, b. Aug. 1, 1661. Five ch. by Mary.

32. A son, b. Sept. 2, 1695, d. Dec. 1, 1695. 33. MARY, b. Oct. 2, 1696; adm. granted Dec. 5, 1780, to Eli Curtis; md. Dec. 19, 1721, Daniel Wilkins, jr.; Will proved Jan. 4, 1742-3; rem'd to Middleton about 1729. Yeoman. Eight ch:—MARY, ABIGAIL and ELIZABETH, bapt. July 18, 1725. RACHEL, bapt. June 4, 1727. SARAH, bapt. Apr. 6, 1729. MERCY, b. Feb. 26, 1731. PRISCILLA and DANIEL mentioned in the Will. 34. JOHN[4]. 35. ABIGAIL, b. Mch. 17, 1702; md. Mch. 5, 1727-28, Benjamin, son of Benjamin and Sarah Putnam, b. Jan 8, 1692; Will proved Oct. 15, 1744. He also md. Bethiah, dau. of Joseph Hutchinson, jr. (see No. 23). Yeoman. One ch:— ABIGAIL, bapt. Jan. 4, 1729-30. 36. EBENEZER[4]. Two ch. by Hannah:—

37. EUNICE, b. Apr. 9, 1712; md. 1731, Holyoke Putnam, of Middleton. 38. WILLIAM[4].

(14) BENJAMIN[3], son of JOSEPH[2] (6), b.——, d. 1733, intestate; no adm. on his estate. Feb. 7, 1733, he sold Sam'l Houlton ten and one-half acres of land for £168, and Oct. 5, same year, his son-in-law, Jona. Buxton, and Jane, his wife, sold to Benj. Hutchinson, jr., all their right and title in the estate of Benj. Hutchinson, late of Salem, dec'd, which certainly fixes nearly the date of his death. He was a farmer, and lived on that part of the homestead he rec'd from his father by deed of gift, containing 30 acres, bearing date Oct. 2, 1691. He afterwards acquired a considerable real estate by purchase, contiguous to the homestead, and owned a tract of 10 acres on the W. side of Ipswich river, which was given by his father to his bro. Robert, June 3, 1708, of whom he bought it Aug. 6, 1713, and sold it the next year to Walter Smith, for £20. Before his decease he had settled a snug little estate upon each of his remaining children, disposing of most of the remainder by deed of sale. While an infant he was adopted into the family of Dea. Nathaniel Ingersoll, his only child, a daughter, having died at an early age. A deed to this effect is recorded in the Probate Rec., which reads as follows:—

"Benjamin Hutchinson, being an infant, when he was given to us by his parents, we have brought him up as our own child; and he the said Benjamin, living with us as an obedient son until he came of one and twenty years of age, he then marrying from us, I, the said Nathaniel Ingersoll, and Hannah my wife, on these considerations do, upon the marriage of our adopted son, Benjamin Hutchinson, give and bequeath to him * * * this deed of gift of ten acres of upland, and also three acres of meadow * * *" dated Oct. 2, 1691. Dea. Ingersoll died in 1719, leaving a Will, wherein, "for the consideration of the great help he had been while living with him, and after he had left," he bequeaths all the remaining part of his whole estate, both real and personal, except a lot of two acres (describing the same), after making provision for the rest of his family.

But little more is known of his personal history, and that through the medium of the witchcraft papers, deposited in the office of the Essex Co. Ct., being at the time quite a youth, about 21 or 22 years of age, with a young wife, both of whom acted their part in this most singular drama, with an apparent air of sincerity, astonishing to all who may read or hear of these performances, the result of which was almost certain conviction of the innocent defendants, and an igno-minious death.

He md. 1st, Nov. 14, 16—, Jane, dau. of Walter and Margaret Phillips, d. —— 7, 1711. He was rec'd into ch. May 7, 1699, and his wife, May 28, following; md. 2d, Jan. 26, 1714-15, Abigail Foster. Eleven ch. by Jane.

39. A son, d. in infancy. 40. Benjamin, b. Aug. 31, 1690, d. Sept. 18, 1690. 41. Hannah, b. May 7, 1692; md. Mch. 6, 1717-18, William, son of William and Elizabeth Henfield, bapt. May 1, 1690. One ch:—William, bapt. Oct. 30, 1720.·

42. BENJAMIN[4]. 43. Bethiah, b. Jan. 5, 1695-6. 44. NATHAN-IEL[4]. 45. Sarah, b. Dec. 26, 1701; md. Nov. 17, 1725, Cornelius, son of Benj. and Sarah Putnam, b. Sept. 3, 1702. Yeoman. No issue. 46. Bartholomew, b. Apr. 27, 1703. 47. Jane, b. Aug. 1, 1705; md. Sept. 8, 1726, Jonathan, son of John and Elizabeth Buxton, b. July 25, 1706; adm. granted his widow, Sept. 23, 1745. He was brother of Benjamin who md. Elizabeth (31), dau. of Joseph Hutchinson, jr. Two ch:—Jonathan, bapt. July 20, 1729; Benjamin, bapt. June 13, 1735.

48. Israel, bapt. Oct. 5, 1708, d. young. 49. John, d. before 1733. One ch. by Abigail.

50. JONATHAN[4].

(16) RICHARD[3], son of JOSEPH[2] (6), b. at Salem Vill., May 10, 1681. He ceased to be taxed in 1738, after which date it is supposed he removed to the State of Maine, where some portion of his family lived and died. Dec. 8, 1707, his father deeded him a farm of 30 acres, joining the homestead, and the "New Dam, so called." From 1707 to 1737, he had accumulated a large estate, portions of which were situated in the town of Middleton, and in the vicinity of the old meeting house. But just previous to the latter date he succeeded in disposing of most of it, preparatory to his supposed removal. He md. Feb. 16, 1713-14, Rachel Bance. Six ch:—

51. STEPHEN[4]. 52. Lydia, bapt. Sept. 2, 1716. 53. Rachel, bapt. Sept. 29, 1723. 54. Elizabeth, bapt. Sept. 29, 1723. 55. Daniel, bapt. Aug. 17, 1729. 56. Joseph.

(18) AMBROSE[3], son of JOSEPH[2] (6), b. at Salem Vill., June 4, 1684. Adm. granted Sept. 26, 1757, to widow, and son George. He was a farmer, and lived and died upon that part of the homestead given him by his father, June 3, 1708, consisting of 30 acres, adjoining land owned by his brother Robert, and the highway. The inventory of his estate was £103, 9s, 2d. He md. June 24, 1709, Ruth, dau. of John and Elizabeth Leach, b. Mch. 31, 1692. Six ch:—

57. AMOS[4]. 58. JAMES. 59. SAMUEL[4]. 60. JOHN, bapt. July 5, 1719, d. Lyndeboro about 1789. 61. JAMES, d. 1752. 62. GEORGE[4].

(19) ROBERT[3], son of JOSEPH[2] (6), b. at Salem Vill., Nov. 13, 1687; adm. granted Apr. 24, 1733, to son-in-law, Wm. Shillaber. Farmer. His homestead was situated near the old meeting house. At the age of 21 he received from his father a farm of 30 acres, on the N. side of Ipswich river, the whole of which he sold in Aug., 1713, to his brothers, Joseph and Benjamin. In 1729, he sold to Peter Hobart, of Braintree, for £1000, two tracts of land situated on Beaver Dam brook, and on or near Thorndike hill. He was, it appears by the inventory of his estate, owner of one-quarter part of a grist mill and a scythe factory, and one sixth of "another mill." Inventory of his estate, £879, 19s, 1d. He md. 1st, Dec. 27, 1711, Elizabeth, dau. of Jonathan and Lydia Putnam, b. Feb. 2, 1686-7; md. 2d, June 6, 1717, Sarah Putnam. ' After the dec. of her husband, she had sett off as part of her dower, "one quarter part of the water mills on N. River, in partnership with Josh. Hicks, of Salem." Two ch. by Elizabeth.

63. SARAH, bapt. Sept. 12, 1712, d. Dec., 1800; md. William Shillaber, d. 1748. Eight ch:—Elizabeth, bapt. 1st ch., middle precinct, Aug. 15, 1731; William, bapt. Sept. 22, 1734, d. Nov. 28, 1804; Robert, bapt. May 16, 1736, d. June 20, 1808; Samuel, bapt. May 21, 1738, d. 1787; Sarah, bapt. Dec. 30, 1739; Elizabeth, bapt. Jan 3, 1741; Hannah, bapt. May 1, 1743; Benjamin, bapt. June 24, 1744.

64. ROBERT, bapt. May 16, 1716, d. before 1733.

FOURTH GENERATION.

(22) JOSEPH[4], son of JOSEPH[3] (12), b. at Salem Vill., Jan. 27, 1689; Will proved June 5, 1781. He was a farmer, and lived several years on the homestead after his marriage. In 1723-4, his father gave him "a tract of upland and meadow with a dwelling house on it," lying on the W. side of Ipswich river, which afterwards, in 1728, was included within the bounds of Middleton when that town was incorporated. In Apr., 1729, he bought of James and David Prince, for £140, two pieces of meadow, "formerly in Salem, now Middleton," situated on the W. side of Ipswich river, one parcel lying on the river and the other on the brook. He removed to Middleton, and was

chosen Selectman for 1741 and 1742, and was also Constable for the latter year. In 1748 he bought of Richard Goldsmith and Hannah, his wife, for £55, seventy-four acres of upland in "Souhegan West," now Amherst, N. H., in "Township No. 3, Lot. 38, 2d Division." He also owned a tract of land in Andover, which he purchased June 19, 1750, of Benj. and Archelaus Fuller. He md. 1st, Oct. 10, 1710, Bethiah Gould; md. 2d, Jan. 19, 1719-20, Abigail, wid. of David Goodale, who d. ———, 1717; he was son of Zechariah and Elizabeth Goodale. Eight ch. by Abigail.

65. JOSEPH[5]. RUTH, bapt. Apr. 29, 1722, d. Aug. 31, 1826, living to the great age of 104 years; md. Dec. 15, 1741, Stephen, son of Francis and Jerusha Elliot. of Middleton, b. June 29. 1717. Three ch:—Stephen, b. July 9, 1742, d. Feb. 12, 1826; Andrew, b. Apr. 13, 1744, d. ———, 1793 (see No. 137); Asa, b. Sept. 23, 1745, d. Mch. 23, 1823.

67. ABNER. 68. JOSIAH. 69 SARAH, bapt. Mch. 31, 1728.

70. ELIZABETH. b. 1730, d. Apr. 27, 1822, aged 92 years; md. Apr. 7, 1752, Stephen Nichols, of Middleton, b. Feb. 10, 1716; adm. granted his wife Elizabeth, June 4, 1776. Yeoman. Ten ch:—Stephen, b. Dec. 1, 1755; Joseph, bapt. Nov, 16, 1760, d. Mch. 4, 1833; Benjamin and Ruth, bapt. Nov. 16, 1760; Asa, bapt. Nov. 4, 1764; Elisha, bapt. Dec. 17, 1769, d. Mch. 3, 1842; Sarah, bapt. Mch. 1, 1772; Hannah, Betsy and Andrew.

71. JOHN, bapt. Jan. 6, 1734, d. young. 72. JOHN.

(25) EBENEZER[4], son of JOSEPH[3] (12), b. at Salem Vill., Feb. 20, 1694; Will signed May 24, 1769, rec'd to Probate, Jan. 2, 1776. son Robert, ex'r. He was a man of considerable affluence, his estate being valued after his decease, at £1610, 8s, 7d. He inherited most of his father's homestead, lands and buildings, and his "personal estate without door." He possessed a valuable farm, "lying within the Province of Hampshire," probably in Amherst, which, in his Will he bequeathed to his son Solomon, who had previously removed there. He was chosen Constable and Assessor for the year 1725. He md. 1st, Aug. 13, 1718, Hannah. dau. of Joseph and Bethiah (Raye) Gould, b. Feb. 20, 1698-9; md. 2d, Apr. 5, 1727, Hannah Shaw (formerly Southwick), wid. of Ebenezer Shaw, whom she md. Mch. 17, 1719-20. She was dau. of John and Hannah (Follet) Southwick, b. 1698. Three ch. by Hannah, 1st:—

73. SOLOMON[5]. 74. EBENEZER, bapt. Mch. 29, 1730, d. young. 75. HANNAH, bapt. Mch. 29, 1730, d. Sept. 23, 1804; md. July 7, 1737, Amos (57), son of Ambrose and Ruth Hutchinson. Four ch. by Hannah, 2d:—

76. BETHIAH, bapt. Mch. 29, 1730; md. Nov. 26, 1751, Joseph, son of Eleazer Brown, bapt. Oct. 9, 1726. Will proved Oct. 6, 1801; wife

Bethiah and son Ebenezer, exec'rs. Both rec'd to ch. July 27, 1755. Yeoman. Seven ch:—Betsy, b. Dec. 9, 1753; Asa, b. July 6, 1756; Ebenezer, b. May 3, 1759; Hannah, b. Mch. 29, 1762; Sarah, b. July 8, 1765; Bethiah, bapt. July 24, 1768; Hitta, bapt. Aug. 25, 1771.
77. ROBERT. 78. JOSEPH⁵. 79. JEREMY⁵.

(30) ELISHA⁴, son of JOSEPH³ (12), d. before 1730. He was a farmer and lived on a farm adjoining his father's homestead. He and his wife were both rec'd into ch. Oct. 8, 1727; md. Jan. 12, 1726-7, Ginger Porter, dau. of Israel and Sarah (Putnam), bapt. Aug. 17, 1707. She survived her husband, and md. 2d, Sept. 20, 1730, Daniel Andrew, son of Daniel and Hannah (Peabody), b. Sept. 28, 1704, by whom she had Sarah, b. Aug. 5, 1731; Daniel, b. July 13, 1734; John, b. Feb. 28, 1736; Nathan, b. Sept. 30, 1739. One child:—
80. ISRAEL⁵.

(34) JOHN⁴, son of JOHN³ (13), b. at Salem Vill., Mch. 31, 1699, d. intestate, and was living as late as Aug. 1726; adm. was granted to his wid. Abigail, Oct. 28, 1726; inventory of his estate, £757, 19s, 9d. He was a farmer and lived on the estate given him by his father, in the vicinity of his homestead. Rec'd to ch. July 10, 1720; md. Nov. 17, 1720, Abigail, dau. of John and Abigail Giles, b. Jan. 3, 1699. Three ch:—
81. ABIGAIL, bapt. July 1, 1722. 82. MEHITABLE, bapt. Apr. 19, 1724.
83. HANNAH, bapt. Sept. 25, 1726.

(36) EBENEZER⁴, son of JOHN³ (13), b. at Salem Vill., June 3, 1705; no Will or adm. of est. Yeoman, and lived on his father's farm; md. Dec. 13, 1726, Mary Bound. Two ch:—
84. WILLIAM. 85. EBENEZER.

(38) WILLIAM⁴, son of JOHN³ (13), b. at Salem Vill., Jan. 16, 1713-14, d. intestate, about 1757; guardianship of his ch., Ebenezer, William and Hannah, above 14 years of age, granted Apr. 14, 1757, to Noah Creesy, of Beverly. He probably lived upon the farm given him by his father, Mch. 1, 1730-7, which consisted of one-half of his land and meadow, including one-third of the orcharding at the W. end of his barn. He also owned rights in the common land at Beverly, which he sold Apr. 17, 1739, to "Randall Preson, taylor, of Beverly." He md. Nov. ——, 1733, Joanna, dau. of Joseph and Elizabeth Trask, bapt. 1st ch., Beverly, Oct. 4, 1713. Four ch:—
86. JOHN. 87. HANNAH. 88. EBENEZER. 89. WILLIAM.

(42) BENJAMIN⁴, son of BENJAMIN³ (14), b. at Salem Vill., Jan.

27, 1693-4. His Will was proved May 10, 1780, being about 86 years of age at his decease. He is one of the first of the numerous descendants of the patriarch Richard, who is known, as far as we have definite knowledge, to have left the land of his fathers for a home in a strange and untried country, all of whom for more than one hundred years, had lived, thrived and died upon the original homestead; and strange to relate, not a stone has yet been discovered to mark the resting place of any who had fallen asleep, in that most interesting locality. The first ancient stones that the compiler has yet found, were erected to the memory of a portion of Benjamin's family, in the burial ground at Bedford, Mass., adjoining the church there.

He ceased to be taxed in Salem in 1734, and it is quite probable he removed to Bedford some time during that year. He and his wife were members of the church, and Nov. 27, 1737, they received letters of dismission to the ch. in Bedford. Benjamin had large possessions at Salem Vill., and after the decease of his father, he bought of all his heirs their rights in the estate left them by inheritance, except that of his brother Jonathan, who was then under age. All of this property he shortly after disposed of prior to his removal, selling his homestead to Joshua Goodale, for £300, Dec. 20, 1733, reserving, however, one-half of his part in the cider mill. In addition to his agricultural pursuits, he appears, from the Registry of Deeds, to have followed the employment of a cooper. He md. Feb. 7, 1715-16, Sarah, dau. of John and Mary (Nurse) Tarbell, b. Oct. 2, 1696. Seven ch : —

90. NATHAN⁵. 91. JANE, bapt. Mch. 20, 1720; md. Feb. 18, 1745-6, Jona. Grimes, of Bedford. One ch : — Elizabeth, b. Bedford, Sept. 7, 1747. 92. BENJAMIN⁵. 93. SARAH⁵, bapt. Feb. 21, 1724-5; md. Jan. 3, 1748-9, Israel, son of Israel and Sarah Putnam, b. Bedford, Mch. 20, 1722-3. Five ch : — John, b. Apr. 23, 1750; Elizabeth, b. Sept. 17, 1751; Sarah, b. July 28, 1753; Israel, b. Apr. 27, 1755; Daniel, b. Oct. 4, 1759.

94. ELIZABETH, b. 1728, d. Mch. 12, 1750, aged 22 years. 95. BARTHOLOMEW, b. July 5, 1734, d. Sept. 20, 1749. 96. MARY, b. July 5, 1734, d. Sept. 14, 1749. 97. JOHN, b. 1737, d. Sept. 1, 1749, aged 12 years.

(44) NATHANIEL⁴, son of BENJAMIN³ (14), b. at Salem Vill., May 3, 1698. His Will was signed May 5, 1756, and proved Oct. 24, 1757.

He and his first wife united with the church at Salem Vill., Mch. 15, 1723-4. He lived on a small farm given him by his father, till 1733, when he removed with his family to Sutton, Worcester Co., and shortly after sold all his lands and right of inheritance, to his bro. Benjamin. He md. 1st, Mary; md. 2d, Joanna, dau. of Lot and Elizabeth Conant, bapt. 1st ch., Beverly, Nov. 27, 1709, d. at Sutton, 1802, aged 93 years. She was great-grand-dau. of Roger Conant, who was b. at Budleigh, in Devonshire, Eng., about 1592, came to America about 1623, and settled first at Cape Ann, and soon after removed to Salem, where, it is said, he built the first house. He removed to Beverly some years before his decease, which occurred Nov. 19, 1679, aged 84 years. Lot Conant's Will was proved June 10, 1745; after making provision for the rest of his children, he gives his dau. Joanna Hutchinson, £20. He had rem'd some time previous to Ipswich, where he died. Three ch. by Mary.

98. MARY, bapt. Mch. 15, 1723-4; md. Jona. Fitts. 99. SUSANNA, bapt. Nov. 28, 1725; md. Daniel Day. Four ch:—Moses, Daniel, Aaron, and Mirriam. 100. BETHIAH, bapt. July 14, 1730; md. Eben'r Fitts; lived in Dudley, Mass., where he d. 1790. Seven ch:—Mehitable, Caleb, Nathaniel, Ebenezer, Mary and Mercy, Seven ch. by Joanna.

101. BARTHOLOMEW[5]. 102. ELIZABETH, b. at Sutton, Nov. 1, 1736. 103. NATHANIEL, d. 1755, in the French war, at Skeensboro, now Whitchall. 104. LOT[5]. 105. BENJAMIN[5]. 106. JONATHAN[5]. 107. SARAH, b. Aug., 1752, d. June 8, 1834; md. late in life to Samuel Rich, of Sutton; no issue.

(50) JONATHAN[4], son of BENJAMIN[3] (14), b. at Salem Vill., July 18, 1716; adm. granted to Abijah Ingalls, of Andover, Oct. 24, 1768. Removed to Andover in 1750, having sold his estate in Salem Vill., for £912, to Timothy Fuller, of Middleton, and the same year bought of Walter Smith, of Andover, for £240, a tract of land in said town, with dwelling house and barn, near "Mill Stone Rock," on the Salem road. He and his wife were members of the ch. at Salem Village, and "received letters of dismission, Jan. 31, 1762, to 1st ch. in Andover, whither they had removed some years previous." He md. Jan. 30, 1734-5, Elizabeth, dau. of John and Abigail (Leach) Ganson, bapt. Feb. 5, 1709-10. Four ch:—

108. BENJAMIN, bapt. Aug. 13, 1738. 109. JONATHAN, bapt. Oct. 26, 1740; killed at the battle of Lake George, Sept. 2, 1758. 110. ELIJAH[5]. 111. SARAH, b. at Andover, June 28, 1753, buried Dec. 9, 1778.

(51) STEPHEN[4], son of RICHARD[3] (16), bapt. Aug. 14, 1715. Removed, 1737, to Penobscot Co., Me., where he lived till the breaking out of the Indian war, in 1780, when he went to Windham, where he d. about 1788. Yeoman. He md. 1st, Feb. 22, 1737-8, Abigail Haskins, d. 1777; md. 2d, Hannah; md. 3d, Ann, wid. of Joseph Legro, of Marblehead, Mass., b. about 1728, d. at Hebron, Me., Aug., 1805. Eight ch. by Abigail.

112. STEPHEN⁵. 113. DANIEL, d. at sea. 114. RICHARD⁵. 115.
LYDIA, d. at Gray, Me., about 1788. 116. ABIGAIL. 117. SAMUEL.
118. JOSEPH⁵.

(57) AMOS⁴, son of AMBROSE³ (18), bapt. June 10, 1710. He
was a mariner, and it is probable he died at sea; md. July 7, 1737,
Hannah (74), dau. of Ebenezer and Hannah Hutchinson, bapt. Mch.
29, 1730, d. Sept. 23, 1804. Three ch:—
119. AMOS, d. young, a cripple. 120. SEVIAH; md. Dec. 4, 1770,
William, son of Ebenezer and Phebe Berry, b. Middleton, Sept. 9,
1749, d. 1786. Yeoman. Three ch:—Hannah, b. 1722, d. Aug. 4,
1800; Amos, d. in N. Carolina; Israel, bapt. June 30, 1776. 121. RUTH,
b. at Danvers, May 23, 1752, d. Apr. 7, 1838; md. Sept. 10, 1795, Benjamin, son of Benjamin and Hannah Russell, b. Mch. 21, 1757, d. Apr.
26, 1838; no issue.

(59) SAMUEL⁴, son of AMBROSE³ (18), bapt. Apr. 24, 1714. In
early life a mariner; removed to Woodstock, Mass., where he engaged
in the manufactory of scythes; md. Nov. 13, 1735, Elizabeth, dau. of
David and Martha Judd. Two ch:—
122. AMOS. 123. SAMUEL.

(62) GEORGE⁴, son of AMBROSE³ (18), b. at Salem Vill., Nov. 1,
1730. He was a farmer, and shortly after his marriage removed, about
1764, to Lyndeboro, N. H. He md. 1st, June 8, 1748, Elizabeth Bick-
ford, of Middleton; md. 2d, Susan Bevins. Twelve ch:—
124. WILLIAM. 125. SAMUEL. 126. GEORGE. 127. MARY. 128.
SUSANNAH. 129. BETSEY. 130. EFFIE, b. at Wilton, N. H., Apr. 2,
1765, d. 1828; md. 1804, Nathan Tuttle, of Wilton, b. Apr. 9, 1769, d.
Aug. 5, 1852. Cooper. One ch:—George H., b. at Wilton, Jan. 22,
1805 (md. Mary Hutchinson, No. 252).
131. EDA. 132. JAMES. 133. AMBROSE. RUTH, b. Nov., 1774.
135. CLARK.

FIFTH GENERATION.

(65) JOSEPH⁵, son of JOSEPH⁴ (22), bapt. 1st ch., Salem Vill.,
Apr. 29, 1722. In his Will, signed Dec. 20, 1794, and proved May 1,
1797, he very liberally provides for his wife's future maintenance, and
gives to his son Elisha, 74 acres of land in Amherst, N. H., joining
that which he already owned. He appoints his son Joseph executor.
The inventory of his estate, appraised July 13, 1797, consisted of the
homestead lands, 110 acres; 5 acres of woodland in Andover; 74 acres
in Amherst; a pew in the Middleton meeting house; stock of cattle;

husbandry tools; furniture, &c., amounting to $3,614 40. He settled on a farm in Middleton, near the boundary line, and at his father's dec., rec'd by Will the westerly half of his estate, meadows and uplands, and one-half of his stock of creatures. He md. 1st., 1746, Hannah, dau. of David and Rebecca Richardson, of Middleton, b. Oct 28, 1724; md. 2d, July 19, 1764, Keziah, dau. of James and Keziah Marble. Five ch. by Hannah : —

136. ELIZABETH, b. Feb. 4, 1747; md. Ebenezer Goodale. Will proved Apr. 5, 1791. Yeoman. 137. HANNAH, b. Feb. 5, 1749, d. before 1794; md. Dec. 26, 1765, Andrew, son of Stephen and Ruth Elliot (No. 66), b. at Middleton, Apr. 13, 1744, d. 1793. Housewright. Ten ch:—Ruth, b. June 29, 1766; Andrew, b. Mch. 23, 1768, d. Sept. 24, 1769; Hannah, b. Sept. 10, 1770; Ruth, b. Nov. 21, 1773; Elias, b. Dec. 17, 1775; Andrew, b. Nov. 27, 1777, d. Jan., 1824; Mary, b. Jan. 24, 1780; Elias, b. 1785; Hannah, b. July 5, 1788; Betsey, b. June 7, 1791, d. about 1810.

138. ELISHA[6]. 139. MARY, b. Apr. 10, 1754, d. before 1797; md. Samuel, son of George and Abigail (Upton) Small, b. May 2, 1753; certificate of marriage given July 1, 1776. 140. JOSEPH[6].

(67) ABNER[5], son of JOSEPH[4] (22), bapt. Sept. 6, 1724. Some time prior to his marriage he removed to N. H., and settled in that part of Amherst afterwards called Milford, where he d. Sept. 2, 1796. Yeoman. He md. Elizabeth, dau. of Elisha and Elizabeth Phelps, b. at Amherst, ———, d. Oct., 1801, in her 72d year. Two ch :—

141. JONATHAN, b. Mch. 5, 1761, d. Jan. 27, 1788. 142. ELIZABETH[6], b. July 25, 1765, d. Feb. 4, 1846; md. 1791, Isaac Bartlett, son of Isaac and Mary (Appleton), b. at Newton, Mass., Oct. 8, 1761, d. Sept. 30, 1806. Yeoman. Five ch:—Abner H., b. Oct. 28, 1792, d. July, 1852; Betsey, b. Oct. 26, 1796; md. Abel Hutchinson (374); Jonathan, b. June 9, 1799; Lydia, b. Sept. 2, 1804, d. Dec. 1845; Sally, b. Mch. 8, 1807, d. Mch. 30, 1807.

(68) JOSIAH[5], son of JOSEPH[4] (22), bapt. July 10, 1726. Lived in Middleton, where he engaged in agricultural pursuits. Adm. granted John Hutchinson, Apr. 2, 1782; inventory of est., £39, 14s., 6d. Two of his ch., Joseph and Philip, were placed under guardianship, Dec. 6, 1781; md. Dec. 8, 1748, Sarah Dean, of Middleton; adm. granted John Hutchinson, May 6, 1782. Eleven ch : —

143. RUTH[6], bapt. Sept. 16, 1750; md. ——— Jonathan Russell, jr.; rec'd to 1st ch., Danvers, May 7, 1775. Four ch : — Huldah and Lydia, bapt. May 21, 1775; Aaron, bapt. Nov. 7, 1777; Jonathan, bapt. Oct. 8, 1780.

144. SARAH, bapt. Nov. 1, 1752. 145. PHEBE, bapt. Oct. 27, 1754, d.

1839; md. June 4, 1777, Jacob McIntire, of Reading; rem'd to Fitchburg, Mass. Three ch:—Josiah, Jessie and Phebe. 146. SARAH, bapt. Oct. 12, 1755. 147. IRENE, bapt. Aug. 12,.1759, d. Sept. 1854; md. Feb. 27, 1781, Daniel McIntire, of N. Reading. Four ch:—Perley, Joseph, James, Susan.

148. JOSIAH⁶. 149. MARY, bapt. June 15, 1766, d. Apr. 17, 1851; md. John McIntire, b. 1759, d. Aug. 25, 1835. Nine ch:—Amos, b. Feb. 5, 1792, d, Jan. 18, 1835; John, b. Mch. 13, 1793; Jeremiah, b. Oct. 30, 1794, d. Dec. 4, 1831; George, b. Feb, 7, 1796; Elisha, b. Sept. 17, 1798, d. Dec. 5, 1798; Elisha, b. Dec. 3, 1801; Jacob, b. Aug. 20, 1802; Mary, b. Jan. 23, 1806, d. July 29, 1809; David, b. Feb. 24, 1807. 150. HANNAH, bapt. Feb. 19, 1769, d. Nov., 1846. 151. PHILIP DEAN, bapt. Aug. 4, 1771, d. ———. 152. An Infant (twin), b. 1771, d. July 10, 1771. 153. BETSY, bapt. June 26, 1774.

(72) JOHN⁵, son of JOSEPH⁴ (22), b. at Middleton, 1736, d. 1830. He and his wife were rec'd to ch. in Middleton, May 2, 1773. Yeoman. He md. Sept. 12, 1766, Lydia, dau. of Abraham and Ruth Goodell, b. May 17, 1741, d. Mch. 30, 1816. Three ch:—
154. JOHN⁶. 155. LYDIA, b. Apr. 9, 1770, d. Oct. 20, 1828. 156. JESSIE⁶.

(73) SOLOMON⁵, son of EBENEZER⁴ (25), b. at Salem Vill., 1721. He lived on his father's farm till about the year 1758, when he removed to Amherst, N. H. He was there chosen, Mch. 8, 1762, Selectman and Surveyor of Highways. At the same time he and Samuel Steward were chosen "a committee to buy a burying cloth and enclose the Grave yard." He removed thence to Fayette, Me., where he d. about 1815. He md. Oct. 22, 1746, Hannah, dau. of Amos Putnam, of Salem Vill., b. 1726, d. at Amherst, N. H., 1802. Five ch:—
157. SOLOMON⁶. 158. EBENEZER⁶. 159. ASA⁶. 160. HITTIE, b. at Amherst, N. H., 1760, d. at Hillsboro, 1799; md. ——— Cram. 161. HANNAH, b. 1778, d. Sept., 1821.

(77) ROBERT⁵, son of EBENEZER⁴ (25), bapt. Feb. 25, 1733, d. Dec., 1785. He inherited his father's homestead, and owned land in Andover and Middleton. Inv. of estate £457, 15s, 9d. Lived in Danvers (formerly Salem Vill). He md. June 16, 1767, Eunice, dau. of Amos Buxton. Nine ch:—
162. DANIEL⁶. 163. EDA, b. Dec. 27, 1769, d. Nov. 19, 1841; md. May, 1796, Asa Putnam, b. at Danvers, Sept. 23, 1765, d. Oct. 9, 1823. Five ch:—Eunice, b. Sept. 17, 1796; Hezekiah, b. Mch. 3, 1799, d. Mch. 20, 1802; Hezekiah, b. Apr. 19, 1802, d. at sea; Robert, b. June 20, 1805; md. Mary Hutchinson (324); Asa, b. May 20, 1808. 164. JOSEPH, b. Apr. 25, 1771, d. young. 165. JOB, b. Oct. 7, 1772,

d. Aug. 23, 1856. 166. ABIJAH⁶. 167. BETSEY, b. June 24, 1778, d.
July 4, 1861. 168. EUNICE, b. Feb. 10, 1780, d. Oct. 4, 1796. 169. EBEN,
b. Mch. 16, 1784, d. July 1, 1844. 170. ROBERT, b. June 4, 1785, d.
Nov. 6, 1828.

(78) JOSEPH⁵, son of EBENEZER⁴ (25), bapt. May 18, 1735; adm.
granted Robert Hutchinson, June 6, 1769. Inv. of est., £125, 5s. 10d.
He was a farmer and shoemaker; md. Jan. 29, 1767, Ruth Pritchard.
One ch : —
171. HANNAH⁶, b. Dec., 1769, d. at Middleton, Aug. 28, 1813; md.
June 28, 1787, Samuel, son of Samuel and Martha White, b. Sept. 2,
1764, d. Sept. 5, 1818. Nine ch : — Hannah, b. Mch. 6, 1789; Ruth, b.
July 30, 1791, d. Mch. 10, 1812; Samuel, b. July 3, 1794; Olive and
Oliver, twins, b. Aug. 21, 1796; Joseph, b. July 11, 1799; Perley, b.
July 28, 1802, d. Feb. 23, 1839; md. Eliza Hutchinson (328); Lydia
and Charlotte.

(79) JEREMY⁵, son of EBENEZER⁴ (25), b. at Salem Vill., June
29, 1738, d. Apr. 7, 1805. He was a farmer, and lived on that portion
of his father's homestead left him by inheritance, consisting of a
dwelling house, barn, and 14 acres on the great road, 22 acres of pas-
ture land, and one-half of the old orchard. He md. Apr. 11, 1760,
Sarah, dau. of Asa and Sarah Putnam, b. Oct. 22, 1739, d. Oct., 1781.
Eight ch : —
172. SARAH, b. Feb. 12, 1762, d. July 14, 1815; md. Oct. 13, 1788,
Jethro Russell, jr., b. Sept. 16, 1764; rem'd to Danville, Vt., where he
d. Apr. 11, 1833. Four ch : — Jeremy, b. at Danvers, Dec. 18, 1788;
Elijah, b. at Danville, Feb. 8, 1792, d. Sept. 25, 1867; md. Eliza, wid.
of Perley Hutchinson (337); Mahala, b. Mch. 30, 1795; Sarah H., b.
Sept. 15, 1797, d. Jan. ———, 1821.
173. EBENEZER⁶. 174. BETHIAH, b. Mch. 8, 1766, d. July 2, 1801.
175. MEHITABLE, b. Jan. 10, 1768, d. Mch. 2, 1835. 176. JOSEPH⁶.
177. HANNAH, b. Mch. 23, 1772, d. Apr. 9, 1813.
178. JEREMY, b. Oct. 28, 1774, d. June 5, 1853; unm'd. Credit is
due him, for the first information we have respecting this branch of
the Hutchinson family. Impelled by curiosity, he drew up a " family
tree," in which he introduced without elaboration, the male descendants of Richard, somewhat in the form of a pedigree. Some time
after his decease this chart was found among other papers of his
which, becoming known outside of the family, prompted the desire to
perpetuate this very brief and imperfect history, in a more elaborate
form. He was a man of much leisure, in consequence of bodily in-
firmities, and possessed in a good degree, a mathematical turn of
mind. Inventory of his est., $2221 84.
179. ASA⁶.

(80) ISRAEL, son of ELISHA (30), bapt. 1st ch., Salem Vill., Nov. 12, 1727. He settled in that part of Danvers known as Danversport, near the Grist Mills, a short distance above, on the opposite side of the road. His homestead, consisting of nearly 3 acres of land, a house and barn, he purchased of Samuel Clark for £260, the deed bearing date Apr. 15, 1762; and on the same day he sold his house on Porter's plain, to the same individual. Prior to this, Mch. 9, 1762, he bought of James Richardson, for 5s., one-eighth part of two Grist Mills, and one Saw Mill on Crane River, and June 19. and Dec. 20, same year, he bought of two other share owners, for £366, 13s., 4d., a quarter more from each. There were three of these mills beside the Saw Mills, which stood on or near the same site of the present Grist Mill, near the Iron Foundry. A very large and commodious Grist Mill has recently been erected, 1868, situated between these two buildings. In early life he evinced an active interest in military affairs, and in the year 1757, he enlisted as a private in a scouting party, under Capt. Israel Herrick, and penetrated the country now included in the State of Maine. During the following year he was appointed Lieut. in Capt. Andrew Fuller's Co., and was actively engaged at Lake George and Ticonderoga. In 1759, we find him at the head of a company, scaling the heights of Abraham, with Gen. Wolfe, which resulted in the entire route of the French under Montcalm. After the news of the Battle of Lexington had reached Danvers, Mr. Hutchinson, who then commanded a company of 60 minute men, hastened immediately with his small force, but before arriving at the scene of action, he met the British in full retreat, and engaged them with signal success, which bravery resulted in a Lieut. Colonel's commission, in Col. Mansfield's Regiment, and subsequently was promoted to a Colonelcy, in which capacity he served during the Revolution. Among other scenes in which he was actively engaged, we find him at the siege of Boston, occupying Fort Hill, Dorchester Heights, Forts Lee and Washington, and crossing the Delaware with Washington on his retreat, from whom he received the strongest proofs of his approbation, and appreciation of his valuable services. After the war he was chosen to the Legislature for twenty-one years in succession. While in that body, he with others, was chosen, Sept. 23, 1779, a committee to confiscate and sell at public auction, the property of William Brown and others, as notorious conspirators against the government. On this committee, he served afterwards in 1782 and 1784. William Brown's fine mansion house, then standing on the site of the present Market House in Salem, was sold, Nov. 6, 1784, to Elias Hasket Derby, for £650. Mr. Hutchinson was affable, social, and generous in his nature, and courteous in his deportment. His death was caused, Mch. 15, 1811, by a fall in his mill, while at work on the water-wheel. He md. 1st, 1748, Anna,

dau. of Robert Cue, of Wenham; md. 2d, Mehitable, wid. of Dea.
Archelaus Putnam, and dau. of Joseph Putnam and Elizabeth (Porter),
b. Jan. 13, 1720. She md. Archelaus Putnam, Apr. 12, 1739, and after
his dec. she and Mr. Hutchinson were joint overseers in the last administration. Four ch. by Anna : —

180. GINGER, b. Sterling, Mass., June 23, 1749, d. Mch. 7, 1831; md.
Mch. 23, 1769, John, son of Bartholomew and Sarah Brown, b. Oct. 20,
1746, d. Aug. 30, 1820. Ten ch : — Nancy, b. Sept. 8, 1772, d. Apr. 14,
1854; John, bapt. Apr. 12, 1775, d. Feb. 4, 1781; Sally, b. Sept. 30, 1777,
d. Sept. 4, 1857; Ellery, b. July 12, 1780, d. Mch. 3, 1846; Samuel Fairfield, b. Apr. 30, 1783; Mira, b. Sept. 30, 1785; John G., b. Sept. 2,
1788; Mary, b. May 26, 1791, d. May 10, 1851; Israel, b. Apr. 4, 1794.

181. ANNA, b. Mch. 26, 1751, d. Sept. 5, 1838; md. May 23, 1771,
Samuel, son of Dr. Jos. Fairfield, of Wenham, b. July 20, 1748, d.
Nov. 26, 1810; no issue. 182. ELIZABETH, b. Apr. 10, 1752, d. Sept. 4,
1775; md. Francis Brown, of Newbury, who d. Sept. 7, 1775. Two
ch : — Betsy, b. Feb. 25, 1773; Samuel, b. Apr. 14, 1775. 183. ELISHA,
b. May 25, 1755, d. 1777, in Halifax prison, having been taken a prisoner of war on board a privateer. One ch. by Mehitable : —

184. ISRAEL⁶.

(86) JOHN⁵, son of WILLIAM⁴ (38). He was a farmer, and lived
on his father's estate; he owned tracts of land both in Middleton and
Andover. Two ch : —

185. ISRAEL. 186. JOHN.

(89) WILLIAM⁵, son of WILLIAM⁴ (38). Adm. granted his wid.
Mary, Oct. 26, 1771; est. appraised five days after, at £60, 3s., 10d.
He was a blacksmith, and lived at Danvers. He md. Jan. 11, 1768,
Mary, dau. of Solomon Martin and Dorothy (Lovejoy), of Andover,
b. Aug. 27, 1737; adm. granted Solomon Martin, Apr. 8, 1777. One
ch : —

187. PHEBE, b. Mch. 26, 1769.

(90) NATHAN⁵, son of BENJAMIN⁴ (42), bapt. 1st ch., Salem Vill.,
Feb. 10, 1717. He was a farmer, and rem'd with his father to Bedford, in 1734; thence to Amherst, now Milford, where he d. Jan. 12,
1795. Md. Rachel Stearns. Six ch : —

188. SAMUEL⁶. 189. NATHAN⁶. 190. BENJAMIN⁶. 191. EBEN-
EZER⁶. 192. BARTHOLOMEW⁶.

193. RACHEL, b. May 19, 1766, d. Sept. 12, 1842; md. Daniel John-
son, d. Nov. 28, 1831. Six ch : — Fanny, b. 1793; Daniel, b. Oct. 19,
1795, d. Aug. 20, 1832; James, b. Jan. 12, 1797; Emily, b. 1781; Thos.
Jefferson, b. 1783, d. Nov. 1, 1834; Rachel, b. 1799, d. Sept. 18, 1821.

(92) BENJAMIN, son of BENJAMIN (42), bapt. Sept. 30, 1722;
rem'd with his father to Bedford, Mass., where he d. 1813. Yeoman.
He was md., July 31, 1750, by Rev. Nicholas Bowes, to Rebecca Lane,
of Bedford. Six ch : —
194. MARY, b. at Bedford. Aug. 21, 1751; md. Nov. 23, 1775, Samuel,
son of John and Rebecca Page, of Rindge, N. H., b. Aug. 1, 1751; no
issue. 195. SUSANNA, b.' Aug. 8, 1754. 196. JOHN, b. June 29, 1757,
d. Aug. 14, 1757. 197. BETSY[6], b. Jan. 20. 1760; md. Feb. 12, 1788,
Sam'l Parkhurst, of Chelmsford. 198. REBECCA, b. Feb. 10, 1762.
199. SARAH, b. Nov. 9, 1765.

(101) BARTHOLOMEW, son of NATHANIEL (44), b. at Sutton,
June 28, 1734. His Will was proved Apr. 4, 1820. He was a thrifty
and enterprising farmer, and owned an estate of nearly 200 acres in
Sutton, a great portion of which he inherited by Will, and succeeded
his father to the homestead. He md. 1st., Aug. 4, 1763, Ruth, dau. of
Dea. John and Susanna Haven, of Framingham, b. 1743, d. 1796; md.
2d, Rebecca Monroe. Ten ch : —
200. NATHANIEL. 201. JOHN[6]. 202. ASA, b. Dec. 24, 1767, d.
young. 203. BARTHOLOMEW[6]. 204. LOIS, b. Jan 18, 1772, d. at
Bellingham, Mass., Aug. 17, 1799; md. Simeon Holbrook. One ch :—
———, d. at birth.
205. TIMOTHY[6]. 206. RUTH, b. June 7, 1776, d. at Douglass, Mass.;
md. ——— Lee; no issue. 207. SIMON[6]. 208. BETSY, b. Apr. 22,
1781; md. Oct. 16, 1804, Jonas, son of Jesse and Mary Cummings, of
Sutton, b. Aug. 14, 1779. Lives in Paris, Me. Four ch : — Chandler,
b. Oct. 30, 1805, d. Aug. 3, 1807; Simon II., b. May 10, 1809. d. May
23, 1857; Calista, b. Dec. 26, 1810; Charles F., b. May 13, 1817.
209. LUCY, b. Apr. 24, 1784, d. June 23, 1812; md. 1808, Sylvester,
son of Dr. Nathaniel F. and Hannah (Gibbs) Morse, b. at Douglass,
Mass., Jan., 1783, d. at Sutton, Nov. 7, 1820. One ch : — Alanson, b.
at New Braintree, Dec., 1809, d. at Sutton, Feb. 6, 1829.

(104) LOT, son of NATHANIEL (44), b. at Sutton, Aug. 1, 1741;
rem'd to Vt., and settled in Braintree, where he d. Mch. 24, 1818.
Yeoman. He md. Hannah Morse, b. 1744, d. Jan. 17, 1815. Six
ch : —
210. JOANNA, b. at Worcester, June 7, 1768, d. at Brookfield, Dec.
26, 1856; md. 1st, Israel Osborn; md. 2d, Amaziah Grover, who d. at
Brookfield, Vt., 1842; no issue. 211. HANNAH, d. So. Hadley; md.
Timothy Jones; no issue. 212. AARON[6]. 213. ASA[6]. 214. POLLY,
d. at Braintree, July 11, 1825; md. Josiah Wellington, of Braintree,
who d. Mch. 22, 1817. Yeoman. Seven ch : — David, b. Apr. 8, 1803;
Ashley; Luther, d. at Lenox, Mich., 1839; Lucy; Polly, d. 1842, in

4

Indiana; Sylvester Levi, b. 1813; Amos Hubbard, b. Mch. 24, 1815.
215. ABIATHAR⁶.

(105) BENJAMIN, son of NATHANIEL (43), b. at Sutton, Jan. 30,
1744, d. at Royalston, Mass., Jan. 7, 1840. He rem'd to Royalston,
prior to 1770, while then a wilderness, and settled upon a tract of
land about one and a half miles distant N. W. from the centre of the
town. The place was first settled in 1754, and named for Col. Isaac
Royall, one of its proprietors. There being no roads in the vicinity
of Mr. Hutchinson's settlement, one was laid out by the Selectmen,
in 1770, leading by the east side of his house. He was a carpenter as
well as farmer, and assisted in building the two first meeting houses
in town. He was a man of industrious habits, kind, benevolent and
useful, and often chosen to fill important town offices, and was ever
ready to assist in forwarding the interests and settlement of the
town. He md. 1st, Judith Libby, b. 1746, d. May 19, 1795; md. 2d,
1797, wid. Mary Partridge (formerly Hill), of Braintree, b. 1748, d.
Aug. 7, 1830. Eight ch. by Judith : —
216. JUDITH, b. July 16, 1771, d. Feb. 20, 1772. 217. BENJAMIN⁶.
218. DANIEL⁶, b. Feb. 15, 1775, d. Aug. 17, 1777. 219. JOSHUA, b. Nov.
7, 1776, d. Aug. 23, 1781. 220. DANIEL, b. July 22, 1779, d. July 11,
1782. 221. JOSHUA⁶. 222. STEPHEN⁶, b. June 22, 1784, d. about 1795.
223. ANNA⁶, b. June 21, 1789; md. Oct. 19, 1819, Patrick McManas, b.
at Dummerston, Vt., 1783. Lives in St. Johnsbury. Two ch : —
Danforth, b. Apr. 22, 1822; d. Aug. 26, 1823; Alhanan, b. Jan. 26,
1824.

(106) JONATHAN, son of NATHANIEL (43), b. at Sutton, Sept. 2,
1746. He was a farmer, and rem'd to Royalston, probably with his
bro. Benjamin, where he lived till March, 1789, when he went to Concord, Vt., where he d. Sept. 1, 1807. He md. Ruth Underwood, b. at
Framingham, Mass., ——, d. at Concord, Vt., May 14, 1834. Five
ch : —
224. DAVID⁶. 225. SAMUEL⁶. 226. BETSY, b. at Royalston, Feb.,
1784, d. at Concord, Vt., Dec. 5, 1855; md. 1812, Buckley, son of Edward and Patty Adams, b. Lincoln, Mass., 1789. Yeoman. Seven
ch : —Mary H., b. at Waterford, Vt., 1814; Amos, b. 1816; Nancy, b.
1819; Laura, b. 1821, d. May, 1851; Rhoda, b. at Concord, Vt., 1823;
Simon H., b. 1825; John Q., b. 1829, d. at N. Y., July, 1848.
227. AMOS⁶. 228. POLLY, b. Jan. 6, 1789. Lived at Royalston,
Mass., Derby, Concord, and at present (1868) in Charleston, Vt.; md.
Jan. 28, 1813, Robert, son of Robert and Polly Hamilton, b. at Conway, Mass., Oct. 4, 1786. Yeoman. Seven ch :—James W., b. at
Concord, Vt., Jan. 14, 1814; William, b. Feb. 2, 1816; Gilbert H., b.

Sept. 9, 1818; Maria, b. Nov. 11, 1821; Mary, b. Dec. 4, 1824; George W., b. July 19, 1828; Benj. Franklin, b. Feb. 10, 1833.

(110) ELIJAH, son of JONATHAN (49), bapt. 1st ch., Salem Vill., June 5, 1743. He rem'd to Andover with his father, 1750, where he d. Sept., 1768. Yeoman. Md. Hannah ——. Two ch:—
229. HANNAH, b. 1766. 230. PHEBE, b. July, 1768.

(112) STEPHEN, son of STEPHEN (51), b. 1741. He was a farmer, and rem'd with his father to Maine, about 1737, and settled in Windham, where he d. Dec. 10, 1826; md. 1st, Sarah Sawyer, who d. at Cape Elizabeth, 1774; md. 2d, wid. Elizabeth Webb, dau. of John and Elizabeth Mabery, of Marblehead, b. 1742, d. Sept. 9, 1827. Four ch. by Sarah:—
231. STEPHEN. 232. JOSIAH, b. Windham, 1769, drowned, 1794. 233. RICHARD⁶. 234. ABIGAIL.
Two ch. by Elizabeth:—
235. SARAH, b. Dec. 23, 1777, d. May 20, 1849; md. Dec. 31, 1795, James, son of James and Mary Fogg, b. at Scarboro, Me., June 17, 1769, d. at Windham, Aug. 21, 1825. Yeoman. Three ch:—Hannah, b. Feb. 4, 1797, d. July 29, 1856; Josiah, b. Mch. 6, 1799; Eliza, b. Sept. 18, 1802. 236. CHARITY⁶, b. Nov. 20, 1784. Lives in Windham, Md., June 1801, Silas, son of James and Mary Fogg, b. at Scarboro, Feb. 22, 1781, d. Apr. 6, 1833. Five ch:—James, b. Dec. 27, 1805; Abigail, b. Feb. 22, 1808; Eliza, b. Jan. 29, 1810; Stephen, b. Oct. 8, 1813; Lydia, b. June 14, 1814.

(114) RICHARD, son of STEPHEN (51), b. ——, Maine; rem'd to Windham, thence to Raymond, where in 1780-1, he was killed by the falling of a tree upon him. Yeoman. Md. Nancy Westcott. Two ch:—
237. DANIEL⁶. 238. JOHN, b. at Windham, 1775, drowned at Hebron, Me., May, 1803.

(118) JOSEPH, Rev., son of STEPHEN (51), b. 1755; rem'd to Windham, thence, about 1794, to Hebron, where he d., Feb., 1800. He was a soldier in the Revolution, and was present at the defeat and capture of Gen. Burgoyne. A few years after his marriage he was ordained to the ministry, and became widely known and distinguished as a travelling preacher; he visited such places especially as were without a settled minister; and so earnest were his efforts in that direction, that his health became seriously enfeebled, and he was obliged to retire from his labors, a short time before his decease. He md., 1778, Rebecca, dau. of Joseph and Ann Legro, b. at Marblehead, Mass., Nov., 1759, d. Buckfield, Me., July, 1843. Eleven ch:—

239. JOSEPH⁶. 240. SAMUEL⁶. 241. ABIGAIL, b. Aug. 16, 1783,
d. 1787. 242. LYDIA, b. July, 1785; md. Nathaniel, son of Joshua and
Abigail Keene, b. at Pembroke, Mass., Mch., 1777. Lives at E. Hebron,
Me. Yeoman. Twelve ch:—Abigail, b. Aug. 8, 1803; Stephen, b.
July 22, 1805, d. Sept. 20, 1805; Rebecca, b. Sept. 18, 1807; Sarah, b.
Apr. 14, 1810; Nancy, b. Apr. 16, 1812, d. Sept. 14, 1812; Nathaniel, b.
Aug., 1814; Daniel H., b. Sept. 30, 1816; Joseph H., b. Oct. 27, 1818;
Isaac H., b. Aug. 27, 1820; Samuel H., b. Mch., 1824; Lydia, b. Jan.
22, 1827; Christopher Columbus T., b. Feb. 21, 1832.

243. STEPHEN⁶. 244. HENRY H⁶. 245. DANIEL⁶. 246. RE-
BECCA, b. Aug. 7, 1793, d. Buckfield, Aug., 1816. 247. BETSY, b. at
Hebron, July, 1795; md. Robert Martin. Four ch:—Hannah, Caroline, Ezekiel, Henry. 248. JOHN⁶. 249. BENJAMIN R., b. Nov., 1799,
d. Aug., 1802.

(132) JAMES, son of GEORGE (62), b. ———. He was a soldier
and patriot in the Revolutionary war, and enlisted, Apr. 8, 1775, under
Capt. Josiah Crosby, in Col. Reed's regiment. He was at the battle of
Bunker Hill, where he was mortally wounded, and d. June 24, 1775.
Adm. of his estate was granted his wid. Sarah, Sept. 27, 1775. Lived
at Lyndeboro. Md. Sarah ———. One ch:—
250. JAMES⁶.

(133) AMBROSE, son of GEORGE (62), b. at Wilton, N. H., Feb.
12, 1773; rem'd, 1802, to Williamstown, Vt., about 1807, to Roxbury,
Vt., thence to Brookfield, Vt., where he d. Aug. 28, 1836. Yeoman.
Md. June 6, 1799, Deborah, dau. of David and Mary Cram, b. at
Lyndeboro, N. H., July 22, 1776. Six ch:—
251. MARY B., b. at Wilton, June 18, 1800; md. 1st, July 28, 1825,
Samuel, son of Samuel and Mary Belcher, b. at Randolph, Mass., Oct.
10, 1786, d. at Roxbury, Vt., Aug. 5, 1830. Carpenter; no issue. Md.
2d, Feb. 19, 1833, George H., son of Nathaniel and Effie (Hutchinson
130) Tuttle, b. at Wilton, Jan. 22, 1805. Live in Wilton, N. H. Two
ch:—Mary C., b. Feb. 4, 1834; Nancy B., b. June 6, 1835.
252. MARTHA, b. Sept. 9, 1802, d. at Williamstown, 1802. 253.
SEWELL⁶. 254. LOIS, b. July 28, 1806; md. Samuel Stearns, of
Peterboro. 255. AMBROSE B⁶. 256. CAROLINE, b. June 21, 1812, d.
Sept. 7, 1813.

SIXTH GENERATION.

(138) ELISHA, son of JOSEPH (65), b. at Middleton, Mass., Dec.
6, 1751, d. at Milford, Oct. 12, 1800. He was a farmer, and as he
ceased to be taxed in 1779, it is supposed that he rem'd, about that
period, to Amherst, N. H., and settled on the banks of the Souhegan

River, in the N. W. part of the present town of Milford, which was set off from Amherst, and incorporated Jan. 11, 1794. He was one of the first settlers, the place then being but a howling wilderness, and the cry of wolves were frequently heard as they passed in close proximity to the rude settlement. Once a moose made his appearance, and Mr. Hutchinson giving the alarm to his neighbors, they grasped their guns, and with a merry shout, gave chase to the huge animal as he bounded away through the woods at lightning speed. It was a long and tiresome chase, and buoyed up by their elated spirits and the novelty of the affair, the animal was at last surrounded, and driven to narrow quarters, when he was quickly dispatched, carried home and equally divided among his pursuers. In addition to his own estate, he rec'd from his father by Will, already referred to, 74 acres joining westerly on his own bounds, being the same piece of upland bought of Richard Goldsmith, Jan. 26, 1742-3, and lying in Township, No. 3. He was one of the first to answer his country's call in the Revolution, and enrolled himself as a private in Capt. Jeremiah Page's Co. of militia, at Danvers, which engaged the British at Lexington, on the 19th of April. He was chosen Surveyor of Amherst, Mch. 12, 1787. He md. Nov. 10, 1772, Sarah, dau. of Amos and Mary Buxton, b. at Middleton, 1751, d. at Amherst, Feb. 5, 1828. Three ch : —

257. ANDREW[7].   258. JESSE[7].   259. SARAH; md. Wm. Marvell.

(140) JOSEPH. son of JOSEPH (65), b. at Middleton, Aug. 3, 1757, d. Dec. 7, 1807. He was a farmer. Lived in Middleton and succeeded to his father's homestead. The inventory of his estate at his dec., was valued at $3,409, including 121 acres of land. He md. 1st, Nov. 2, 1780, Hannah, dau. of Archelaus and Hannah Fuller, b. 1757; md. 2d, Rebecca, wid. of Jacob Goodale, of Middleton, and dau. of ——— Newhall. Four ch. by Hannah : —

260. ELIJAH[7].   261. JOSEPH[7].   262. ARCHELAUS[7].   263. LEVI[7].
Three ch. by Rebecca : —
264. REBECCA, b. Sept. 21, 1797, d. Aug. 27, 1821; md. Mch. 3, 1818, Amos King, 3d, of Peabody (formerly So. Danvers), b. Mch. 3, 1788. Lives in Peabody. Yeoman. One ch : — Rebecca Hutchinson, b. July 3, 1820; md. Samuel Hutchinson (614). 265. SALLY, b. Apr. 5, 1799, d. July 4, 1816. 266. BENJAMIN[7].

(148) JOSIAH, son of JOSIAH (68), bapt. at Middleton, Feb. 26, 1764, d. Dec. 1814. Lived in Middleton and succeeded to his father's estate. Yeoman. Md. Apr. 29, 1788, Elizabeth, dau. of Benjamin Peters, of Reading, Mass., b. 1766, d. June 17, 1852. Nine ch : —

267. RUFUS, d. 1837, at Fayal. 268. DAVID[7]. 269. ISRAEL[7].
270. HANNAH CHICKERING, b. Mch. 24, 1795; md. Dec. 31, 1817,

Joseph, son of Jonathan and Mary Neal, b. at Salem, Dec. 31, 1793, d. Sept., 1866. He was a descendant of John Neal, of Salem; admitted freeman, May 18, 1642. Mason, and lived in Salem. Ten ch:—Hannah, b. Sept. 7, 1818; Elizabeth H., b. July 21, 1820; Sarah H., b. Sept. 28, 1822, d. Nov. 20, 1823; Caroline A., b. May 10, 1824; Joseph W., b. Feb. 7, 1827; Rufus B., b. Mch. 9, 1829; Charles H., b. Nov. 2, 1831; George L., b. Jan. 8, 1834; Mary E., b. Nov. 12, 1836, d. Sept., 1867; James M., b. Oct. 19, 1839.

271. IRA[7]. 272. SARAH DEAN, b. Oct. 5, 1800; md. Sept. 28, 1824, Joseph, son of Aaron and Margaret Wallis, b. Sept. 25, 1802. Lives in Salem. Cabinet maker. Four ch:—Joseph, b. Oct. 24, 1825; Samuel, b. Oct. 28, 1827, d. July 6, 1833; John Peirson, b. May 25, 1832; Caddie Matilda, b. Aug. 14, 1840. 273. NAAMAH, b. July 5, 1803, d. Nov. 13, 1868; md. July 23, 1835, David Peirce, b. Jan. 23, 1800. Lives in Peabody. Morocco Dresser. Six ch:—Eunice Pope, b. Jan. 12, 1836; Charles Page, b. June 25, 1837, d. July 13, 1837; Charles Page, b. July 16, 1838; David Hutchinson, b. Mch. 17, 1840; Michael Shepard, b. June 23, 1845; Samuel Wallis, b. Aug. 14, 1847. 274. ELIZA, b. Dec. 5, 1805; md. Feb. 15, 1834. Four ch:—George Warren, b. July 12, 1828; Emma, b. Feb. 9, 1830; Frederick Augustus, b. Feb. 1, 1832; Matilda Shepard, b. Jan. 4, 1834. 275. JOSIAH, b. Oct., 1813.

(154) JOHN, son of JOHN (72), b. at Middleton, Apr. 25, 1767, d. July 10, 1850; rem'd to Danvers. Yeoman. Md. Mch. 31, 1795, Patty Holt, of Andover, b. July 25, 1777. Nine ch:—

276. PERLEY, b. May 19, 1795. 277. SALLY, b. Aug. 19, 1797; md. Apr. 27, 1828, Saus Standley, of Marblehead, b. Oct. 15, 1804. Three ch:—Samuel A., b. June 2, 1829; Robert B., b. Feb. 21, 1831; Sarah J., b. Jan. 18, 1836.

278. LYDIA, b. Jan. 27, 1799, d. Dec. 15, 1844; md. May 1, 1818, James Crowell, of Danvers, b. Nov. 12, 1799. Twelve ch:—Harriet, b. Sept. 24, 1818; Elizabeth, b. Aug., 1822, d. May 10, 1823; Louisa, b. Aug. 10, 1824; James, b. June 18, 1826; Henry, b. Mch. 22, 1828, d. May 27, 1850; Augustus, b. Mch. 11, 1830, d. Feb. 8, 1853; Eliza, b. Feb. 25, 1832, d. Oct. 11, 1833; Sarah Ann, b. Dec. 21, 1833; George, b. Dec. 7, 1835; Hannah, b. Jan. 12, 1838; Benjamin, b. Mch. 31, 1840, d. Aug. 5, 1841; Benjamin, b. Feb. 21, 1842.

279. WILLIAM[7]. 280. ELI, b. Oct. 27, 1806. 281. MARY HOLT, b. May 23, 1809; md. 1st, Apr. 13, 1828, Frederick Dale, son of Ebenezer and Hannah (Very), b. Mch. 13, 1808, d. Dec. 2, 1833; md. 2d, Oct. 23, 1836, David R. Howard, son of Benjamin F. and Mary (Martin), b. May 17, 1814. Three ch. by Frederick:—Mary Ann, b. Oct. 11, 1829; Martha Jane, b. Nov. 12, 1831; a son b. at Middleton, d. at Danvers, June 4, 1833. One ch. by David R:—Nancy Ellen, b. May 22, 1837.

282. EBENEZER, b. Sept. 19, 1814. 283. NANCY, b. June 2, 1816. 284. JACOB.

(156) JESSE, son of JOHN (72), b. at Middleton, Feb. 4, 1779; rem'd to Danvers, where he d. July 10, 1853. Carpenter. He md. May 24, 1804, Mehitable, dau. of Ephraim and Mehitable Lacy, b. May 25, 1784. Twelve ch:—
285. INFANT, b. May 18, 1806, d. May 22, 1806. 286. JEREMIAH L., b. Nov. 2, 1807, d. Feb. 23, 1848. 287. CLARISSA, b. Dec. 16, 1809; md. Mch. 20, 1832, Cornelius M. Roundy, of Boston, b. May 1, 1808. Lives in Danvers. Two ch:—George, b. Nov. 10, 1833; Alfred R., b. June 28, 1837. 288. INFANT, b. Dec. 23, 1811, d. Dec. 30, 1811. 289. IN-FANT, b. Jan. 25, 1813, d. Mch. 26, 1813.
290. KIMBALL[7]. 291. OSGOOD[7]. 292. MEHITABLE, b. Jan. 18, 1819; md. Nov. 13, 1838. Josiah, son of Jacob and Mary Welch, b. Sept. 29, 1814. Two'ch:—George Thomas, b. May 1, 1840; Albert, b. Apr. 7, 1849. 293. EPHRAIM, b. Jan. 27, 1821, d. Apr. 15, 1832. 294. BETSY FARNUM, b. Mch. 23, 1823, d. Dec. 3, 1842. 295. ANDREW, b. May 18, 1826, d. Sept. 7, 1830. 296. ANDREW, b. June 28, 1830, d. Aug. 9, 1834.

(157) SOLOMON, son of SOLOMON (73), b. at Salem Vill., Nov. 10, 1750; rem'd with his father to Amherst, in 1758, and thence to Fayette, Me., where he d. about 1821. He was at one time Town Clerk at Amherst. Yeoman. Md. Susan Riddle, of Bedford, N. H. Five ch:—
297. SUSAN. 298. SAMUEL. 299. DAVID. 300. SOLOMON. 301. HANNAH.

(158) EBENEZER, son of SOLOMON (73), b. at Danvers, Mch. 22, 1753. He went to Amherst with his father, in 1758, and thence to N. Paris, Me., where he erected saw mills on the Little Androscoggin River, and engaged in the lumber business till about 1812, when he sold his mills, and removed with his family to Ohio, where he d. about 1828. He md. —— Littlefield. Nine ch:—
302. POLLY. 303. EBENEZER. 304. ABRAHAM. 305. SOLOMON. 306. NATHANIEL. 307. ASA. 308. JOHN. 309. ROBERT. 310. HAN-NAH.

(159) ASA, son of SOLOMON (73), b. at Amherst, Nov. 17, 1759. He was a farmer, and rem'a to Fayette, Me., Feb., 1799, where he d. June 27, 1848. Md. July, 1784, Eunice, dau. of Andrew Davis, b. at Amherst. May, 1764, d. at Fayette, Mch. 30, 1855. Ten ch:—
311. EUNICE, b. Oct. 16, 1785; md. Apr. 2, 1809, Daniel W., son of

Moses and Lydia Whittier, b. at Raymond, N. H., Sept. 9, 1783. Resides in S. Chesterville, Me. Yeoman; no issue. 312. MARY, b. Nov. 13, 1786, d. at Winthrop, Me., Apr., 1839. 313. ASA. 314. HITTIE, b. Oct. 16, 1789, d. at Madrid, Me, Feb., 1849; md. 1810, John, son of William and Martha Hankerson, of Madrid, b. at Readfield, Sept. 10, 1774, d. at Madrid, Sept., 1861. Yeoman. Five ch:—William, b. Dec. 18, 1810; Asa, b. Sept. 20, 1813; John, b. Feb., 1817; Hiram, b. Sept., 1820, d. 1824; Myrinda, b. Sept. 23, 1824. 315. DANIEL, b. Dec. 17, 1791; rem'd to Fayette with his father, thence to Winthrop, Me., where he d. Oct., 1833. Yeomen. Md. Achsah Higgins; no issue. 316. LUTHER, d. at Fayette, Dec., 1815.

317. JOSEPH[7]. 318. SARAH, b. at Fayette, July 16, 1800; md. Nov. 25, 1828, Comfort, son of Thomas and Elizabeth Smith, b. at Readfield, Me., Sept. 20, 1800. Lives in Troy, Me. Yeoman. Four ch:— George, b. Nov. 23, 1830; Octavie, b. Mch. 4, 1833; John, b. Nov. 16, 1835; Jane, b. June 1, 1841. 319. FANNY, b. May 29, 1803, d. at Winthrop, 1803. 320. HIRAM[7].

(162) DANIEL, son of ROBERT (77), b. at Danvers, May 22, 1768, d. Nov. 6, 1844. Lived in Danvers and Greenfield, N. H. Yeoman. Md. Aug. 19, 1790, Ruth, dau. of Richard and Lydia Whittridge, b. Sept. 22, 1771, d. Nov. 8, 1843. Seven ch:—

321. NANCY, b. Nov., 1791, d. at Nashua, Oct. 16, 1854; md. Jan. 26, 1819, Amos, son of Benjamin and Mary Ball, b. at Hancock, N. H., Sept. 19, 1795. Lives in Nashua. Carpenter. Five ch:—Francis Newton, b. Nov. 9, 1820; William Horace, b. Jan. 19, 1823; Susan Mariah, b. Jan. 23, 1825; Alfred Augustus, b. Jan. 9, 1829, d. Dec. 19, 1830; Alfred A., b. May 7, 1831. 322. EUNICE, b. Feb., 1797, d. at Jaffrey, N. H., Nov. 6, 1828; md. Feb. 20, 1823, Joseph, son of Joseph and Elizabeth Hodge, b. at Jaffrey, Nov. 9, 1786. Lives in Jaffrey. Two ch:—William Harvey, b. at Hancock, N. H., Aug. 4, 1824; Joseph Jackson, b. at Jaffrey, Feb. 11, 1828.

323. WILLIAM[7]. 324. MARY[7], b. at Greenfield, N. H., Apr. 24, 1808; md. June 20, 1832, Robert Putnam, son of Asa and Eda (Hutchinson, 163), b. June 20, 1806. Lives in Danvers. Shoemaker. Four ch:—Eunice, b. at Groton, N. H., Oct. 8, 1832; William, b. at Danvers, Apr. 14, 1837; Elmira, b. July 15, 1840; Robert, b. Aug. 18, 1848, d. same day. 325. BETSEY, b. Dec. 11, 1811, d. Oct. 14, 1834. 326. JAMES LAWRENCE, b. at Danvers, July 7, 1813. 327. JOSEPH, d. young, aged 11 years.

(166) ABIJAH, son of ROBERT (77), b. at Danvers, Nov. 28, 1774, d. Jan. 3, 1861. Lived in Danvers. Yeoman. Md. Mch. 18, 1800, Irene, dau. of Robert Badger, b. Lyndeboro, N. H., Jan. 20, 1780, d. Mch. 30, 1864. Ten ch:—

328. ELIZA, b. Oct. 25, 1800, d. Nov. 6, 1845; md. Archelaus Hutchinson (262). 329. REBECCA, b. Mch. 19, 1803, d. May 6, 1846; md. Dec. 24, 1834, George W. Priest. Two ch:—George F., b. June 8, 1838; Rebecca F., b. Mch. 29, 1843; 330. RUTH, b. July 26, 1805, d. June 10, 1814. 331. ELIAS, b. Aug. 2, 1806. 332. IRENE, b. Nov. 28, 1810, d. at Lowell, Sept. 22, 1832. 333. EUNICE, b. May 4, 1813. 334. EDITH, b. Oct. 26, 1816, d. Nov. 24, 1868. 335. RUTH, b. Apr. 10, 1819.

336. BENJAMIN F[7]. 337. LUCINDA[7], b. Apr. 21, 1824; md. July 23, 1854, Lewis, son of Darius and Mary (Keyser) Dickerson, b. Feb. 25, 1816. Lives in Ipswich. Farmer and Shoemaker. One ch:—John Lewis, b. July 24, 1855.

(172) EBENEZER[7], son of JEREMY (78), b. at Danvers, July 10, 1764, d. at Danville, Vt., Aug. 25, 1849; rem'd thence, Feb. 19, 1801, about fifteen years after its first settlement, and when the town was a wilderness, and infested with wild beasts. His farm consisted at first of fifty acres; afterwards he added fifty more, living for some length of time in the most primitive style. About 1801-2, rem'd to Gilmanton, N. H., and then six years after to Barnston, Canada, residing there till 1810, when he returned to Danville. Yeoman. Md. June 4, 1792, Anna Caves, of Danvers, b. at Chebacco, Apr. 14, 1760, d. Oct. 27, 1842. Three ch:—

338. PERLEY[7]. 339. JEREMY, b. at Danvers, Mch. 30, 1795; rem'd to Danville, Vt., where he now resides. Md. Sept. 4, 1849, Eunice Huse, b. at Enfield, N. H., Feb. 25, 1800; no issue. 340. SARAH H., b. Mch. 4, 1800; md. Dec. 19, 1838, Hiram Merritt, b. at Derby, Vt., May 23, 1799, d. Oct. 1, 1853. Lived in Danville; no issue. She md. 2d, Jan. 4, 1864, John Drew, b. at Pittsfield, N. H., Feb. 17, 1799. Yeoman.

(176) JOSEPH, son of JEREMY (79), b. at Danvers, Apr. 9, 1770, d. Jan. 1, 1832. He was a farmer and lived in Danvers. Md. Feb. 9, 1806, Phebe, dau. of George Upton, of N. Reading, b. Mch. 2, 1777, d. Jan. 27, 1861. Five ch:—

341. ELIJAH[7]. 342. BENJAMIN, b. at Danvers, Feb. 28, 1810. He is a farmer and lives in Danvers. Md. Jan. 26, 1838, Catherine Elizabeth Fuller, dau. of John and Anna (Symonds), b. at Middleton, Aug. 15, 1816, d. Feb. 7, 1863; no issue.

343. JEREMY, b. Aug. 12, 1813, d. Sept. 4, 1815. 344. AMOS, b. Nov. 15, 1814, d. Mch. 13, 1818. 345. AMOS, b. Apr. 2, 1818, d. Jan. 27, 1831.

(179) ASA, son of JEREMY (79), b. at Danvers, Mch. 4, 1777, d.

May 11, 1854. Lived in Danvers. Yeoman. Md. Jan. 23, 1814, Ruth Putnam, b. Mch. 25, 1786. Five ch:—

346. EBEN, b. Oct. 15, 1814. 347. JAMES PUTNAM, b. Dec. 15, 1816. Lives in Danvers. Shoe Manufacturer. Md. Dec. 4, 1854, Jerusha W. Dale, b. Dec. 29, 1826. 348. HANNAH, b. Apr. 17, 1820. 349. MARY POPE, b. June 26, 1823; md. June 17, 1856, James A., son of James A. S. and Betsy F. Bartlett. One ch:—Mary Putnam, b. June 18, 1857. 350. SARAH, b. Oct. 3, 1828.

(184) ISRAEL, son of ISRAEL (80), b. at Danvers, Sept. 27, 1760, and lived in that part of the town called the Port. He was a farmer, and also carried on the grist mills after his father's decease. He md. 1st, Dec. 15, 1785, Susannah, dau. of William and Abigail Trask, b. at Beverly, Nov. 22, 1766, d. Dec. 5, 1794; md. 2d, July 18, 1795, Eunice Putnam, b. at Danvers, Jan. 3, 1766, d. Mch. 20, 1817; md. 3d, Aug., 1820, at Newton, to Abigail French, of Portsmouth, N. H., d. at Roxbury, Dec., 1832. Four ch. by Susannah:—

351. HANNAH, b. Oct. 3, 1786, d. Apr. 9, 1857; md. July 5, 1807, Nicholson, son of Zebulon and Jerusha Marcy. He was first a storekeeper and afterwards a farmer. Nine ch:—William N., b. Apr. 16, 1808, d. June 23, 1808; Zebulon C., b. May 2, 1809; Susan T., b. May 22, 1811; Albert N., b. Nov. 3, 1813; Israel H., b. Nov. 17, 1815; Porter; Olive P., b. Feb. 2, 1818; Harriet, b. Nov. 29, 1819; Eunice.

352. SUSANNAH, b. Sept. 1, 1789, d. Nov. 20, 1845. 353. BETSY[7], b. Jan. 14, 1791, d. Mch. 31, 1850; md. May 21, 1809, Briggs R. Reed, son of Ezekiel and Mary (Rogers), b. at Bridgeport, Conn., May 2, 1784, d. at Danvers, Sept. 28, 1835. Resided in Boston, Weymouth, Pembroke, and Danvers. The father of Mr. Reed was inventor of a patent for making tacks, at Abington, Mass. Eleven ch:—Mary Ann, b. at Boston, Jan. 1, 1810; Elizabeth, b. at Weymouth, Dec. 17, 1811; Susan J., b. at Pembroke, May 11, 1814; William Briggs, b. at Danvers, Dec. 15, 1816; Edward R., b. Mch. 14, 1819, d. at Topsfield, Nov. 5, 1838; Augustus, b. Apr. 13, 1821; George W., b. Aug. 5, 1823; John, b. Aug. 13, 1825, d. Apr. 4, 1847; James H., b. Jan. 28, 1828; Joseph W., b. May 7, 1830, d. July 27, 1856. His death was caused by the explosion of a boiler on board the steamer "Empire State," at Fall River. Baptist Clergyman. Cornelius H., b. Aug. 28, 1832. 354. ISRAEL, b. Apr. 3, 1794, d. Nov. 5, 1815.

Four ch. by Eunice:—

355. MEHITABLE P., b. July 22, 1796, d. Oct. 22, 1796. 356. EUNICE, b. Dec. 19, 1797, d. Mch. 11, 1866; md. May 3, 1839, Capt. John, son of John and Rachel Kenney, b. at Danvers, Nov. 26, 1807, d. ———. Lived in Gloucester. Mariner; no issue. Have an adopted ch., Susan Putnam Davenport, dau. of her sister, Mehitable P. (358).

357. ELISHA[7]. 358. MEHITABLE PUTNAM, b. Apr. 23, 1805, d. Apr. 22, 1837; md. Sept. 9, 1830, Daniel Davenport, of Andover. One ch: —Susan Putnam, b. June 21, 1831; adopted by her aunt, Eunice (356).

(188) SAMUEL, son of NATHAN (90), b. at Amherst, N. H., 1749. He was a farmer, and rem'd to Wilton, N. H., where he d. Sept. 27, 1821. He md. about 1773, Mary Wilkins, b. 1752, d. June 29, 1841, aged 89 years. Nine ch:—
359. SAMUEL[7]. 360. MARY[7], b. at Wilton, Sept. 18, 1777, d. Sept. 18, 1838; md. —— Dea. Joshua, son of Joshua and Elizabeth (Keyes) Blanchard, b. at Wilton, July 10, 1771, d. July 23, 1810. Yeoman. Four ch:—Abel, b. Oct. 10, 1802; Lydia, b. July 9, 1805, d. Nov. 8, 1821; Ezra, b. Aug. 25, 1808, d. Sept. 8, 1851; Joshua, b. June 29, 1810. 361. RACHEL, b. June 3, 1779, d. Dec. 20, 1865; md. Mch. 17, 1803, David Lovejoy, son of Samuel and Lydia (Abbot), b. at Wilton, July 16, 1779, d. May 22, 1833. Lived in Wilton. Yeoman. Ten ch:—Lydia, b. Dec. 30, 1803, d. Jan. 10, 1844; Samuel, b. Feb. 20, 1806, d. July 26, 1844; Mary, b. June 21, 1808; Abiel, b. May 25, 1810; William, b. Mch. 3, 1814; Isaac, b. June 29, 1816; Clarissa, b. Sept. 10, 1818, d. Dec. 27, 1853; David, b. Mch. 1, 1821; Rachel, b. Apr. 9, 1823; Sarah, b. Aug. 4, 1826, d. Nov. 3, 1854.
362. JOTHAM[7]. 363. FREDERICK[7]. 364. BETSY, b. July 31, 1785; md. Mch., 1808, Richard, son of Pierce and Eunice Gage, b. at Pelham, N. H., Mch. 20, 1784, d. July 17, 1854. Lived in Wilton. Yeoman. Nine ch:—David, b. Dec. 1, 1809; Samuel, b. Sept. 6, 1811, d. Apr. 21, 1851; Pierce, b. Sept. 4, 1813; Isaac N., b. June 12, 1815; Mary, b. June 1, 1817; Elvira, b. July 11, 1819; Charles, b. July 16, 1821, d. June 24, 1856; George W., b. Sept. 7, 1823; Sidney R., b. Oct. 14, 1826.
365. ABIEL[7]. 366. SOLOMON[7]. 367. FANNY, b. May 5, 1790; md. June 12, 1811, Putnam Wilson, son of Abiel and Abigail (Putnam), b. at Lyndeboro, Oct. 9, 1795. Resides at Newport, Me.; rem'd thence from Wilton, Oct., 1826. Farmer and Lumberman. His father, Abiel, was b. at Andover, Mass., and served seven years in the Revolution, and rem'd afterwards to Lyndeboro. He md. Abigail, dau. of Philip Putnam, Esq., of Wilton. Ten ch:—Abiel, b. Sept. 27, 1812; Harriet, b. Dec. 6, 1814; Putnam, b. Oct. 26, 1816; Philip, b. Sept. 10, 1818; George, b. Sept. 26, 1820; Lydia, b. Aug. 8, 1823, d. Dec. 12, 1838; Fanny, b. Jan. 3, 1825; Joseph, b. at Newport, Jan. 18, 1827, d. Oct. 13, 1838; Charles Edwin, b. May 16, 1829; Hollis B., b. Nov. 21, 1832.

(189) NATHAN, son of NATHAN (90), b. in that part of Amherst, now Milford, Feb., 1752, d. Dec. 26, 1831. He was a farmer and lived

in Milford. Md. 1778, Rebecca Peabody, dau. of William and Rebecca (Smith), b. Jan. 2, 1752, d. Feb. 25, 1826. Seven ch:—

368. NATHAN[7]. 369. REBECCA S., b. Oct., 1781, d. at Maryland, Sept. 9, 1850; md. Nehemiah Hayward, b. 1779, d. May 16, 1849, aged 70. Two ch:—George M., b. 1809, d. Apr. 7, 1840; Betsy, b. Mch. 19, 1807; md. David Hutchinson (589).

370. REUBEN[7]. 371. IRA, b. 1785, d. Jan. 5, 1833, unm'd. 372. OLIVE, b. 1789, d. Apr. 16, 1828; md. ——, 1809, Dr. John, son of John and Mary Wallace, b. at Milford, 1781, d. Aug. 4, 1837. One ch:—Robert Burns, b. Oct. 7, 1810. Dr. Wallace md. 2d, Sept. 15, 1829, Eliza, dau. of Moses and Betsy Burns, b. 1807. One ch:—John James, b. 1830. Lives at Union Co., Ohio. She md. 2d, Joseph Davis, of Hancock, N. H.

373. JONAS[7]. 374. ABEL[7].

(190) BENJAMIN, Lieut., son of NATHAN (90), b. at Amherst, June 9, 1744, d. at Milford, Sept. 12, 1832. Lived in Milford. Yeoman. Md. —— Susanna, dau. of William and Rebecca (Smith) Peabody, b. at Amherst, Nov. 4, 1755, d. Aug. 23, 1834. Six ch:—

375. BENJAMIN[7]. 376. SARAH, b. Mch. 16, 1779, d. Nov. 9, 1865; unm'd. She was a woman endowed with superior faculties of mind, a very retentive memory, and to whom the compiler is indebted for much valuable information connected with this work. 377 SUSAN, b. Apr. 20, 1781, d. Aug. 2, 1783. 378. LUTHER[7]. 379. EUGENE[7]. 380. CALAOPE, b. Apr. 7, 1787, d. Sept. 25, 1848.

(191) EBENEZER, son of NATHAN (90), b. at Amherst, Sept. 10, 1756, d. Jan. 31, 1831. Lived in E. Wilton. Yeoman. Md. Feb. 3, 1780, Phebe, dau. of Hezekiah and Margaret Sawtell, b. at Shirley, Dec. 11, 1759, d. Apr. 5, 1835. Ten ch:—

381. EBENEZER[7]. 382. PHEBE[7], b. at E. Wilton, June 21, 1782, d. Oct. 11, 1824; md. her cousin, Jotham Hutchinson (363). 383. JOHN[7]. 384. HEZEKIAH[7]. 385. SYLVESTER[7]. 386. SYLVANUS[7]. 387. ASENATH, b. Aug. 16, 1793, d. Feb. 5, 1826. 388. JAMES[7].

389. STEARNS[7]. 390. PEGGY, b. Nov. 4, 1802; md. Apr. 6, 1819, Benjamin, son of Peter and Hannah (Burnam) Hopkins, b. at E. Wilton, Oct. 15, 1797. Lives in E. Wilton. Farmer and Miller. Four ch:—Benjamin, b. Nov. 12, 1820; Herman, b. Aug. 6, 1825; Phebe, b. Nov. 15, 1829; William, b. Aug. 30, 1838.

(192) BARTHOLOMEW, son of NATHAN (90), b. at Amherst, 1758, d. Sept. 23, 1841. Lived in Milford. Yeoman. Md. Oct. 14, 1784, Phebe, dau. of Jacob Haggett, of Andover, Mass., bapt. May 10, 1767, d. Aug. 27, 1849. Thirteen ch:—

391. JACOB[7]. 392. Lucy, b. Dec. 20, 1786; md. Reuben Hutchinson (370). 393. ALFRED[7].

394. Acтacy, b. Nov. 6, 1790, d. Oct. 20, 1852; md. Mch., 1808, Jona. Buxton, b. Mch. 18, 1787, d. Sept. 16, 1844. Lived in Milford. Twelve ch:—Mara Ann, b. Nov. 16, 1808; Annette M., b. July 16, 1810; Achacy, b. July 22, 1813, d. Jan. 2, 1850; George, b. Sept. 21, 1815; Caroline, b. Oct. 20, 1817; William, b. Oct. 1, 1819; Jonathan, b. Aug. 4, 1821, d. Mch. 25, 1844; Rhoda H., b. June 24, 1823; Charles, b. Oct. 11. 1825, d. Nov. 6, 1848; James, b. July 25, 1828; Henry Clay, b. June 17, 1830. d. Feb. 19, 1831; Henry Clay, b. Nov. 29, 1832.

395. Minerva. b. Jan. 31, 1792. d. June 14, 1831; md. 1808, Samuel Henry, b. at Milford, 1786, d. about 1828. Two ch:—Christiana, b. Mch. 25, 1810, d. Feb. 4. 1829; George W.. b. Aug. 20, 1812. 396. Nancy, b. May 19, 1794, d. Oct. 11, 1821; md. 1820, Luther Jones, b. Dec. 13, 1796. He was son of Luther Hoar, of Worcester. After the decease of his parents he was. while an infant, adopted into the family of Jona. Jones, and assumed their name. Yeoman. One ch:—Nancy, b. Dec. 2, 1820.

397. Augustus, b. July 25, 1796, d. 1800. 398. Rnoda, b. July 2; 1798, d. Mch. 20, 1822. 399. Alvan, b. Jan. 25, 1800, d. July 6, 1826; 400. Myra, b. Dec. 24, 1801, d. Dec. 3, 1837; md. Oct. 19, 1823, Dr. William Darracott, jr., b. June 22, 1799. Lives in Milford. Dentist. Five ch:—Samuel. b. Feb. 12, 1825, d. Feb. 16, 1825; William, b. Dec. 8, 1826, d. June 5. 1852; Christiana Henry, b. Jan. 31, 1829, d. Dec. 13, 1853; George Lafayette, b. July 17, 1831; Albert M., b. Aug. 7, 1834.

401. Eliza, b. Oct. 4, 1803; md. Feb. 3, 1823, Holland Hopkins, b. Apr. 4, 1802, d. at Illinois, Nov. 17, 1857. Lived in Milford. Seven ch:—Henry A., b. May 9, 1824, d. June 8, 1831; Harriet E., b. July 30, 1826, d. Oct. 30, 1854; John H., b. Feb. 7, 1832, d. Feb. 22, 1853; Jane M., b. Feb. 25, 1835; Frye, b. April 23, 1839; James B., b. Jan. 31, 1845, d. Dec. 29, 1852; Ellen J., b. June 6, 1846.

402. AUGUSTUS[7]. 403. Albert S., b. Dec. 8, 1807, d. Aug. 20, 1834.

(200) NATHANIEL, son of BARTHOLOMEW (101), b. at Sutton, Mass., Apr. 13, 1764. He was a farmer, and rem'd to Braintree, Vt., in 1785, where he d. Aug. 3, 1794. He was one of the first settlers of that town, and his wife's mother-in-law, Abigail, "was the first female that moved into Braintree, and, in consideration of that circumstance, the town voted to her, Sept. 16, 1788, a grant of 100 acres of land." (Gen. of Flint family.) Md. 1786, Lucy, dau. of Silas and Sarah (Norton) Flint, b. at Windham, Conn., Aug. 21, 1762, d. ———. Four ch : —

404. NATHANIEL[7]. 405. LUCY, b. 1790, d. Apr., 1794. 406. IN-FANT, b. and d. 1792. 407. INFANT, b. and d. 1794.

(201) JOHN, son of BARTHOLOMEW (101), b. at Sutton, Jan. 18, 1766. He was a farmer, and rem'd to Braintree, Vt., in the fall of 1793, where he d. May 29, 1845. He was a man of more than ordinary abilities and was chosen seventeen times to the Vermont Legislature. Md. Feb., 1792, Lucy, dau. of Asa and Mehitable Kenney, b. at Sutton, Sept. 23, 1771, d. Nov. 2, 1868. Nine ch : —

408. RUFUS[7]. 409. POLLY, b. at Braintree, Vt., Mar. 24, 1795, d. July 4, 1845; md. Sept., 1814, Nathan Morse, b. Nov. 3, 1791. Four ch :—Nathan, b. June 30, 1816, d. Jan. 18, 1832; Polly, b. Jan., 1818, d. Apr. 12, 1849; Betsey, b. Jan., 1820; Lucy, b. Nov. 3, 1825, d. Jan. 18, 1832. 410. JAMES[7].

411. SALLY, b. Aug. 19, 1799, d. Northfield, Vt., May 18, 1853; md. Dec. 5, 1823, Amersa Nichols, b. July 10, 1791, d. Mch. 28, 1835. Lived in Northfield, Vt. Yeoman. Three ch :—Amersa, b. June 27, 1825, d. Sept. 2, 1826; Sarah, b. Jan. 17, 1828, d. Jan. 27, 1832; George A., b. Aug. 9, 1834.

412. BETSEY, b. Dec. 2, 1801, d. Aug. 4, 1848; md. June 10, 1836, Warren Harlow, b. Feb. 28, 1805. Lived in Randolph, Vt. Yeoman. Four ch :—Elizabeth M., b. Sept. 3, 1837, d. July, 1843; Celia, b. Jan. 11, 1845; Alvin and Alonzo, twins, b. Aug. 4, 1847.

413. KELITA, b. Mch. 6, 1804; md. ——— Isaac Allen, b. July 29, 1788. Lived in Braintree, Vt. Yeoman; no issue. 414. LUCY, b. Feb. 1, 1806; md. Dec. 29, 1829, Alvin Braley, b. Nov., 1807. Yeoman. Three ch :—George, b. Oct. 8, 1832, d. Dec., 1833; George, b. Apr. 2, 1835; Lucy, b. Apr. 2, 1847. 415. JOHN, b. Mch. 19, 1808, d. July 26, 1816. 416. RUTH, b. May 8, 1813; md. Jan. 5, 1837, Cassim B. Hawes, b. Feb. 18, 1812. Lives in Randolph, Wis. Yeoman. Three ch :—Alban, b. Jan. 5, 1838; Marion L., b., Jan. 11, 1840; Celia E., b. Aug. 26, 1841.

(203) BARTHOLOMEW, son of BARTHOLOMEW (101), b. at Sutton, Mass., Jan. 7, 1770. Farmer and Carpenter; rem'd to Dixfield, Me., Feb., 1800, where he d. Feb. 14, 1855. He md. Jan., 1797, Olive Kenney, dau. of Stephen and Mary (Bartlett), b. at Sutton, Mch. 20, 1777, d. Dec. 6, 1847. Seven ch : —

417. FANNY F., b. July 13, 1797; md. Sept. 12, 1814, Thomas Morse, son of Nathan and Abigail (Staples), b. July 26, 1794. Resides in E. Dixfield. Yeoman. Eight ch :—B. Franklin, b. Apr. 5, 1816; Abigail S., b. Feb. 14, 1818; Russell S., b. Jan. 17, 1820; W. Harris, b. Sept. 29, 1822; Gilbert A., b. Oct. 10, 1824; Sylvester H., b. Feb. 10, 1828; Olive H., b. Mch. 20, 1830; Bartholomew H., b. June 1, 1832.

418, Susan, b. Dec. 29, 1798; md. May 28, 1818, Spencer Thomas, son of Holmes and Mary (Dingley), b. Mch. 31, 1787. He served five years in the war of 1812. and was wounded in the mouth at the battle of Lundy's Lane. He is a farmer. and lives in E. Dixfield. Ten ch: —Diantha J., b. Mch. 31, 1819; Spencer, b. Jan. 13, 1821; Nathaniel T., b. Nov. 29, 1823; Abbie II., b. Sept. 23, 1825; Rebecca M., b. Jan. 20, 1827, d. Dec. 16, 1829; Salome D.. b. Mch. 28, 1829; James M., b. Apr. 20, 1831; Ripley, b. Feb. 11, 1833. d. Oct. 1, 1848; Fanny H., b. Nov. 11, 1837; Sylvander M., b. Dec. 25, 1839.

419. Rebecca M.. b. at Dixfield, Aug. 29, 1800; md. Jan. 18, 1830, Ansel, son of Joseph and Patience (Joy) Staples, b. at Sanford, Me., May 4, 1795. Lives in Dixfield. Yeoman. Four ch:—Susan H., b. May 7, 1831; Hannibal H., b. Mch. 10, 1834; Ellen R., b. Nov. 18, 1837; Rebecca C., b. Sept. 22, 1842.

420. JAMES H[7]. 421. SYLVESTER M[7]. 422. Ruth B., b. May 19, 1816; md. Mch. 15, 1842, Sylvester S. Kidder, son of Jacob and Esther (Waite), b. June 13, 1818. Lives in E. Dixfield. Yeoman. Two ch:—Hialmer A., b. May 24, 1844; F. Linette, b. Aug. 22, 1850. 423. Horace L., b. Mch. 25, 1821.

(205) TIMOTHY, son of BARTHOLOMEW (101), b. at Sutton, July 31, 1774. He was a farmer, and rem'd 1st, to Paris, Me., and thence about 1818, to Albany, Me., where he d. Mch. 14, 1867, aged 93 years. Feb. 17, 1818, after he removed to Paris, he sold to his bro. Simon, for $85, all his right and title in the estate bequeathed to him by Dea. John Haven, situated in the W. part of the town of Sutton. In early life he fitted himself for a teacher, and for twenty years, during a portion of the year, he served in that capacity with much success. In Albany he was chosen for many years to offices of honor and trust; was an ardent supporter in the cause of temperance and all other moral reforms, besides leading a life of strict piety for over seventy years. He md. Mch., 1796, Nizaula, dau. of Ebenezer and Sarah (Chase) Rawson, a descendant of Secretary Rawson, b. at Sutton, Apr. 18, 1777. Fourteen ch:—

424. LEWIS[7]. 425. GALEN[7]. 426. Nizaula, b. Jan. 13, 1801, d. at Portland, Sept. 2, 1855; md. 1822, Herman, son of Samuel and Lydia Town, b. at Salem, Mass., Aug. 16, 1797. Lives in Albany. Yeoman. Two ch:—Arabella R., b. Dec. 7, 1824; Clara D., b. July 26, 1830. 427. MARMADUKE RAWSON[7]. 428. James Sullivan, b. Nov. ——, d. young. 429. Charlotte, b. May ——, d. young. 430. HAVEN[7]. 431. TIMOTHY HARDING[7].

432. Arvilla[7], b. Feb. 19, 1812; md. Jan. 29, 1837, William, son of Simeon and Mehitable Evans. b. at Shelburne, N. H., Jan. 21, 1812. Lives in Milan, N. H. Yeoman. Seven ch:—Edwin F., b. at Berlin,

N. H., Jan. 29, 1838; Caroline, b. at Milan, Aug. 17, 1839, d. Oct. 2, 1850; Virgil P. b. Oct. 29, 1841; Rawson H., b. Aug. 2, 1845; William S., b. June 27, 1847; Osmon C., b. Mch. 21, 1850; Clara Emily, b. Aug. 18, 1854. 433. CLARISSA, b. Feb. 8, 1813; md. June 20, 1833, William H., son of Samuel and Esther Pingree, b. at Norway, Me., Dec. 20, 1804. He is a farmer, and lives in Norway. Six ch:—Edwin F., b. at Albany, Me., July 14, 1834, d. Aug. 28, 1837; Harriet, b. Jan. 20, 1836, d. Sept. 8, 1837; Rosanna, b. at Norway, Feb. 25, 1838; Mary E., b. Apr. 2, 1840; Roena, b. Jan. 20, 1843; Caroline, b. May 4, 1852. 434. EDWIN F⁷. 435. MARY, b. Feb., 1816, d. Feb., 1843; md. Sept. 5, 1839, Dustin P., son of John and Hannah Ordway, b. at Conway, N. H. Lives in Milan, N. H. Yeoman. One ch:—Sumner H., b. Mch. 31, 1842. 436. DIANTHA, b. Oct. 12, 1819; md. June 8, 1841, Prescott, son of David and Abigail Lovering, b. at Poland, Me., Feb. 1, 1816. Residence at Greenwood, Me. Yeoman. Five ch:—Eliza, b. May 6, 1842, d. Nov. 12, 1842; Sabra Rawson, b. Feb. 8, 1845; Lewis H., b. Apr. 18, 1848; Francis Hill, b. Jan. 17, 1850; Dustin Ordway, b. June 5, 1851, d. Sept. 23, 1853. 437. EBENEZER SUMNER⁷.

(207) SIMON, son of BARTHOLOMEW (101), b. at Sutton, Apr. 26, 1779. Lives in Sutton, at an advanced age. He bought, Jan. 10, 1806, for $1,666.66, one-half of his father's lands, 160 acres, and buildings; the first piece containing 123 acres, being the homestead, with the buildings upon it. He md. 1st, Nov. 27, 1806, Vandalynda, dau. of Nathaniel F. and Hannah (Gibbs) Morse, b. at Sutton, Apr. 28, 1785, d. Aug. 18, 1839; md. 2d, Jan., 1841, Mrs. Sophia, wid. of Lewis Batchelder, and dau. of Abel and Loreno (Rice) Newton, b. at Southboro, Mass., July 20, 1800. Twelve ch:—

438. ALAXA ANN, b. Sept. 7, 1807; md. Nov. 1, 1830, Alanson A. Lombard, b. at Millbury, Mass., Jan. 25, 1803. Lives in Sutton. Three ch:—Frances Ann, b. Apr. 5, 1832, d. Apr. 29, 1837; Henry F., b. Jan. 19, 1834; Edwin, b. Dec. 22, 1837, d. May 6, 1838. 439. SYLVANDER, b. Mch. 7, 1809. Grad. Amherst Coll. in the class of 1836, and entered the Theological Seminary at Princeton, N. J., where, after remaining a short time, he was directed by his medical adviser to try a warm climate for the benefit of his health. He accordingly went to Athens, Ga., and engaged as a tutor in the College at that place; he however continued to decline, and d. June 15, 1838. 440. DEXTER, b. Mch. 14, 1811, d. July 24, 1813. 441. LUCY MORSE, b. Sept. 24, 1812; md. May 4, 1853, Jona. D. Holbrook, b. at Upton, Mass., Mch. 11, 1808; no issue. 442. CHARLES DEXTER⁷. 443. HORACE⁷. 444. HANNAH GIBBS, b. July 23, 1818, d. July 16, 1845. 445. BARTHOLOMEW, b. Sept. 3, 1820, d. Sept. 14, 1820. 446. EDWARD HAVEN⁷.

447. EMELINE BEMIS[7], b. July 23, 1823; ınd. Aug. 30, 1853, Amos Brown, b. at Charlton, Mass., Apr. 13, 1813. Two ch:—Clara Elizabeth, b. at Brooklyn, N. Y., July 9, 1854; Helen Herrick, b. July 2, 1856. 448. MARY LEE, b. Sept. 23, 1828, d. July.28, 1844. 449. MARGARET, b. Oct. 12, 1830, d. June 3, 1831.

(212) AARON, son of LOT (104), b. at Sutton, Oct. 1, 1771; rem'd early to Pembroke, western N. Y., and afterwards, Feb. 11, 1815, to Darien, N. Y., where he d. Feb. 12, 1836; also lived in Randolph and Williamstown, Vt. Yeoman. Md. Feb. 15, 1796, Hannah, dau. of Jacob and Mehitable (Flint) Parish, b. at Windham, Conn., May 21, 1779. After the dec. of her husband, Mrs. Hutchinson rem'd to Wauwatora, Wis., where she d. Dec. 13, 1863. Six ch:—
450. DANIEL PARISH[7]. 451. CHESTER FLINT[7]. 452. HANNAH M.[7], b. at Williamstown, Vt., May 19, 1809; md. June 14, 1827, Alexander L., son of John and Rachel Munroe, b. at Springfield, Mass., Dec. 2, 1799. Lives in Milwaukie. Four ch:—Emeline, b. at Darien, May 19, 1828; Marshal E., b. Feb. 18, 1830; John H., b. Dec. 5, 1833; Edward L., b. at Milwaukie, Dec. 4, 1844.
453. RODOLPHUS ALBINUS[7]. 454. AARON PARISH[7]. 455. HELENA M., b. at Randolph, Vt., May 15, 1814; md. Apr. 3, 1836, Sanford, son of Jacob and Hannah Wheeler, b. at Watertown, N. Y., Nov. 4, 1811. Lives in Rockland, Ill. Two ch:—Julia Rosilla, b. at Milwaukie, Dec. 27, 1841; Parish H., b. Feb. 26, 1846.

(213) ASA, son of LOT (104), b. at Sutton, Sept. 15, 1780. Farmer. Removed to Vt., and md. Mch. 3, 1808, Christiana Churchill, of Chittenden, and immediately rem'd to Shoreham, Vt. Lived in Shoreham, Braintree, Chittenden and Shrewsbury, Vt. Eight ch:—
456. ELECTA[7], b. at Shoreham, May 11, 1809, d. at Lyons, N. Y., Aug. 30, 1850; md. Jan. 1, 1835, Miles S., son of Jacob and Sarah Leach, b. at Lyons, Aug. 17, 1810. Lives in Lyons. Trader. Seven ch:—Rosabella, b. Oct. 3, 1835; Theodore A., b. Jan. 15, 1837, d. Feb. 5, 1855; Deborah E., b. Nov. 30, 1838, d. July 25, 1847; Gerald R., b. Dec. 21, 1840, d. Aug. 8, 1841; Sarah C., b. Oct. 22, 1842; John H., b. June 4, 1845; Esbon B., b. July 10, 1847. 457. PHILANCIA[7], b. Feb. 27, 1811; md. Apr. 22, 1835, Thadeus O. Warner, of Lyons, N. Y.; rem'd to Lyons, Mich. Seven ch:—Harriet A., b. at Lyons, Mich., Feb. 10, 1836; Frances H., b. June 11, 1837, d. Feb. 28, 1839; Martha F., b. Oct. 7, 1839; Lawson S., b. Oct. 7, 1841; Lucius C., b. Apr. 25, 1844; Emily E., b. Oct. 1, 1846; Electa M., b. Nov. 17, 1848.
458. ALZINA, b. July 16, 1813, d. May 23, 1827. 459. AARON, b. at Braintree, Sept. 6, 1816. 460. DRUCILLA, b. at Shrewsbury, Jan. 21, 1819. 461. ISRAEL, b. Mch. 10, 1822. 462. ELIZA ANN, b. at Chitten-

den, June 18, 1825, d. Jan. 25, 1826. 463. CHRISTIANA, b. at Shrewsbury, Oct. 28, 1826; md. Mch. 30, 1830, Thomas Rudgers, at Lyons,
Mich. One ch:—Nancy Lane, b. at Portland, Mich., Oct. 6, 1852.

(215) ABIATHER, son of LOT (104), b. at Sutton, ——, 1787;
rem'd to Braintree with his father, where he d. Mch. 17, 1844. House
joiner. Md. 1st, Susannah Hall; md. 2d, Polly Gleason; md. 3d,
Betsy Moses, or Mosier, b. at Gilmanton, N. H., Feb. 13, 1804, d. at
Braintree, Mch. 23, 1837; md. 4th, wid. Eunice Curtis. Lives in
Braintree. Four ch. by Susannah :—
464. ARMINA. 465. CALEB. 466. GEORGE. 457. BETSY; all d.
young. One ch. by Betsy :—
468. RUFUS M., b. at Braintree, Aug. 3, 1834. Lives in Calais, Vt.;
unm'd.

(217) BENJAMIN, son of BENJAMIN (105), b. at Royalston,
Mass., Apr. 18, 1773; rem'd to Waterford, Vt., about 1801, where
he d. Jan. 18, 1827. Yeoman. Md. ——, 1800, Nabby, dau. of Eli-
phalet Rogers, of Royalston, b. 1776, d. July 5, 1848, aged 72. Four
ch :—
469. FARWELL J⁷. 470. BENJAMIN⁷. 471. POLLY, b. at Waterford, 1805, d. young. 472. ABIGAIL⁷, b. Nov. 18, 1808; md. Jan. 6,
1831, Robert P., son of Samuel and Perces Porter, b. at Pomfret, Vt.,
Apr. 13, 1808. Lived in Charleston and Burke, Vt. Resides at present
in Waukau, Wis. Yeoman. Four ch:—Mary and Martha, twins, b.
at Charleston, Aug. 31, 1831; Lyman, b. Sept. 1, 1836, d. July 10, 1838;
Robert P., b. June 5, 1842.

(221) JOSHUA⁷, son of BENJAMIN (105), b. at Royalston, Mass.,
Apr. 13, 1782; rem'd to Sutton, where he d. Feb. 16, 1854. It is said
that he was a man of excellent christian character, an industrious and
hard working farmer; and that his wife was a woman of unusual
executive powers, skill and beauty, combined with a pure and chris-
tian-like deportment throughout life. Md. Jan. 6, 1822, Betsey, dau.
of Jona. and Lucy (Lilly) King, b. at Sutton, Feb. 22, 1801, d. Oct. 23,
1855. Three ch :—
473. ORVILLE K⁷. 474. OTIS K. A⁷.
475. ELIZABETH M., b. at Royalston, Aug. 23, 1835; md. Aug. 4,
1856, Admiral P., son of Simon J. and Mary B. Stone, b. at Piermont,
N. H., Aug. 14, 1820. Entered Dartmouth Coll., N. H., 1840. Sick-
ness compelled him to leave before his class grad. in 1844. Finished
his course by private study. He taught an Academy in Southbridge,
also in Millbury. Went to Plymouth, Apr., 1856, where he officiated
as Principal of the High School for several years, when he removed

to Portland, Me., and has present charge of the High School there. One ch:—Willie Carloss, b. at Plymouth, Oct. 9, 1859.

(224) DAVID, son of JONATHAN (106), b. at Royalston, Dec. 10, 1773; rem'd to Concord. Vt., about 1820, where he d. Aug. 4, 1828. Yeoman. Md. May 2, 1796, Olive, dau. of Jona. and Mary Ames, b. at Natick, Mass., Nov. 2, 1778, d. Mch., 1860. Twelve ch:—
476. Nancy, b. at Royalston, July 20, 1796, d. Jan. 16, 1868. 477. John, b. Dec. 23, 1797, d. Oct. 13, 1822. 478. Ruhama, b. July 17, 1801, d. Apr. 27, 1814. 479. Magdalena W., b. May 1, 1803. 480. Betsy, b. Mch. 27, 1805, d. Dec. 30, 1862; md. ——, John, son of Jedediah and Anna Smith, b. at Acworth, N. H., Aug. 1, 1791, d. Dec. 28, 1862. Lived in St. Johnsbury, Vt. Farmer; no issue.
481. JONATHAN A[7]. 482. TITUS[7]. 483. Mary Ann[7], b. Apr. 20, 1813, d. at Waterford, Vt., June 15, 1841; md. Jan. 15, 1840, Luther, son of Sylvanus and Elizabeth Hemmingway, b. at Waterford, Sept. 13, 1808. Yeoman. One ch:—An infant, buried with its mother. 484. Sally Ann[7], b. July 10, 1816; md. May 20, 1839, Solomon, son of Solomon and Betsy Gee, b. at Lunenburg, Vt., Oct. 16, 1819. Lives at St. Johnsbury. Yeoman. Four ch:—Alzina, b. Dec. 20, 1840; Henry, b. Nov. 7, 1842; Charles, b. Apr. 9, 1844; Helen E., b. Aug. 17, 1855.
485. Ruhama[7], b. Aug. 16, 1818; md. Mch. 3, 1844, Willard, son of Samuel and Martha Adams, b. at Concord, Vt., Sept. 28, 1816. He is a farmer and lives in Concord. Five ch:—Mary Ann H., b. at Concord, Dec. 26. 1844; Edward, b. Feb. 24, 1847; Jerome, b. May 30, 1848, d. Mch. 27, 1851; Emora, b. Mch. 7. 1849; David H., b. Feb. 7, 1853. 486. HORATIO S[7]. 487. GEORGE R[7].

(225) SAMUEL, son of JONATHAN (105), b. at Royalston, Apr. 10, 1775; rem'd with his father to Concord, Vt., where he d. Feb. 11, 1855. Yeoman. Md. ——, 1796, Delight, dau. of Jesse and Delight Woodbury, b. at Royalston, Mch. 9, 1777, d. at Concord, Aug. 10, 1839. Seven ch:—
488. Philena, b. at Concord, Apr. 23, 1798; md. Apr. 22, 1835, Moses, son of Charles and Hannah Greenfield, b. at Henniker, N. H., June 9, 1785. Resides in Concord. Yeoman; no issue. 489. Rox-anna[7], b. Jan. 28, 1800; md. Mch. 20, 1823, Jonas, son of Jonas and Elizabeth Warren, b. at Bethlehem, N. H., Apr. 25, 1796. He is a farmer and resides at Charleston, Vt. Six ch:—Annah, b. Jan. 18, 1824; Abigail, b. Aug. 28, 1825, d. Feb. 26. 1833; Otis W., b. Dec. 28, 1829; Charles, b. Dec. 26, 1832; Abby J., b. June 12, 1835; Myron, b. July 12, 1845. 490. HIRAM[7]. 491. Malinda[7]; md. John Smith, of Moira, N. Y.

492. MARY, b. Feb. 26, 1806; md. Nov. 16, 1830, Hiram, son of Enos and Rhoda Harvey, b. at Waterford, Vt., Mch. 24, 1804. He is a miller, and lives in Charleston, Vt. Four ch:—Aurelia M., b. Mch. 13, 1830, d. Dec. 11, 1830; Cordelia, b. Apr. 23, 1836, d. Nov. 13, 1838; Samuel Enos, b. May 23, 1838; Sumner F., b. Aug. 1, 1841. 493. RUTH, b. ———; md. Joseph Gray, of Charleston, Vt. Eight ch:— Riley, Marcus, William, Charles, Alonzo, Augusta, Amelia, and Milo. 494. SARAH, b. July 28, 1815; md. Jan. 19, 1848, Stephen S. P., son of Stephen S. and Mercy (Paine) Mathewson, b. at Lyndon, Vt., Aug. 23, 1807. Lives in Lyndon. Yeoman. Three ch:—Thomas P., b. Jan. 6, 1852; Edy H., b. Aug. 23, 1854; Mercy M., b. Jan. 29, 1856.

(227) AMOS, son of JONATHAN (106), b. at Royalston, Dec. 29, 1778; rem'd to Concord, Vt., 1790, where he d. Jan. 22, 1860. Yeoman. Md. Aug. 10, 1807, Ruth, dau. of Soloman and Ruth Babcock, b. at Royalston, Mass., Dec. 2, 1785, d. at Concord, Apr. 6, 1859. Eight ch:—

495. POLLY, b. at Concord, Vt., Mch. 12, 1808; md. June 16, 1834, Stephen, son of Nathaniel and Susan Reed, b. May 10, 1811, d. July 1, 1854. Lived in W. Concord. Yeoman. Seven ch:—Ruth B., b. at W. Concord, Apr. 7, 1835, d. July 17, 1852; Stephen H., b. Oct. 7, 1836; Nathaniel G., b. July 27, 1839; Lucius S. F., b. June 27, 1842; Winthrop T., b. Oct. 5, 1844; Amos H., b. Oct. 5, 1847; Celia M., b. July 18, 1850. 496. SARAH, b. Oct. 19, 1811; md. Jan. 24, 1855, Jacob F., son of Leonard and Phebe (Farr) Dean, b. at Bradford, Vt., May 12, 1802. Lives in St. Johnsbury. Farmer and Mechanic; no issue. 497. SOPHRONIA[7], b. Feb. 5, 1814; md. May 3, 1840, Lucius S., son of Arad and Desire Freeman, b. at Waterford, Vt., July 11, 1812. Lives in Waterford. Yeoman. Two ch:—Lorenzo Dow, b. Aug. 31, 1843; Lucilla S., b. Oct. 30, 1848. 498. STEPHEN[7]. 499. HIRAM, b. Apr. 30, 1821, d. Aug. 19, 1827. 500. RUTH, b. Mch. 17, 1825, d. Mch. 17, 1833. 501. JUDITH B., b. July 4, 1827; md. Apr. 3, 1853, Nathaniel, son of Reuben and Mary Gilbert, b. at St. Johnsbury, June 11, 1811, d. May 23, 1868. Lived in Concord, Vt. Yeoman. Three ch:—Sarah Ella, b. May 9, 1854; Florence E., b. Feb. 13, 1857; George N., b. Apr. 28, 1859. 502. HIRAM N[7].

(233) RICHARD, son of STEPHEN (112), b. at Windham, Me., Nov., 1770. He was a farmer, and rem'd about 1790-1, to Chebeague Isl., where he d. Jan., 1822. This island is situated in Casco Bay, about ten miles N. E. of Portland, three and one-half miles long, and one and a half miles broad, containing about five hundred inhabitants.

Md. 1793, Deborah, dau. of Ambrose and Deborah (Soule) Hamilton, b. at Chebeague, Aug. 8, 1767, d. Nov., 1852. Six ch : —

503. STEPHEN⁷. 504. SAMUEL⁷. 505. SARAH, b. Sept. 27, 1798; md. James Hamilton, jr., b. at Chebeague, June, 1800. Six ch : — Lovena, b. Nov., 1826; Louisa, b. Sept., 1829, d. 1850; Julia, b. Apr., 1834; Deborah, b. Aug., 1837; two ch., d. at birth. 506. SIMEON, d. young. 507. WILLIAM, b. Sept., 1804, d. Aug., 1822.

508. EMMA, b. Sept. 30, 1806: md. ———, 1823, Samuel, son of Alexander and Patience (Stowell) Ross, b. at Gray, Me., June 9, 1802. Lives at Chebeague Isl. Yeoman. Eleven ch : — Lovina, b. June 1, 1823; Mellen, b. Oct. 29, 1824, d. Feb. 1, 1846; Elias, b. July 9, 1827; Alexander, b. Feb. 25, 1829, d. June 1, 1851; Samuel, b. Jan. 29, 1831; Luther, b. Jan. 27, 1833; Charles, b. Nov. 17, 1834, d. Jan., 1835; Susan, b. Dec. 21, 1836; Edward, b. June 28, 1839; Ellen, b. Dec. 13, 1842; George, b. July 28, 1844.

(237) DANIEL, Rev., son of RICHARD (114), b. at Windham, Me., Jan. 8, 1773, d. at Hartford, Me., Dec. 13, 1853. Lived in Hebron, Buckfield, Turner, and Hartford. He was regularly ordained as a Baptist Clergymen. He md. 1st, 1798, Mercy, dau. of Joshua and Abigail (Ames) Keene, b. at Hebron, May 2, 1776, d. at Hartford, July 27, 1840; md. 2d, Jan., 1844, Catherine, dau. of Nathan Crafts, Esq., b. at Jay, Me., where she now resides. Nine ch : —

509. JOSEPH⁷. 510. MARCIA, b. at Hartford, Mch. 7, 1804; md. Feb. 4, 1827, Robert Bates, b. at Abington, Mass., July 10, 1802. Lives in Hartford, Me. Yeoman. Two ch : — William Hervey, b. Sept. 28, 1828, d. Jan. 30, 1831; Elizabeth Lincoln, b. July 3, 1832. 511. RICHARD⁷. 512. JESSE D⁷. 513. ABIGAIL, b. at Buckfield, Mch. 17, 1809; md. Jan. 30, 1843, Sumner F., son of Timothy and Leah Fernald, b. at Buckfield, June 18, 1818. Lives in Livermore, Me. Cabinet Maker. Three ch : — Mercy Ellen, b. June 13, 1844; Charles Edwin, b. Feb. 16, 1850; Adelia Jane, twin, b. same time, d. Feb. 20, 1850.

514. NANCY, b. May 2, 1811; lives at Canton Mills. 515. RODNEY⁷. 516. HANNAH, b. at Turner, May 2, 1815; md. Oct. 7, 1839, Benjamin, son of Seth and Julette Foster, b. at Livermore, Sept. 27, 1812. Lives in So. Livermore, Me. Housewright. Four ch : — Sarah H., b. Oct. 14, 1840, d. Sept. 30, 1841; Frances E., b. Aug. 21, 1842; George M., b. Apr. 17, 1845; Carroll C., b. at Brunswick, Jan. 21, 1853.

517. PERSIS S., b. at Hartford, Me., July 25, 1818; md. ———, 1842, William, son of Thomas and Phebe Coolidge, b. at Livermore, Aug. 21, 1811. Residence, Canton Mills, Me. Merchant. Two ch : — Emily N., b. at Livermore, Aug. 5, 1845; Edward E., b. Feb. 19, 1849.

(239) JOSEPH, Rev., son of JOSEPH (117), b. at Windham, Me., Nov. 2, 1779; rem'd with his father to Hebron, about Mch., 1795, where he d. Jan. 21, 1840. He was a farmer, and also a Freewill Baptist preacher. For a number of years a Selectman, and once a Representative to the Legislature. Md. July, 1801, Deborah, dau. of Jesse and Ruth Fuller, b. at Hebron, Oct. 2, 1780. Five ch:—

518. JOSEPH[7]. 519. RUTH, b. at Hebron, June 13, 1809; md. Mch. 1, 1834, Stafford S., son of Samuel and Lucy Bridgham, b. at Minot, Me., Mch. 29, 1807. Lives in Lewiston, Me. Inn Keeper. One ch:— Derrick S., b. at Hebron, Dec. 24, 1834.

520. WEALTHY, b. Aug. 2, 1811; md. Sept. 8, 1839, William P., son of William and Araminta Allen, b. at Minot, Dec. 26, 1811. He is a farmer and mechanic, and lives in W. Minot. Four ch:—Levi, b. Mch. 24, 1841. d. Sept. 9, 1848; Stafford B., b. Oct. 2, 1843, d. Sept. 3, 1848; Albion P., b. Nov. 30, 1845; William Henry, b. Oct. 10, 1850. 521. NANCY[7], b. Dec. 5, 1813; md. May 11, 1836, Seth, son of William and Hannah Loring, b. at Turner, Apr. 3, 1807. He is a farmer, and lives in Turner. Five ch:—Lucy, b. Jan. 26, 1838; Maria, b. May 6, 1843; John M., and Isaac N., twins, b. Oct. 24, 1847; Frederick M., b. Jan. 31, 1850. 522. LYDIA[7], b. May 7, 1816; md. Nov. 28, 1839, Alvan, son of William and Mary Howard, b. at Gloucester, Me., Sept. 23, 1811. Residence, Lewiston, Me.; no issue.

(240) SAMUEL, Rev., son of JOSEPH (118), b. at Windham, Me., Aug. 8, 1780, d. at Buckfield, Mch. 7, 1828. He was first a Freewill Baptist Clergyman, but afterwards changed his views to Universalism. Lived in Gorham, Me. He md. Mch. 15, 1803, Mercy, dau. of Seth and Sarah Randall, b. May 24, 1780, d. Oct. 7, 1828. Ten ch:— .

523. BENJAMIN R., b. at Gorham, Aug. 16, 1804; rem'd to Wis., where he d. 1844. 524. REBECCA, b. Jan. 8, 1805, d. Sept. 24, 1839; md. Phelps Ames, and rem'd some years since to Texas. 525. SAMUEL, b. Aug. 15, 1807, drowned, Apr. 9, 1832, in "twenty mile stream;" md. ——, Rebecca Bicknell.

526. BUZZELL[7]. 527. JOSEPH[7]. 528. STEPHEN, b. Mch. 25, 1815, d. Aug. 16, 1854; unm'd. 529. EBENEZER[7]. 530. BETSY, b. Mch. 19, 1819; living in Texas. 531. MERCY, b. Feb. 25, 1822; living in Texas. 532. ASA FOSTER[7].

(243) STEPHEN, son of JOSEPH (118), b. at Windham, Me., Aug. 10, 1787, d. at Buckfield, Sept., 1850. Lived in Windham, Hebron and Buckfield. Yeoman. He md. 1st, 1809, Asenath D., dau. of Samuel Gilbert, b. at Leeds, Me., 1790, d. 1828; md. 2d, Jennette Alden. Six ch. by Asenath:—

533. STEPHEN D[7]. 534. CHANDLER[7]. 535. HORACE[7]. 536.

MARK[7]. 537. BETSEY, b. at Buckfield, Dec. 1821, d. July, 1823. 538. ALBION PARRIS[7].

Four ch. by Jennette :—

539. JENNETTE A., b. Mch., 1830; md. Oct. 20, 1849, Samuel F., son of Simon and Catherine Record, b. at Buckfield, Jan. 1, 1822. Resides in Norway, Me. Boot and shoe manufacturer. Three ch :—Milton LaRoy, b. at Auburn, Me., Sept. 20, 1850; Nelson Burgess, b. Jan. 18, 1852; Royal Benton, b. Dec. 20, 1854. 540. AUGUSTA H., b. Feb., 1831, d. at Lewiston, Feb., 1853. 541. VESTA A., b. Apr., 1833, d. Apr., 1835. 542. ASENATH, b. Jan., 1836; md. June 17, 1857, Lewis O'Brien, b. at Quebec, Canada, May 5, 1829. Lives in Norway, Me. Merchant Tailor. Three ch :—Alton, b. at Buckfield, 1852; a dau., b. at Turner, 1854, d. 1855; Emma J., b. at Norway, 1857.

(244) HENRY H., son of JOSEPH (118), b. at Windham, Aug. 13, 1789. Lived in Hebron, and resides at present in Buckfield, Me. Was Rep. to the Maine Legislature, and for a number of years Selectman. He md. Mch., 1812, Caroline, dau. of Edmund and Hannah Landers, b. at Minot, Me., Jan. 30, 1791. Four ch :—

543. BENJAMIN R., b. at Hebron, Nov., 1812, drowned in Merrimack river, at Amesbury, N. H., June, 1834. 544. HENRY H[7]. 545. HANNAH[7], b. at Buckfield, Mch. 23, 1816, d. Nov. 20, 1821. 546. EDMUND[7].

(245) DANIEL, son of JOSEPH (118), b. at Windham, Aug. 8, 1791; rem'd to Turner, Me., where he d. Apr., 1851. He was a farmer, and held the office of Selectman and Assessor for a number of years, and was several times chosen Rep. to the Legislature. Md. Charlotte, dau. of Tobias and Abigail Ricker. Two ch :—

547. CHARLOTTE, b. June, 1818. 548. DANIEL, b. 1822.

(248) JOHN, son of JOSEPH (118), b. at Hebron, Me., Nov. 15, 1797, d. at Buckfield, Apr. 6, 1846. Yeoman. Md. Apr. 21, 1823, Hannah, dau. of Edmund and Hannah (Sebra) Landers, b. at Minot, Sept. 2, 1802. Three ch :—

549. JOHN COLBY[7]. 550. JOSIAH[7]. 551. JAMES F., b. at Hebron, Oct. 10, 1829, d. at Buckfield, May 25, 1830.

(250) JAMES, son of JAMES (132), b. at Amherst, N. H., Apr. 28, 1772. He removed to Wilton, N. H., where he now resides. He is a person of a very dignified appearance, being nearly, or quite, six feet tall, and proportionably large other ways; very communicative, and interesting in narrations pertaining to history of his times, and to whom I am much indebted for many valuable facts concerning this work. Yeoman. Md. 1st, July 4, 1797, Ruth Stiles, b. Oct. 7, 1772;

d. Aug. 7, 1823; md. 2d, Sept. 23, 1824, Anna Spalding, b. Nov. 30, 1777. Four ch. by Ruth: —
552. JAMES, b. Nov. 20, 1800. 553. ABNER S., b. Dec. 10, 1803. 554. SARAH, b. Sept. 23, 1806. 555. JOHN[7].

(253) SEWELL, son of AMBROSE (132), b. at Williamstown, Vt., Oct. 1, 1803; rem'd with his father to Roxbury, Vt., Nov., 1805, where he now resides. Yeoman. Md. Apr. 3, 1827, Nancy, dau. of Bernard and Phebe Blanchard, b. at Brookfield, Vt., Mch. 30, 1808. Ten ch: —
556. TIMOTHY LEWIS, b. at Brookfield, June 26, 1829, d. Feb. 26, 1850. Md. Betsey Hemmingway, Apr. 3, 1848; no issue. 557. BERNARD, b. at Roxbury, Dec. 13, 1830, d. Jan. 18, 1831. 558. JEDSON MATTHEW[7]. 559. SEWELL STEARNS, b. Oct. 9, 1835. 560. NANCY ELVIRA, b. Mch. 16, 1837; md. Mch. 16, 1854, Luther G. Tracy. Two ch: —Luther F., b. 1854; Clarence F., b. 1856.
561. WILLIAM ALPHONSO, b. Nov. 21, 1839. 562. HANNAH URSULA, b. Aug. 30, 1840, d. Sept. 11, 1844. 563. ASENATH VICTORY, and 564. TAMAR VILORA, twins, b. July 21, 1842. 565. AMASA JACKSON, b. July 24, 1845.

(255) AMBROSE B., son of AMBROSE (133), b. at Roxbury, Vt., Nov. 25, 1808, d. Sept. 1, 1857. Lived in Roxbury. Yeoman. Md. May 5, 1831, Sarah, dau. of Amos and Polly Blanchard, b. at Brookfield, Vt., Mch. 7, 1809. Twelve ch: —
566. EZRA BARTLETT[7]. 567. INFANT, b. June 11, 1833, d. same day. 568. GEORGE D., b. Mch. 7, 1834, d. Sept. 19, 1837. 569. SAWEN G., b. June 19, 1835, d. Apr. 19, 1847. 570. BETSY D., b. Nov. 29, 1836, d. Apr. 25, 1847. 571. GEORGE D., b. Sept. 29, 1838, d. Apr. 23, 1847.
572. J. FRANCIS, b. July 22, 1840, d. Apr. 30, 1847. 573. JAMES CARLOSS, b. Apr. 22, 1842. 574. AMOS B., b. Jan. 11, 1844, d. Apr. 22, 1847. 575. BETSY D., b. Jan. 8, 1848. 576. GEORGE F., b. Sept. 9, 1849, d. July 25, 1851. 577. S. ORLANA, b. June 18, 1852, d. Dec. 21, 1854.

SEVENTH GENERATION.

(257) ANDREW, son of ELISHA (138), b. at Middleton, Feb. 1, 1775. When quite young he rem'd with his father to Amherst (now Milford), where he settled, and d. Oct. 22, 1862. He and his brother Jesse succeeded to their father's estate, situated on the Souhegan river. He was deacon of the Baptist ch. in Milford. He md. Martha, dau. of Nathaniel and Phebe Rayment, b. at Hamilton, Mass., Feb. 6, 1777, d. at Milford, Mch. 10, 1858. Ten ch: —

578. NATHANIEL⁸. 579. ELISHA, b. Oct. 25, 1799, d. Nov. 9, 1800. 580. ELISHA, b. Feb. 6, 1801, d. Feb. 9, 1843. 581. JONATHAN, b. Jan. 17, 1804, d. Sept. 9, 1805. 582. SALLY, b. Oct. 11, 1804, d. Dec. 20, 1806. 583. SALLY, b. Sept. 7, 1806, d. Dec. 28, 1807. 584. STILL-MAN.⁹ 585. PHEBE D., b. Mch. 25, 1814. 586. MARY G., b. Dec. 11, 1817, d. July 24, 1854. 587. MARTHA C., b. Dec. 30, 1819.

(258) JESSE, son of ELISHA (138), b. at Middleton, Feb. 3, 1778, and rem'd the year following with his father to Amherst (now Milford), where he lived till about 1823-4, when he, with his family, excepting David and Noah, rem'd from their mountain residence to a farm in one of the valleys below, through which ran the Souhegan river. Prior to their removal, the old home had been the birth-place of fourteen children, some of whom, endowed with remarkable musical gifts, have left an ineffaceable impression upon the public mind, both in this country and England. Jesse Hutchinson was a very religious man through life; and he with his brother Andrew, erected the first Baptist meeting house in Milford, where they with their families, forming the greater proportion of the audience, met for some time, and worshipped God, and sang praises from full and overflowing hearts. Before his conversion, Jesse was considered an adept in the use of the violin, and was passionately fond of secular music, to a degree which, after his religious emotions were awakened, he repented of, throwing aside his violin, and finding solace alone in the melody of vocal sounds. Mrs. Hutchinson herself gave early indications of musical talent, and it was while singing one day in a village choir, that she first, by her voice, attracted the attention of her future husband. Her father, Andrew Leavitt, is said to have been very fond of psalmody, from whom the musical talent of the Hutchinsons may have been hereditary. He lived a very exemplary life, and died at the ripe age of ninety-three years. Mr. Hutchinson was by turns a farmer, carpenter, and cooper, as circumstances seemed to favor. He md., Aug. 7, 1800, Polly, dau. of Andrew and Sarah (Hastings) Leavitt, b. at Amherst, N. H., June 25, 1785, d. at Milford, Sept. 20, 1868. Her husband d. Feb. 16, 1851, aged 73. Sixteen ch :—

588. JESSE, b. Feb. 25, 1802, d. Apr. 5, 1811. His death was caused by the overturning of a pile of boards upon him, near a saw mill, being blown down by a sudden gust of wind. 589. DAVID⁹. 590. NOAH B⁹. 591. POLLY, b. June 7, 1806, d. Sept., 1809. 592. ANDREW B⁹. 593. ZEPHANIAH K⁹. 594. CALEB⁹. 595. JOSHUA⁹. 596. JESSE⁹. 597. BENJAMIN P., b. Oct. 3, 1815, d. Dec. 23, 1844. 598. JOSEPH JUDSON⁹.

599. SARAH RHODIA, b. Mch. 14, 1819; md. 1st, Isaac A., son of Abner H. and Sally (Fisher) Bartlett, and grand-son of Isaac and

7

Elizabeth (Hutchinson) Bartlett (142), b. Feb. 28, 1817, d. Dec. 22, 1844; md. 2d, May 26, 1855, Matthew Gray, b. May 22, 1800. Yeoman. Lives in Milford. One ch. by Isaac: — Marietta Caroline, b. Mch. 17, 1844. Three ch. by Matthew: — The first two dying in infancy; Nellie, b. Jan. 2, 1860.

600. JOHN WALLACE⁹. 601. ASA BURNHAM⁹. 602. Elizabeth, b. Nov. 14, 1824, d. Sept. 27, 1828. 603. Abby J., b. Aug. 29, 1829; md. Feb. 28, 1849, Ludlow, son of Rev. William Patton, D.D. and Mary (Weston), b. at N. Y., Aug. 3, 1825. Resides in N. Y. city. Banker and broker; no issue.

(260) ELIJAH, son of JOSEPH (140), b. at Middleton, Feb. 8, 1781, d. at Danvers, Sept. 10, 1818. Housewright. Md. Feb. 3, 1808, Nancy, dau. of Simeon and Elizabeth (Whittridge) Mudge, b. at Danvers, Apr. 7, 1785, d. Sept. 17, 1815. Three ch: —

604. Simeon, b. Oct. 22, 1808, d. Aug. 27, 1816. 605. Elizabeth W., b. Mch. 27, 1811; md. June, 1833, Joseph Porter, jr., b. at Mt. Vernon. N. H., Aug. 23, 1809. Lives in Danvers. Six ch:—Melville A., b. Dec. 12, 1834, d. June 14, 1839; Leverett H., b. Sept. 11, 1837, d. June 11, 1839; Melville A., b. Dec. 26, 1839; d. Sept. 10, 1844; Leverett H., b. June 23, 1843; Lucilla A., b. Apr. 7, 1847; Elizabeth J., b. May 10, 1851. 606. Nancy, b. July 6, 1813, d. Feb. 9, 1815.

(261) JOSEPH, son of JOSEPH (140), b. at Middleton, Mch. 18, 1782; rem'd to Danvers, where he d. May 10, 1842. Yeoman. Md. 1st, June 28, 1808, Sally, dau. of Samuel and Elizabeth Curtis, b. Oct. 16, 1782, d. 1815. Md. 2d, June 21, 1820, Rhoda Mackintire, d. at Danvers, Nov. 10, 1830. Four ch. by Sally: —

607. HIRAM⁹. 608. Joseph, b. Aug. 13, 1810, d. Apr. 6, 1825. 609. Mary, b. Feb. 15, 1812; md. June 24, 1841, George Putnam (613), son of Levi and Betsy Hutchinson. 610. ELISHA PUTNAM⁹.

One ch. by Rhoda: —

611. Sally, b. Feb. 15, 1821.

(262) ARCHELAUS, son of JOSEPH (140), b. at Middleton, Feb. 28, 1784, d. June 5, 1825. Lived in Middleton and Danvers. Yeoman. Md. June 8, 1818, Eliza, dau. of Abijah (166), and Irene Hutchinson, b. Oct. 25, 1800, d. Nov. 6, 1845. Two ch:—

612. Eliza Ann Jane, b. Apr. 20, 1819, d. at Reading, Aug. 22, 1840; md. Dec. 25, 1839, Charles Higbee, b. Nov. 13, 1817; no issue. 613. Archelaus Eustis, b. Dec. 28, 1825.

After her husband's dec., Mrs. Hutchinson md. 2d, Nov. 30, 1826, Perley, son of Samuel and Hannah White, b. July 28, 1802, d. Feb.,

1838. Three ch : — Albert H., b. Dec. 2, 1827; William J., b. Aug. 22, 1830; Irene Augusta, b. Sept. 8, 1836, d. young.

(263) LEVI, son of JOSEPH (140), b. at Middleton, May 13, 1786; rem'd to Danvers, where he d. Mch. 10, 1844. Yeoman. Md. May 5, 1811, Betsy, dau. of Benjamin and Hannah (Putnam) Russell, b. Jan. 21, 1780. Mr. Russell md. for his 2d wife, Ruth (121), dau. of Amos Hutchinson. Six ch : —
614. GEORGE PUTNAM³. 615. SAMUEL³. 616. BENJAMIN R., b. Oct. 10, 1816, drowned Oct. 13, 1850, in San Francisco Bay, Cal.; unm'd. 617. SIMON, b. Aug. 17, 1818, d. July 12, 1845; unm'd. 618. LEVI RUSSELL³. 619. ALVEN ELIJAH, b. Jan. 22, 1826.

(266) BENJAMIN, son of JOSEPH (140), b. at Middleton, May 5, 1802; rem'd with his father to Danvers; afterwards settled in So. Danvers, where he now resides. Lived a few years in Lowell. Yeoman. Md. Dec. 4, 1826, Martha A., dau. of Amos and Abigail King, b. at So. Danvers, Jan. 25, 1805. Nine ch : —
620. CLEAVES KING³. 621. SUSAN ELIZABETH, b. Feb. 2, 1829. 622. REBECCA NEWHALL, b. Oct. 9, 1831; md. May 7, 1863, William N., son of Dr. Joseph and Maria Osgood, of So. Danvers, b. Apr. 12, 1835. Lives in Thompson, Conn. Cashier of the bank there. One ch : — William Henry, b. Mch. 14, 1865.
623. EDWIN AUGUSTUS³, b. at So. Danvers, Jan. 1, 1834; rem'd, Sept., 1853, to Cincinnati, O., where he now resides. Importer and dealer in Hardware. Md. Feb. 25, 1863, Cate D., dau. of James B. and Cate D. Ferguson, b. at Salem, Mch. 10. 1839; no issue. 624. BENJAMIN FRANKLIN, b. at So. Danvers, Jan. 19, 1836, where he now lives. Dealer in W. I. Goods. Md. Apr. 12, 1865, Susan A., dau. of Tobias and Margaret Hanson, b. at Salem, Mch. 30, 1841; no issue.
625. WILLIAM H³. 626. MARTHA MARIA, b. Dec. 10, 1840. 627. AMOS KING, b. Dec. 7, 1843. 628. FRANK DUDLEY, b. Mch. 14, 1848.

(268) DAVID, son of JOSIAH (148), b. at Middleton, Feb. 13, 1790; rem'd to Cambridgeport, where he d. Mch., 1825. Housewright. Md. May 27, 1819, Fanny, dau. of David and Eunice Peabody, b. at Middleton, July 14, 1798. d. May 7, 1832. Two ch : —
629. AUGUSTUS RICHARDSON³. 630. DAVID.

(269) ISRAEL, son of JOSIAH (148), b. at Middleton, July 29, 1792; rem'd to Lynn, where he d. ———, 1849. Md. Eliza, dau. of ——— and Rebecca French, b. 1799, d. at Boston. Dec. 7, 1851. Four ch : —
631. ELIZA ANN, b. Mch. 14, 1818; md. 1st, June 16, 1835, John Furber, b. Mch. 29, 1814, d. at Lynn, Sept., 1843; md. 2d, Nov. 15, 1846,

David Low, b. ———, 1805. Three ch. by John : — Arianna, b. Dec. 18, 1836; John C., b. Sept. 6, 1839, d. Nov., 1839; John C., b. Jan. 9, 1842. One ch. by David : — David, b. Mch. 6, 1854. 632. HANNAH SILSBEE, b. Dec. 26, 1819; md. Feb. 16, 1835, John Lufkin, b. Apr. 7, 1815. Lives in Lynn. Shoemaker. Three ch : — Caroline Augusta, b. Mch. 17, 1836; Sally Ann, b. July 11, 1838; Emma Eddy, b. Mch. 7, 1843. 633. REBECCA, d. young. 634. JOSIAH, b. 1823.

(271) IRA, son of JOSIAH (148), b. at Middleton, Apr. 5, 1797. Yeoman. Md. May 10, 1824, Hannah, dau. of Stephen and Mary (Mansfield) Wilson, b. Oct. 8, 1801, d. in the fall of 1866. Nine ch : —
635. AUGUSTUS LUCAS⁸. 636. BENJAMIN PETERS, b. Jan. 27, 1827, d. Mch. 2, 1827. 637. BENJAMIN PETERS⁸. 638. SAMUEL FLINT, b. Mch. 27, 1831. 639. SARAH DEAN, b. June 7, 1833.
640. ADELINE WILSON, b. Oct. 1, 1835. 641. RUBY GRIFFIN, b. Apr. 11, 1839; md. Oct., 1856, John Henry Crowley, of Salem. 642. OLIVE ELIZABETH, b. Feb. 5, 1840. 643. HORACE MANSFIELD, b. Nov. 5, 1841.

(279) WILLIAM, son of JOHN (154), b. at Danvers, July 9, 1803. Resides in Danvers. Yeoman. Md. Apr. 24, 1825, Lucy, dau. of Ebenezer and Lydia Berry, b. Aug. 20, 1806. Four ch : —
644. LUCY JANE, b. Nov. 25, 1826, d. June 8, 1848; md. Apr. 13, 1846, Richard Goss, of Marblehead, b. Apr. 17, 1821. One ch : — William Putnam, b. July 9, 1848.
645. WILLIAM HENRY⁸. 646. JAMES AUGUSTUS⁸. 647. MARY ANN, b. Apr. 6, 1833; md. Nov. 25, 1852, John 2d, son of Josiah and Betsy Gould, b. at Topsfield, Dec. 5, 1826. Lives in Topsfield. Butcher. Two ch : — Josiah Loring, b. Dec. 22, 1854; Charles Augustus, b. May 17, 1858.

(284) JACOB, son of JOHN (154), b. at Danvers, Aug. 8, 1819. Lives in Danvers. Shoe manufacturer. Md. Sept. 24, 1844, Sarah Colony, b. at New Durham, N. H., Aug. 22, 1820. Four ch : —
648. SARAH JANE, b. June 13, 1845. 649. JACOB AUGUSTUS, b. Apr. 1, 1847. 650. GEORGE KILBURN, b. May 28, 1851. 651. CHARLES, b. Apr. 28, 1860, d. Apr. 29, 1863.

(290) KIMBALL, son of JESSE (156), b. at Danvers, Jan. 14, 1814. Lives in Danvers. Shoe manufacturer. Md. Jan. 20, 1847, Emily Helen Prentiss, b. at Marblehead, Sept. 27, 1821. Three ch : —
652. HORACE KIMBALL, b. Jan. 11, 1851. 653. MELLEN PRENTISS, b. June 14, 1852, d. Aug. 13, 1854. 654. EMILY, b. July 12, 1857.

(291) OSGOOD, son of JESSE (156), b. at Danvers, Sept. 5, 1816;

rem'd to Lawrence, where he now resides. He md. June 7, 1850, Hannah Tappan Berry, b. Feb. 24, 1824, d. at Lawrence, Nov. 22, 1856.
Two ch : —

655. CHARLES C., b. June 7, 1851. 656. FRANK OSGOOD, b. Sept. 12.
1853.

(313) ASA, son of ASA (159). b. at Amherst, July 8, 1788. He was
a farmer, and rem'd with his father, Feb., 1799, to Fayette, Me., where
he now resides. He md. 1st, Feb. 27, 1816, Betsy, dau. of Jonathan
and Abigail Woodman, b. at Candia, N. H., Oct. 29, 1786, d. at Fayette,
Oct. 23, 1833; md. 2d, Hannah B., dau. of Daniel and Mary Tewks-
bury, b. at Amesbury, Mass., Dec. 22, 1804. Two ch. by Betsy : —

657. ABIGAIL WOODMAN, b. Dec. 18, 1820, d. Oct. 26, 1832. 658.
MARY JANE, b. Oct. 2, 1822: md. Oct. 2, 1843, Rev. Frederick Augustus, son of John and Miriam T. Wadleigh, b. at Salisbury, Mass., May
25, 1814. Resides in Arlington, Vt. Three ch : — Abby Elizabeth, b.
at Guilford, Vt., June 16, 1845; John F., b. at Arlington, Jan. 23, 1850;
George H., b. Aug. 5, 1852.

(317) JOSEPH, son of ASA (159). b. at Amherst, Aug. 12, 1794;
rem'd with his father to Fayette, where he now lives. Has lived in
Readfield and Winthrop, Me. Yeoman. Md. ——, 1814, Sarah,
dau. of Robert and Sarah Waugh, b. at Fayette, Sept. 6, 1793. Four
ch : —

659. SARAH JANE W., b. Sept. 16, 1816, d. June 9, 1832. 660. SULLI-
VAN A., b. Jan. 12, 1825. 661. HORACE W., b. Mch. 7, 1829. 662.
HORATIO D³.

(320) HIRAM, son of ASA (159), b. at Fayette, May 20, 1806.
Shoe manufacturer and Apothecary. He rem'd. Jan. 28, 1837, to Burn-
ham, Me., where he now lives. Md. Mch. 18, 1829, Abigail B., dau. of
Asabel and Deborah Chandler, b. at Sandwich, Mass., July 16, 1803.
Four ch : —

663. GEORGE M., b. Feb. 10, 1830, d. Apr. 11, 1831. 664. ELIZA
ANN, b. Dec. 14, 1832; md. Oct. 23, 1853, Rufus B., son of Rev. Otis
and Betsy B. Williams, b. at Burnham, Jan. 2, 1831. Yeoman. Two
ch : — Edwin W., b. Oct. 9, 1854; Adelia Ida, b. Oct. 10, 1856. 665.
ELLEN ORVILLA, b. Sept. 5, 1836, d. Feb. 1, 1858. 666. JULIA EMELINE,
b. Sept. 6, 1839, d. July 9, 1855.

(323) WILLIAM, son of DANIEL (162) b. at Danvers, 1801; rem'd
to Lynn, where he d. Oct. 30, 1824. Shoemaker. Md. ——, 1823,
Mary Cammal. One ch : —

667. MARIAH D., b. June 8. 1824, d. Jan. 27, 1848; md. Dec. 22, 1844,

Henry D., son of Edmund and Grace F. Gilman, b. at Lynn, Oct. 17, 1824. Shoemaker. One ch:—A son, b. Mch., 1847, d. same day.

(336) BENJAMIN FRANKLIN, son of ABIJAH (166), b. at Danvers, June 23, 1821. He is a lawyer, and rem'd to Provincetown, Mass., Feb. 22, 1860, where he now lives. Began the practice of law, Apr., 1859. Md. Sept. 30, 1858, Mary Jane, dau. of Samuel and Sarah DeMerritt, b. at Lee, N. H., July 15, 1823. She was formerly a school teacher a number of years in Danvers. Two ch:—
668. ANNA EDITH, b. June 12, 1861, d. July 24, 1863. 669. FRANKIE STURGIS, b. Dec. 18, 1866, d. Sept. 3, 1867.

(338) PERLEY, son of EBENEZER (173), b. at Danvers, Apr. 9, 1793. He was a farmer, and rem'd to Danville, Vt., where he d. Sept. 21, 1820. He md. Feb. 29, 1817, Eliza Huse, b. at Enfield, N. H., Feb. 27. 1796, d. July 19, 1867. After her husband's dec., she md. 2d, Mch., 1821, Elijah, son of Jethro Russell, jr. and Sarah (172), b. Feb. 8, 1792, d. Sept. 25, 1867. Two ch:—
670. JEREMY[6]. 671. ANN ELIZA, b. at Danville, Vt., Feb. 28, 1820; md. Aug. 26, 1845, Nathan Porter, b. at Danville, Aug. 15, 1819. Lives in Jericho, Vt. Two ch:—Julia A., b. July 31, 1847; Alice Rosa, b. Apr. 13, 1851.

(341) ELIJAH, son of JOSEPH (176), b. at Danvers, Mch. 22, 1808. He is a farmer, and lives in that portion of Danvers called Bramanville, west of the common, a tract of land originally owned, and given to the town for a training field, by Dea. Nathaniel Ingersoll, in the early settlement of the place. A deacon of the Congregationalist ch. in that part of the town. Md. Dec. 5, 1832, Ruthey, dau. of Allen and Ruth (Putnam) Nourse, b. at Danvers, Dec. 6, 1803. Eight ch:—
672. EDWARD[9]. 673. ALFRED, b. Oct. 3, 1835. Resides in Danvers. Shoe manufacturer, at Boston. Md. May 9, 1867, Abby, dau. of Eben and Sarah T. Colcord, b. at Danvers, May, 1844; no issue. 674. WARREN PUTNAM, b. Feb. 16, 1837. Resides in Danvers. Shoe manufacturer. Md. Dec. 13, 1865, Daphney C., dau. of Daniel and Pauline F. Towne, b. at Danvers, Dec. 22, 1841; no issue. 675. EMILY, b. Aug. 28, 1838. 676. HARRIET ENDICOTT, b. July 20, 1841; md. Feb. 13, 1867, William Henry, son of William and Serena Preston, b. at Danvers, Sept. 9, 1840. Lives in Danvers. Shoe manufacturer; no issue. 677. MARY, b. Dec. 20, 1842. 678. MARTHA ELLEN, b. Sept. 30, 1844. 679. ALMIRA PUTNAM, b. July 27, 1847, d. Aug. 27, 1849.

(357) ELISHA, son of ISRAEL (184), b. at Danvers, Sept. 27, 1799; rem'd to Haverhill, where he d. Aug. 30, 1860. Shoe manufacturer.

Md. June 10, 1823, Harriet, dau. of Thomas and Sarah (Carr) Morrison, b. at Newburyport, Dec. 14, 1801. Six ch : —

680. SARAH M., b. Mch. 4, 1824; md. June 15, 1844. John W., son of John W. and Sarah Clark, b. at Truro, Mass., Dec.. 1821, d. from a wound rec'd at the battle of Antietam. Lived in Haverhill. Mason; no issue. 681. WILLIAM AUGUSTUS⁹. 682. EUNICE PUTNAM, b. Feb. 11. 1828. 683. HARRIET FRANCES, b. June 30, 1833, d. Dec. 17, 1867; md. July 20, 1856, George H., son of Humphrey and Alice Hoyt, b. at W. Newbury, June 10. 1833. Resides in Haverhill. Leather dealer, One ch : — Georgia Frances, b. Nov. 3, 1866, d. Jan. 9, 1867.

684. THOMAS MORRISON, b. May 7, 1835, d. Apr. 4, 1836. 685. MARY ELIZABETH THETELLE, b. June 15, 1848; md. Nov. 22, 1866, John N., son of Nahum and Almira Witham, b. at Newbury, Aug. 11, 1844. Lives in Haverhill. Grocer.

(359) SAMUEL, son of SAMUEL (188), b. at Wilton, N. H., Nov. 19, 1776, d. Nov. 5, 1852, Yeoman. Md. June 5, 1798, Martha, dau. of Silas and Sybil (Reed) Howard, b. at Westford, Mass., Sept. 4, 1774, d. Sept. 21, 1856. Thirteen ch : —

686. MELINDA, b. at Wilton, Nov. 21, 1798. 687. SARAH, b. Nov. 24, 1799; md. Dec. 25, 1828, John Patten, b. at Bedford. N. H., May 3, 1805, d. Dec. 20, 1835. Blacksmith. His widow resides at present in Charlestown, Mass. Four ch : — James G., b. at Nashua, July 18, 1829; David, b. July 1, 1831, d. Aug. 25, 1833: Andrew J., b. Aug. 3, 1833, d. Aug. 25, 1835; Sarah S., b. Apr. 2, 1836.

688. MARTHA, b. at Milford, Feb. 25, 1801; md. June 3, 1821, Andrew Burnham, b. at Lyndeboro, Nov. 14, 1800. Lives in Mt. Vernon, N. H., where he rem'd in 1843. Yeoman. Eight ch : — William T., b. at Lyndeboro, Feb. 11, 1823; George. b. May 23, 1824; Jane, b. Sept. 14, 1827; Lavina and Louisa, twins, b. Mch. 4, 1828; James, b. July 6, 1834, d. June 25, 1851: Israel, b. Nov. 1, 1838; Albert, b. Jan. 7, 1840.

689. MARY, b. Mch. 20, 1802; md. Mch. 4, 1823. Robert, son of James and Sarah Ritchie, b. at Peterboro, N. H., July 27, 1798. Lives in Jeffry, N. H. Yeoman. Twelve ch : — James, b. at Peterboro, Jan. 11, 1824; Samuel, b. July 19, 1825; John, b. June 21, 1827; William R., b. Sept. 16, 1829; George C., b. May 5, 1831; Mary J., b. Jan. 20, 1833; Alvin, b. Feb. 24, 1835; Darius, b. at Jeffry. Aug. 12, 1836, d. Aug. 28, 1863; Henry, b. Nov. 7, 1837, d. Sept. 30, 1864; Edmund F., b. Dec. 10, 1839, d. Nov. 26, 1862; Sarah M., b. May 27, 1842; Adelbert, b. Feb. 13, 1846.

690. RACHEL, b. Aug. 25, 1803. 691. FREEMAN⁹. 692. FRANCIS, b. Oct. 24, 1805. 693. LAVINA, b. 1807; md. Austin George. Twelve ch.

694. CYRENE, b. 1809, d. 1835. 695. SAMUEL, b. 1811, d. ———.

696. Sybil, b. Mch. 17, 1812, d. Nov., 1840. 697. Harriet N., b. Mch. 10, 1814; md. Feb. 10, 1864, Earl C., son of Joshua and Mary (Saunders) Gordon, b. at Salem, N. H., Aug. 15, 1804, where he now resides. Yeoman; no issue. 698. Jane, b. 1819, d. 1825.

(362) JOTHAM, son of SAMUEL (188), b. at Wilton, N. H., Apr. 11, 1781, d. June 12, 1839. Lived in Wilton. Yeoman. Md. 1810, Phebe (382), dau. of Ebenezer (191) and Phebe (Sawtell) Hutchinson, b. at E. Wilton, June 21, 1782, d. Oct. 11, 1824. Three ch : —
699. Mariah, b. Feb. 14, 1811, d. Apr. 27, 1855. 700. HARVEY[8]. 701. Alathena, b. May 4, 1819.

(363) FREDERICK, son of SAMUEL (188), b. at Wilton, July 10, 1783, d. ———. Lived in Wilton. Yeoman. Md. Aug. 8, 1811, Mary, dau. of John and Rhoda (Holt) Dale, b. at Wilton, Sept. 10, 1783. Seven ch : —
702. CHARLES[8]. 703. Mary, b. Oct. 20, 1813; md. Apr. 28, 1840, Nathan Hazelton. Two ch : — Mary Adeline, b. at Wilton, Apr. 23, 1842; Timothy Center, b. Sept. 23, 1845.
704. Lydia Dale, b. Feb. 5, 1816, d. Oct. 2, 1818. 705. ABEL FISK[8]. 706. Lyman, b. Oct. 28, 1820, d. Mch. 16, 1822. 707. Lydia Dale, b. Feb. 27, 1823, d. July 12, 1825. 708. FREDERICK LYMAN[8].
(365) ABIEL, son of SAMUEL (188), b. at Wilton, Nov. 1, 1787. Rem'd to Nashua, N. H., Mch. 6, 1846, where he d. Yeoman. Md. 1st, Nov. 2, 1813, Sophia, dau. of William R. Pettingill, b. 1790, d. at Wilton, Aug. 23, 1826. Md. 2d, Jan. 22, 1828, Sarah, dau. of Sardis and Mehitable Miller, b. at Alstead, N. H., Feb. 9, 1806. Four ch. by Sophia : —
709. Sophia A., b. at Wilton, Aug. 10, 1815, d. Sept. 6, 1852. 710. Abiel P., b. June 22, 1817. 711. Orin, b. Aug. 25, 1819. 712. Laorsa, b. Aug. 26, 1821.
Eight ch. by Sarah : —
713. Sarah Melissa, b. Sept. 25, 1828; md. July 10, 1857, Richard Ewes, of Providence, R. I. 714. SARDIS MILLER[9]. 715. STEPHEN BARNARD[9]. 716. ANDREW JACKSON[8]. 717. William Dustin, b. Apr. 9, 1835, d. May 31, 1839. 718. Oscar, b. Aug. 12, 1836. 719. Albert, b. Mch. 11, 1838, d. May 16, 1839. 720. Aman, b. Aug. 25, 1839. 721. George Dwight, b. Apr. 6, 1844.

(366) SOLOMON, son of SAMUEL (188), b. at Wilton, N. H., Mch. 27, 1792; rem'd to Nashua, N. H., 1835, where he d. Apr. 14, 1849. Musician. Md. May 10, 1812, Catherine P., dau. of Jacob and Mary (Pearsons) Flynn, b. at Milford, Oct. 7, 1795. Nine ch : —
722. ROBERT[8]. 723. JACOB F[8]. 724. GEORGE W[8]. 725. Cather-

INE, b. at E. Wilton, July 3, 1820; md. Oct. 9, 1888, Stephen F., son of Stephen and Amity Shirley (Lamb) Atwood, b. at Worcester, Dec. 5, 1816. Resides in Nashua. Surveyor. Seven ch:—Loretto M., b. Apr. 9, 1840; Adeline F., b. Oct. 1, 1842; Albert F., b. Dec. 28, 1844; Frank W., b. Dec. 3, 1847; George S., b. Dec. 4, 1850; Katy J., b. May 8, 1853, d. Sept. 20, 1854; Carrie J., b. Mch. 20, 1856.

726. HARRIET, b. July 3, 1823, d. Sept. 16, 1824. 727. HENRY O^8. 728. HARRIET E., b. May 5, 1829; md. July 26, 1864, Obadiah H., son of William and Fanny Peters, b. at Bradford, Apr. 4, 1825. Lives in Nashua. Machinist. One ch:—Emma L., b. Mch. 5, 1868. 729. LUCY A. F., b. July 17, 1832, d. Sept. 7, 1851; md. July 19, 1850, Henry H., son of Joseph and Abigail Law, b. at Brookline, N. H., Apr. 27, 1828. Lives in Nashua. Coachman; no issue. 730. SAMUEL, b. Jan. 28, 1838, d. Sept. 28, 1839.

(368) NATHAN, son of NATHAN (189), b. at Milford, N. H., Apr. 25, 1779. Lived in Milford and Temple, N. H., and Boston, Mass., where he d. Sept. 12, 1823. He was a farmer, and subsequently a trader. Md. Apr. 26, 1807, Lydia, dau. of Jona. and Abigail (Wyman) Jones, b. at Woburn, Mass., Feb. 13, 1788. She lives at present, in Derry, N. H. Four ch:—

731. OLIVIA, b. at Milford, Feb. 20, 1808; md. Dec. 6, 1832, Abijah Spalding, of Wilton. Three ch:—Horatio A., b. Sept. 10, 1833; Theresa A., b. Sept. 6, 1836; Henry E., b. Jan. 12, 1840. 732. ERASTUS^9. 733. HORATIO, b. Nov. 16, 1817, d. 1819. 734. AUGUSTUS STUART, b. May 9, 1823, d. 1866; md. —— Willoughby.

(370) REUBEN, son of NATHAN (189), b. at Milford, Sept. 9, 1782, d. Aug. 25, 1861. Lived in Milford. Yeoman. Md. June 7, 1804, Lucy (392), dau. of Bartholomew and Phebe Hutchinson, b. at Milford, Dec. 20, 1786, d. July 15, 1858. Twelve ch:—

735. LUCY C., b. at Milford, Jan. 17, 1805, d. Oct. 15, 1813. 736. ROBERT^9. 737. SOPHIA, b. Sept. 12, 1810; md. Dec. 30, 1828, James B., son of Jona. and Sybil Farwell, b. at Groton, Mass., May 11, 1805. Lives in Milford. Yeoman. Eight ch:—Adelia Sophia, b. July 20, 1833; Henry, b. Feb. 19, 1835, d. Feb. 13, 1857; Caroline Jennette, b, Feb. 21, 1837; George Clifton, b. Apr. 3, 1839; Lucy Ann, b. Apr. 10, 1841; Josephine H., b. May 16, 1843; James N., b. Apr. 8, 1846; Hannah Elizabeth, b. Aug. 15, 1849.

738. SOPHRONIA, b. at Milford, Aug. 31, 1812; md. 1st, Mch. 11, 1847, Abner, son of Nathaniel and Rebecca (Mason) Holt, b. at Temple, N. H., Oct. 11, 1810, d. July 30, 1851, without issue. Wheelwright. Md. 2d, Apr. 29, 1852, Ira, son of Nehemiah and Mary (Wright) Holt, b. at Temple, July 26, 1815. Lives in Milford. Box

8

and Pattern maker; no issue. 739. REUBEN⁹. 740. NATHAN R, b.
Nov. 7, 1816. Lives in Milford. Yeoman. Md. Nov. 17, 1842, Abby
Maria, dau. of Benjamin and Betsy Conant, b. Oct. 25, 1823; no issue.
741. EDMUND P⁹. 742. CLIFTON, b. Oct. 11, 1820, d. Jan. 15, 1822.
743. LUCY C., b. Apr. 8, 1823; md. Feb. 14, 1843, Holland Prouty, b.
at Milford, Apr. 8, 1823. Lives in Milford. Yeoman. Two ch:—
Charles Albert, b. Sept. 9, 1848, d. Aug. 5, 1849; Charles Holland, b.
July 11, 1850. 744. CLIFTON, b. Mch. 14, 1825, d. ———. 745. RE-
BECCA P., b. Aug. 13, 1826; md. Aug. 27, 1846, Christopher C. Shaw,
b. Mch. 20, 1824. Lives in Milford. Clerk. Two ch:—Horatio C.,
b. July 31, 1847; Charles J., b. Dec. 15, 1851. 746. JENNETTE, b. Oct.
11, 1828; md. Feb. 1, 1848, John, son of Adam and Mary (Gordon)
Dickey, b. Apr. 8, 1820, d. Mch. 6, 1868. Lived in Milford. Tin and
sheet-iron worker. Three ch:—Frank Gordon, b. June 24, 1852;
Kate Alice, b. Feb. 1, 1858; Hattie Frances, b. Nov. 28, 1867.

(373) JONAS, son of NATHAN (189), b. at Milford, June 2, 1792,
d. Sept. 13, 1857. Physician. He attended medical lectures and com-
pleted his studies at the medical school connected with Dartmouth
Coll., Dec., 1814. Rem'd to Hancock, N. H., where he commenced
practice, and continued his residence there till Nov., 1841, when he
rem'd to Milford. Represented the town of Hancock in the Legislature during the years 1833-4-5. Md. Sept. 5, 1815, Nancy, dau. of
John and Mary (Bradford) Wallace, of Milford, b. June 5, 1794. Five
ch:—
747. ROBERT BRUCE WALLACE, b. at Hancock, Nov. 14, 1816, d. Dec.
12, 1819. 748. ISABEL ANN BRAIDFOOT, b. Nov. 11, 1820; md. Oct. 11,
1866, Dr. Francis P., son of Samuel F. and Eunice F. Fitch, b. at
Greenfield, N. H., Oct. 2, 1806. Lives in Milford; no issue.
749. LUCRETIA JOSEPHINE, b. May 16, 1823, d. Oct. 26, 1839. 750.
HELEN CURTIS, b. Nov. 22, 1828, d. July 30, 1830. 751. CATHERINE
FRANCES, b. Aug. 9, 1831; md. Mch. 10, 1852, Clinton S., son of Calvin
and Eunice Averill, b. at Milford, Sept. 22, 1827. Lawyer. One ch:
—Catherine Isabella, b. June 23, 1859, d. Aug. 30, 1859.

(374) ABEL, son of NATHAN (189), b. at Milford, Aug. 8, 1795,
d. Feb. 19, 1846. Yeoman. Md. Jan. 22, 1816, Betsy, dau. of Isaac
and Elizabeth Bartlett (141), b. at Amherst, Oct. 26, 1796. Nine
ch:—
752. ELIZABETH, b. June 18, 1816. 753. ABEL FORDYCE⁹. 754.
GEORGE CANNIN⁹. 755. JERUSHA PEABODY, b. Apr. 20, 1825; md.
Joseph Judson Hutchinson (see 598). 756. ANDREW JACKSON⁹.
757. ISAAC BARTLETT⁹. 758. HELEN AUGUSTINE, b. Nov. 16, 1832,
d. Apr. 12, 1855. 759. NATHAN⁹. 760. JONAS, b. Jan. 10, 1840.

(375) BENJAMIN, son of BENJAMIN (190), b. at Milford, Aug. 5, 1777, d. Oct. 14, 1857. Lived in Milford. Yeoman. Md. Nov., 1803, Azubah Tarbell, b. at Mason, N. H., Oct. 9, 1780, d. Apr. 24, 1863. Seven ch:—

761. BENJAMIN, b. Aug. 5, 1804, d. Aug. 28, 1813. 762. SALLY D., b. Nov. 2, 1805; md. Oct. 24, 1834, Emri Clark, of Heath, Mass. Lives in Milford. One ch:—Miranda Frances, b. Sept. 27, 1835. 763. MIRANDA, b. June 11, 1808, d. Sept. 25, 1849. 764. WILLIAM P., b. May 16, 1811, d. July 31, 1811. 765. BENJAMIN F⁸. 766. LUCY, b. May 14, 1820; md. Dec. 31, 1845, George W. Royleigh, b. Sept. 6, 1823. Lives in Milford. Yeoman. Two ch:—Ella Miranda, b. June 1, 1847; Kate Emilyette, b. Nov. 7, 1856, d. Mch. 9, 1857.

(378) LUTHER, son of BENJAMIN (190), b. at Milford, N. H., Apr. 2, 1783. Lives in Milford. Yeoman. Md. 1st, May 2, 1809, Sarah, dau. of Joshua Mear, b. ———, d. Jan. 6, 1857. Md. 2d, Nov. 12, 1857, wid. Betsy (Tay) Crosby, b. Mch. 14, 1792. Four ch:—

767. CASSANDANA, b. June 20, 1812; md. Dec. 25, 1837, John B., son of John and Orphia Hopkins, b. Sept., 1803. Rem'd to Waltham, Mass., 1837. Dealer in Dry Goods for two years; followed farming till 1850, when he went to California, where he d. Apr. 11, 1857; no issue. 768. EVELYN MILTON⁸. 769. ELBRIDGE⁸. 770. GERRY⁸.

(379) EUGENE, son of BENJAMIN (190), b. at Milford, Mch. 11, 1785, d. Feb. 7, 1854. Lived in Milford. Yeoman. Md. 1812, Susan Danforth, b. ———, d. Feb. 16, 1855. Three ch:—

771. EUGENE, b. Mch. 25, 1813. 772. SUSAN, b. Feb. 3, 1816; md. Jan. 4, 1848, George Savage, b. Jan. 8, 1823. Lives in Auburn, N. H. Yeoman. Three ch:—Eugene Alphonzo, b. Dec. 6, 1850; Georgianna Arabel, b. Mch. 4, 1853, d. May, 1854; Susan Rosabel, b. Feb. 20, 1855. 773. ELIZA, b. May 16, 1820; md. Sept. 6, 1842, George W., son of Henry and Hannah Moore George, b. at Goffstown, N. H., Nov. 8, 1817. Lives in Manchester, N. H. Yeoman. Six ch:—Lydia Vilany, b. Nov. 6, 1843; Eugene Alphonzo, b. Aug. 4, 1845, d. Apr. 2, 1848; Eliza Josephine, b. Oct. 29, 1847; Mary Almaretta, b. Feb. 20, 1850; Rebeckah Little, b. Sept. 6, 1854; Frank Westley, b. Oct. 30, 1857.

(381) EBENEZER, son of EBENEZER (191), b. at Wilton, Sept. 18, 1780; rem'd to Weld, Me., Jan., 1804, where he d. Jan. 23, 1845. Yeoman. Md. 1803, Rhoda, dau. of Eben and Rhoda Dale, b. at Wilton, ———, d. at Weld, June 27, 1852. Eleven ch:—

774. RHODA DALE, b. Oct. 18, 1804; md. Oct. 20, 1828, Jacob A. Whitney, of Weld, b. ———, d. Oct. 13, 1852. Yeoman. Five ch:—Emily H., b. Aug. 27, 1830; Ebenezer H., b. Feb. 28, 1832; Amasa H.,

b. July 27, 1834; Jacob A., b. Sept. 11, 1838; Lucy B., b. Nov. 8, 1844.
775. EBENEZER⁸. 776. ANNA, b. Apr. 13, 1808; md. Sept. 21, 1826,
William Winter, b. at Carthage, Me., Mch. 23, 1802. Yeoman. Four
ch:—Betsy, b. Mch. 11, 1827, d. Mch. 1, 1833; Mary Ann, b. Apr. 23,
1830; Melvin L., b. Oct. 21, 1835; Juliett, b. Mch. 3, 1840; md. Luther
Hutchinson (1243). 777. ACHSAH, b. Apr. 13, 1808; md. Nov. 12,
1826, Abel Holt, of Weld, b. May 10, 1805, d. Feb. 20, 1853. Ten ch:
—Sylvanus, b. July 10, 1827; Amos, b. Oct. 16, 1829; Lydia, b. Sept.
10, 1831; Daniel, b. Mch. 5, 1834; Eliza, b. Mch. 5, 1836; Rhoda Dale,
b. Mch. 26, 1843; Nancy, b. Nov. 1, 1846; Hezekiah, b. May 13, 1848;
Mandana, b. Oct. 5, 1852, d. Feb. 17, 1853.

778. JOHN⁸. 778. LYDIA DALE, b. May 22, 1812; md. Jan. 8, 1834,
Abner C. Holman, of Carthage, b. ———, d. in the fall of 1866. Five
ch:—Hannibal, b. July 3, 1836, d. May 14, 1852; Lydia Dale, b. Feb.
4, 1838; Belinda Marcilla, b. Jan. 10, 1841; Daniel Gording, b. Dec.
21, 1844; Sylvester Henry, b. Oct. 14, 1847. 779. REUBEN⁸. 780.
PHEBE, b. Dec. 18, 1816, d. July 17, 1867; md. Nov. 26, 1840, Reuben,
son of William and Rachel French, b. at Livermore, Me., Jan. 11,
1819. Resides at Boston. Railroad waste cleaner and bleacher. Five
ch:—William H., b. at Jay, Me., Aug. 26, 1841; Rachel Ann, b. Feb.
19, 1843; Luther A., b. Sept. 14, 1845; Harriet A., b. at Boston, Dec.
22, 1847; George O. E., b. Mch. 16, 1850.

781. LUTHER⁸. 782. BELINDA, b. Dec. 7, 1821; md. Mch. 10, 1846,
Hezekiah S. Taylor. Lives in Mexico, Me. Carpenter. Four ch:—
Daniel G., b. at Dixfield, Apr. 10, 1847; Livonia F., b. Feb. 7, 1849;
Eugene F., b. Dec. 1, 1851; Leonah C., b. June 9, 1855. 783. ELIZA,
b. Sept. 25, 1825, d. Apr. 11, 1831.

(382) JOHN, son of EBENEZER (190), b. at Wilton, July 10,
1784, d. Oct. 28, 1853. Yeoman. Md. Sept. 25, 1813, Esther, dau.
of Winslow and Rebecca (Sawtell) Lakin, b. at Francistown, N. H.,
Jan. 22, 1784, drowned in Souhegan river, Nov. 28, 1850. Five
ch:—

785. JOHN SAWTELL, b. at Wilton, July 1, 1814. 786. WINSLOW, b.
Jan. 14, 1816. 787. ELVIRA, b. July 14, 1820; md. May 8, 1838, George,
son of George and Lydia Whitfield, b. at Wilton, Me., Oct. 17, 1818.
Lives in Francestown, N. H. Yeoman. Seven ch:—George Edward,
b. June 1, 1840; Alvirah Mariah, b. June 18, 1842; Emer Francis, b.
Aug. 17, 1845; James Harrison, b. Oct. 15, 1848; Almira Augusta, b.
Apr. 22, 1851; William Wilson, b. Oct. 24, 1853; Charles Warren, b.
at Lowell, May 12, 1856. 788. ALMIRA, b. July 14, 1820; md. Apr. 6,
1840, Justice, son of Benjamin and Mary Felch, b. at Weare, N. H.,
Aug. 1, 1820. Lives in No. Weare, N. H. Mechanic. Two ch:—
Hosea B., b. Feb. 23, 1845; Elvira F., b. Jan. 30, 1848.

(384) HEZEKIAH, son of EBENEZER (191), b. at Wilton, N. H.,
May 14, 1786. Lived in Wilton, Bedford, and Lowell, Mass., where
he d. Mch. 18, 1852. Carpenter. Md. Oct. 6, 1807, Rachel, dau. of
Ebenezer and Ann Gould, b. at Rindge, N. H., June 7, 1785. Nine
ch : —

789. SELINA ANN, b. Mch. 3, 1808, d. Apr. 14, 1808. 790. HEZEKIAH
ALVIN⁹. 791. BENJAMIN⁶. 792. BETSY S., b. June '2, 1814; md.
May 19, 1836, Samuel, son of Samuel and Sally Rugg, b. at Lancaster,
Mass., July 6, 1807. Resides in Lowell. Machinist. Two ch : —
Mary Ann, b. Mch. 21, 1837, d. Oct. 23, 1844; Emily Newhall, b. Nov.
14, 1851, d. Oct. 26, 1852.

793. ELMIRA, b. Apr. 10, 1816, d. at Lowell, Oct. 9, 1832. 794.
RACHEL ANN, b. July 2, 1818; md. Apr., 1852, John L. Jones, of Pelham, N. H. Yeoman. One ch : —Emma C., b. at Pelham, July 14,
1856. 795. LUCY, b. Sept. 20, 1820; md. May 31, 1853, David B., son
of Edward and Eunice (Hazen) Weston, b. at Derry, N. H., May 29,
1815. Resides in Charlestown, Mass. House and Sign painter; no
issue. 796. JOHN GOULD⁹. 797. ELIZA SUSANNAH, b. Sept. 27,
1826, d. at Lowell, Dec. 30, 1850.

(385) SYLVESTER, son of EBENEZER (191), b. at Wilton, N. H.,
June 21, 1789. Lives in Wilton. Yeoman. Md. Dec. 15, 1815, Charlotte Blanchard, b. Nov. 4, 1796. Seven ch : —
798. EMILY, b. Feb. 27, 1816; md. Samuel Brown, b. Feb. 8, 1808.
799. ISAIAH⁹. 800. FERDINAND⁹. 801. EDWARD B⁹. 802.
ISAAC B⁹. 803. APPLETON⁹. 804. ALBERT, b. June 17, 1833.

(386) SYLVANUS, son of EBENEZER (191), b. at Wilton, Aug.
12, 1791, d. Apr. 17, 1855. Yeoman. Md. Aug. 4, 1818, Hannah, dau.
of Peter and Hannah (Burnham) Hopkins, b. at Milford, Aug. 19,
1790. Four ch : —
805. SYLVANUS⁹. 806. BETSY R., b. Oct. 26, 1826, d. ——, 1843.
807. EMELINE H., b. Apr. 7, 1829; md. Sept. 25, 1850, Henry H., son
of Jesse Travers, b. at Hillsboro, N. H., July 12, 1828. Lives in
Nashua. Mechanic. One ch : —Henry Frank, b. Mch. 6, 1854. 808.
JANE L., b. Oct. 12, 1829; md. Apr. 5, 1855, Isaac P., son of Isaac
and Chloe Abbot, b. at Jackson, Me., Mch. 1, 1826. Lives in Milford.
Mechanic.

(388) JAMES, son of EBENEZER (191), b. at Wilton, June 12,
1797. Lives in Wilton. Yeoman. Md. Jan. 26, 1836, Lucinda, dau.
of Hollis and Polly (Wright) Read, b. at Hollis N. H., Nov. 8, 1800.
One ch : —
809. JAMES HARRISON, b. Aug. 14, 1840.

(389) STEARNS, son of EBENEZER (191), b. at Wilton, N. H., June 13, 1800; rem'd to Francistown, N. H., Jan., 1827, where he d. Dec. 26, 1860. Yeoman. Md. Nov. 11, 1824, Nancy H., dau. of Caleb and Nancy H. Houston, b. at Lyndeboro, Nov. 3, 1804. Eight ch : —

810. PHEBE, b. at Wilton, Nov. 11, 1825; md. Nov. 9, 1842, Willard N. Harraden, b. at New Boston, N. H., Nov. 26, 1820; rem'd to Manchester, thence to Boston, Mass., where he now resides. Four ch : — George N., b. Aug. 10, 1843, d. Sept. 8, 1844; Charles N., b. Oct. 27, 1844. Taken prisoner June 22, 1863, at the raid on the Weldon R. R., and conveyed to the Andersonville prison, where he d. the Nov. following. George W., b. Mch. 13, 1849; Eugene C., b. Aug. 25, 1850, d. Apr. 2, 1857. 811. MINOT STEARNS, b. at Francistown, Aug. 26, 1827, d. at Concord, May 11, 1860.

812. NANCY HOLMES, b. Mch. 10, 1830; md. Rev. Henry S., son of Newman S. and Abigail (Stark) White, b. at Hoosic, N. Y., Apr. 7, 1828. Lived in N. Bedford, Mass., and rem'd thence to Ann Arbor, Mich., where he is now pastor of a newly dedicated church in that place, Three ch : — Abby Frances, b. June 4, 1853, d. June 30, 1853; Frank Newman, b. Aug. 15, 1854; Charles Henry, b. Aug. 12, 1856. 813. MARY ANGELINE, b. Oct. 13, 1832; md. May 27, 1853, Charles C. Mills, b. at Boston, Mch. 18, 1827. Resides in Manchester. Two ch : — Abby Davis, b. Nov. 12, 1855; Flora Estella, b. July 31, 1857. 814. LAURINDA, b. Mch. 15, 1836. 815. EMILY, b. Nov. 20, 1838. 816. RODNEY HOUSTON, b. Dec. 3, 1841, drowned at Manchester, Aug. 14, 1859. 817. GEORGE LEWIS, b. Oct. 18, 1844, d. Mch. 13, 1861.

(391) JACOB, son of BARTHOLOMEW (192), b. at Milford, N. H., Feb. 5, 1785, d. Mch. 23, 1859. Yeoman. Md. 1st, Elizabeth Burnham, b. Sept. 5, 1788, d. Jan. 18, 1839. Md. 2d, June 2, 1839, Esther, dau. of Phineas and Susan Whitney, b. Sept. 29. 1788, d. Feb. 6, 1867. Five ch. by Elizabeth : —

818. BETSY, b. Mch. 21, 1808; md. Nov, 20, 1823, Dr. William Shaw, b. Jan. 4, 1803. Lives in Milford. Four ch : — Christopher Columbus, b. Mch. 20, 1824; Luthera Adaline, b. Oct. 17, 1837, d. Oct. 4. 1854; Mary Jane E., b. Nov. 13, 1841, d. Sept. 29, 1843; Ella F., b. July 12, 1846. 819. JANE, b. Mch. 21, 1814, d. Jan. 23, 1841; md. Oct., 1833, Milton V. Wilkins; rem'd to California, where he d. ———. Two ch : — A child, d. nameless; Milton V., d. young. 820. HARRIET, b. Nov. 13, 1817; md. Nov. 23, 1847, Luther S. Bullard, b. Nov. 18, 1819. Lives in Milford. Yeoman. One ch : — Frances Jane A., b. Aug. 29, 1848. 821. MARIA A., b. Nov. 13, 1826, d. Aug. 30, 1854; md. Apr., 1846, Timothy C. Center. Lives in Wilton. Inn-holder. Two ch : — Ella M., b. Sept. 28, 1848; Charles T.

(393) ALFRED, son of BARTHOLOMEW (192), b. at Milford, Aug. 27, 1788. Resides in Milford Village. Yeoman. Md. May 8, 1810, Lydia, dau. of Jonathan and Rachel Foster, b. Nov. 11, 1789. Ten ch:—

822. PAULINA, b. Mch. 6, 1811, d. at Lawrence, Mass., Oct., 1865; md. Mch. 4, 1834, William T. Little, b. ———, d. at Wethersfield, Ill., aged 36 years. Four ch:—Lydia D., b. Jan. 17, 1835; Nancy T., b. Apr. 26, 1837; Adeline P., b. Aug. 27, 1842; Ruth Maria F., b. Jan. 16, 1844. 823. RODNEY K⁹. 824. JONATHAN D⁸. 825. ROXANNA, b. Nov. 21, 1815, d. Mch. 31, 1854; md. Oct. 8, 1839, John G. Raymond. Lives in Milford. Blacksmith. Two ch:—Rebecca J., b. Aug. 27, 1840, d. Aug. 12, 1854; Abby J., b. Aug. 31, 1848. 826. FRANCIS P⁸. 827. CHARLOTTE E., b. July 30, 1819; md. Aug. 29, 1837, Thomas M., son of Mansfield and Rachel King, b. at Amherst, Sept. 28, 1812. Lives in So. Merrimack, N. H. Blacksmith. Six ch:—Helen, b. May 23, 1840; Charlotte, b. Feb. 13, 1843, d. Jan. 12, 1845; Newton M., b. Sept. 2, 1845; Mary Ann, b. Sept. 23, 1852; Frank P., b. Feb. 1, 1855; Emma R., b. Jan. 13, 1857, d. Dec. 31, 1863. 828. RACHEL F., b. Dec. 21, 1821, d. Sept. 1, 1854; md. Aug. 13, 1844, Sumner Constantine. Lives in Clinton, Mass. Blacksmith. Two ch:—William Sumner, b. Sept. 9, 1848, d. Oct., 1853; Clara Ione, b. Apr. 28, 1851. 829. ALFRED A., b. May 26, 1825, d. Nov. 24, 1834. 830. NATHAN C⁸. 831. RHODA F., b. Dec. 4, 1832; md. Oct. 27, 1851, William R. Peirce, b. ———, 1831, d. Sept. 19, 1854. One ch:—Cora Adeline, b. Sept. 21, 1852.

(397) AUGUSTUS, son of BARTHOLOMEW (192), b. at Milford, Aug. 5, 1805, d. Mch., 1866. Md. June, 1836, Adelaide Smith, who d. Jan. 10, 1856. Eight ch:—

832. ALBERT S., b. Nov. 21, 1836. 833. WILLIAM A., b. Mch. 31, 1839, d. Mch. 31, 1843. 834. PHEBE JANE, b. May 26, 1841. 835. MARY ADELAIDE, b. June 15, 1843. 836. SARAH ANTOINETTE, b. Nov. 1, 1846. 837. ANN A., b. June 14, 1849, d. Sept. 11, 1851. 838. WILLIE O., b. June 5, 1851, d. May 2, 1856. 839. LIZZIE A., b. Oct. 20, 1854, d. Sept. 21, 1856.

(404) NATHANIEL, son of NATHANIEL (200), b. at Braintree, Vt., Apr. 22, 1787, where he now lives. Yeoman. Md. 30, 1808, Nancy, dau. of Jesse and Hannah Stearns Kenney, b. at Barnard, Vt., Mch. 12, 1789, d. Aug. 24, 1864. Seven ch:—

840. ELIZA ANN, b. Dec. 14, 1810; md. Nov. 26, 1835, Daniel, son of Robert and Hannah (Webster) Cram, b. at Roxbury, Vt., Mch. 26, 1809. Lived in Braintree, Vt., and Burns, La Crosse Co., Wis.; rem'd thence, Nov. 8, 1866, to Salisbury, Mo., where he now resides. Yeo-

man. Five ch:—Eliza Jane, b. Oct. 30, 1836; Ellen Maria, b. Apr. 18, 1838; Azro D., b. Oct. 4, 1841, d. June 21, 1863; Vasco Haws, b. Aug. 13, 1844; Lucius Lawson, b. Aug. 8, 1850.

841. A SON, b. Jan. 9, 1810, d. same day. 842. ALDEN, b. June 28, 1813, d. Mch. 24, 1814. 843. SYLVANDER⁸. 844. JOHN⁸. 845. AZRO, b. Jan. 12, 1823, d. Jan. 31, 1823. 846. HARRIET NEWELL, b. Oct. 25, 1824; md. Apr. 13, 1847, Lucius, son of Belcher and Nancy (Lawson) Salisbury, b. at W. Randolph, Vt., June 11, 1824; rem'd to Keytesville, Mo., thence to Salisbury, Mo. For thirteen years a merchant; since then engaged in farming. Five ch:—Mary E., b. Jan. 17, 1849, d. May 13, 1852; Alice C., b. Sept. 3, 1851; Lucius W., b. July 3, 1857, d. Mch. 2, 1866; Arthur V., b. Mch. 28, 1861; Hattie H., b. Mch. 14, 1864.

(408) RUFUS, son of JOHN (201), b. at Sutton, May 9, 1793; rem'd with his father to Braintree, Vt., in the fall of 1793, where he has since lived. Yeoman. Md. July 2, 1818, Abigail, 4th dau. of Henry and Elephal Brackett, b. at Braintree, Mch. 24, 1797. Seven ch:—

847. JOHN B⁸. 848. CHARLES⁸. 849. RUFUS⁸.

850. MINORA A., b. Sept. 16, 1826, d. Apr. 10, 1848; md. Nov. 30, 1847, Seth Mann, now living at Freeport, Ill.; no issue. 851. ELEPHAL, b. Jan., 1831, d. Sept., 1832. 852. GEORGE⁸. 853. SAMUEL, b. Feb. 26, 1835.

(410) JAMES, son of JOHN (201), b. at Braintree, Vt., Feb. 27, 1797, d. Mch. 3, 1861. Lived in W. Randolph. Yeoman. Md. 1st, Nov. 16, 1820, Sophia, dau. of Henry and Dinah F. Brown, b. at Randolph, Vt., Nov. 12, 1801, d. at Braintree, Mch. 3, 1861; md. 2d, Mch., 1862, Mrs. Julia B. Cady. Eight ch:—

854. WILLIAM⁸. 855. JAMES⁸. 856. HENRY⁸. 857. JOHN⁸.

858. SOPHIA, b. Mch. 26, 1832; md. Jan. 9, 1854, Harvey Spaulding. Resides in Lawrence, Kansas. 859. RUTH E., b. Oct. 12, 1834; md. 1865, Henry Leis. Resides in Lawrence, Kansas. 860. LYMAN⁸. 861. EDWIN, b. Nov. 2, 1840, d. at Lawrence, Kansas, Oct. 26, 1864.

(420) JAMES H., son of BARTHOLOMEW (203), b. at Dixfield, Me., Aug. 2, 1805; rem'd to Fayette, Me., Mch., 1835, where he is at present engaged in agricultural pursuits. Md. Feb. 1, 1831, Martha, dau. of Joseph and Hannah (Walton) Davis, b. at Fayette, Aug. 7, 1806. Five ch:—

862. JOSEPH D., b. Dec. 3, 1832, d. Mch. 3, 1833. 863. CYNTHIA C., b. May 3, 1834. 864. HELEN A., b. July 30, 1836. 865. HENRY J., b. Aug. 19, 1840. 866. ALBERT C., b. Dec. 12, 1846.

(421) SYLVESTER M., son of BARTHOLOMEW (203), b. at Dix-field, Me., Feb. 17, 1812; rem'd to Jay Bridge, Me., Apr. 17, 1848, where he now resides. Mill owner. Md. July 23, 1840, Lydia, dau. of Israel and Betsy (Paine) Bean, b. at Jay, Me., Sept. 2, 1814, d. Mch. 20, 1852. Two ch:—

867. CHARLES A., b. June 24, 1846. 868. FRANK W., b. June 23, 1851, d. Apr. 23, 1852. •

(424) LEWIS⁸, son of TIMOTHY (205), b. at Sutton, Mass., Oct. 3, 1797; rem'd with his father to Albany, Me., thence to Norway, Me., and afterwards to Milan, N. H., in 1835, where he now resides. Yeo-man. Md. 1st, Jan. 12, 1820, Abigail, dau. of Enoch and Martha (Wood) Merrille, b. at Andover, Mass., Nov. 1, 1789, d. Nov. 6, 1851. Md. 2d, Feb. 21, 1852, Caroline, dau. of Ichabod and Rachel (Cole) Packard, b. at Hebron, Me., Jan. 12, 1809. Four ch. by Abigail.

869. ALMON⁹. 870. ANGELINE, b. at Norway, May 19, 1825; md. Jan., 1852, Stephen, son of Edmund and Susan Merritt, b. at Norway, Jan., 1825. Yeoman. Two ch:—Georgianna, b. Nov., 1853; Isabel, b. May, 1855. 871. FREELAND⁹. 872. ARVILLA, b. Nov. 24, 1833; md. Ransom F., son of Ransom and Julia (Swan) Twichel, b. at Milan, N. H., Jan., 1832. Lives in Milan. Yeoman. One ch:— Ervin, b. May 26, 1858.

(425) GALEN, son of TIMOTHY (205), b. at Sutton, Mass., Jan. 8, 1798; rem'd with his father to Albany, Me., thence to Milan, N. H., where he is engaged in farming and lumbering. Md. June 10, 1821, Olive, dau. of Benjamin and Elizabeth (Merrill) Flint, b. at Norway, Me., Jan. 26, 1799. Four ch:—

873. ELIZABETH, b. Dec. 31, 1821, d. Oct. 15, 1839. 874. SULLI-VAN⁹. 875. GALEN, b. Dec. 31, 1829, d. Jan. 29, 1831. 876. TIMOTHY, b. Nov. 21, 1831.

(427) MARMADUKE RAWSON⁹, son of TIMOTHY (205), b. at Sutton, Feb. 12, 1802; rem'd with his father to Albany, Me., where he now resides, engaged in farming. Md., Feb. 27, Sophia, dau. of Asa and Lydia Cummings, b. at Albany, Me., Dec. 19, 1802. Five ch:—

877. LYMAN⁹. 878. CHARLES⁹. 879. DANIEL, b. Apr. 19, 1834. 880. MIRANDA, b. Sept. 24, 1837; md. Oct. 30, 1861, Peter, son of James and Fanny Wardwell, b. at Albany, May 16, 1829. Lives in Albany. Yeoman; no issue. 881. ROENA, b. Sept. 9, 1845.

(430) HAVEN⁹, son of TIMOTHY (205), b. at Sutton, Nov. 1, 1808. Resides in Albany, Me. Yeoman. Md. Dec. 23, 1834, Laurinda, dau.

of David and Milly Kimball, b. at Waterford, Me., Apr. 27, 1806.
Four ch: —
882. HORACE[8]. 883. INFANT, b. ———, d. 1840. 884. FREDERICK,
b. Dec. 31, 1842. 885. AUSTIN, b. Nov. 29, 1846.

(431) TIMOTHY HARDING[8], son of TIMOTHY (205), b. at San-
gerville, Me., Mch. 5, 1810. From 1822 till 1846, a mill builder.
Afterwards erected a mill on the Androscoggin river, and followed
lumbering till 1855, when he disposed of his property, and rem'd Mch.,
1856, to Gorham, Me., where he still resides. Md. Dec. 22, 1856, Eliza
Amelia, dau. of James and Betsy Hazelton, b. at Orford, Me., June 6,
1824; No issue.

(434) EDWIN F.[8], son of Timothy (205), b. Nov. 16, 1815; rem'd
in 1840, to Milan, N. H., thence to Auburn, Me., where he now lives.
Yeoman. Md. July 23, 1843, Eliza Ann, dau. of Benjamin and Elizabeth (Merrill) Flint, b. at Norway, Apr. 6, 1821. Seven ch: —
886. LIBERTY HAVEN, b. at Milan, Mch. 1, 1844. 887. HARLON, b.
Nov. 21, 1845. 888. FREEDOM, b. Aug. 6, 1847. 889. LUELLA, b. June
18, 1849, d. Dec. 17, 1854. 890. MELVIN, b. Aug. 27, 1851. 891. ARA-
BELLA LIBBY, b. June 26, 1853. 892. HENRIETTA, b. Mch. 26, 1855.

(437) EBENEZER SUMNER, son of TIMOTHY (205), b. at Albany,
Me., Dec. 1, 1822. Lives in Albany. Yeoman. Md. June 15, 1845,
Betsy Flint, dau. of William and Eleanor Pingree, b. at Norway, Me.,
Oct. 4, 1824. · Four ch: —
893. MARY URSULA, b. Sept. 30, 1846; md. Nov. 28, 1866, John E.
Saunders. Lives in Mechanic Falls, Me. One ch: — Mary Annette, b.
Dec. 7, 1867. 894. ORINDA, b. May 28, 1853. 895. LUELLA ANGELINE,
b. June 22, 1857. 896. AMBROSE BURNSIDE, b. June 2, 1862.

(442) CHARLES DEXTER, son of SIMON (207), b. at Sutton,
Mass., Oct. 18, 1814; rem'd to Northbridge, thence to Dudley, Mass.,
where he d. June 9, 1849. Yeoman. Md. Apr. 24, 1844, Elizabeth W.
Pope, b. at Dudley, May 26, 1818. Two ch: —
897. CHARLES POPE, b. at Northbridge, Aug. 4, 1845, d. Jan. 3, 1847.
898. MARY ELIZABETH, b. at Dudley, May 23, 1847.

(443) HORACE, Rev., son of SIMON (207), b. at Sutton, Aug. 10,
1816. Grad. Amherst, 1839; studied theology at Andover, and after
completing his studies, settled in the ministry at Burlington, Iowa,
where he d. Mch. 7, 1846. Md. Sept., 1844, Susan Bacheller; no issue.

(446) EDWARD HAVEN, son of SIMON (207), b. at Sutton, Aug.

22, 1821. Lives in Sutton. Md. Dec. 12, 1844, Mary Ann Waters, b. at Millbury, Mass., Dec. 12, 1820. Four ch :—

899. WILLIAM HORN, b. Feb. 28, 1846. 900. MARY ELIZABETH, b. Aug. 30, 1848. 901. CHARLES EDWIN, b. Feb. 3, 1851. 902. MARTHA ANNE, b. Mch. 30, 1854.

(450) DANIEL PARISH, son of AARON (212), b. at Randolph, Vt., Aug. 1, 1797; rem'd to Darien, N. Y., thence to Wheatland, Ill., where he now lives. Yeoman. Md. Jan. 9, 1820, Urania, dau. of Richard and Mary Pray, b. at Richfield, N. Y., Apr. 24, 1800. Nine ch :—

903. MARY SUSANNA, b. at Darien, N. Y., Mch. 15, 1821; md. William Brown. Lives in Lawrence, Ill, Yeoman. Two ch :—Anna and George.

904. HANNAH URANIA, b. July 19, 1822, d. Aug. 10, 1822. 905. LOT PERRY⁸. 906. LOVINA, b. Jan. 29, 1828, d. at Waupaca, Wis., Nov. 4, 1854; md. William Thompson, who lives at present in Waupaca. Merchant. Three ch :—Urania, Hettie and Perry.

907. ANDELUCIA, b. Mch. 1, 1829, d. at Wheatland, Ill., Feb. 2, 1846. 908. AMANDA, b. Jan. 11, 1832, d. Sept. 19, 1838. 909. HANNAH MINERVA, b. July 11, 1834, d. Feb. 7, 1842. 910. JOHN, b. July 25, 1839, d. at Harvard, Ill., Dec. 10, 1857. 911. AMANDA MINERVA, b. at Wheatland, July 3, 1842, d. Dec. 12, 1844.

(451) CHESTER FLINT, son of AARON (212), b. at Randolph, Vt., July 19, 1799; rem'd to Genesee Co., N. Y., thence to Johnstown, Wis., and thence, Apr. 2, 1855, to Waupaca, Wis., where he d. Jan. 20, 1867. Yeoman. Md. Feb. 29, 1824, Susannah, dau. of Richard and Mary Pray, b. at Richfield, N. Y., Apr. 24, 1800. Three ch :—

912. DELOSS⁸. 913. GEORGE⁸. 914. DENISON PALMER, b. at Darien, N. Y., Feb. 15, 1837.

(453) RODOLPHUS ALBINUS, son of AARON (212), b. at Williamston, Vt., Jan. 6, 1806; rem'd to Big Foot, Ill., where he d. Aug. 20, 1860. Yeoman. Md. 1st, at Orangeville, N. Y., Jan. 22, 1833, Julia, dau. of John and Rachel Middick, b. ———, d at Alden, N. Y., May 17, 1838. Md. 2d, wid. Lydia Finch, of Alden. dau. of George and Susannah Hunt. Two ch. by Lydia :—

915. ORRIN FINCH. 916. GEORGE ALBINUS.

(454) AARON PARISH, son of AARON (212), b. at Williamstown, Vt., Feb. 11, 1812. Resides in Darien, N. Y., whither he rem'd with his father, Feb. 11, 1815. Yeoman. Md. 1st, Mch. 1, 1842, Maria Louisa, dau. of Jabis and Asenath Backus, b. at Hebron, Conn., Nov. 7, 1818, d. at Darien, Feb. 7, 1852. Md. 2d, Jan. 2, 1853, at Alden,

wid. Ruth Miles, dau. of Jonathan and Bridget Beardsell, from Hinch-
liffe, Eng., b. at Marsdin., Eng., Jan. 3, 1820. Three ch. by Maria L:—
917. AMANDA MARIA, b. June 18, 1843. 918. HENRY PARISH, b. Aug.
7, 1846. 919. CHARLES BACKUS, b. July 9, 1849.

Three ch. by Ruth:—
920. GEORGE ALFARD, b. Oct. 28, 1853. 921. ELLA BEARDSELL, b.
July 9, 1857. 922. GRACE, b. June 14, 1858.

(469) FARWELL J., son of BENJAMIN (217), b. at Waterford,
Vt., Oct. 23, 1801; rem'd to W. Concord, Vt., where he now resides,
Mch. 17, 1854. Yeoman. Md. Apr. 3, 1823, Mary, dau. of Edward
and Esther L. (Rice) Nichols, of Brookfield, Vt., b. Dec. 19, 1802, d.
Feb. 17, 1868. Four ch:—
923. MILO^9. 924. JANE JOSEPHINE, b. at Waterford, Oct. 4, 1828;
md. Dec. 3, 1851, Edwin R., son of Henry and Charity Turner, b.
July 22, 1826. Lives in Concord, Vt. Yeoman. One ch:—Frank
H., b. Oct. 9, 1859.

925. MARY ANN, b. Dec. 29, 1831, d. Apr. 9, 1853. 926. IDA M., b.
Nov. 22, 1848.

(470) BENJAMIN, son of BENJAMIN (217), b. at Waterford, Vt.,
Oct. 10, 1803, d. Mch. 18, 1865. Lived in Waterford. Yeoman. Md.
May 15, 1834, Sophronia, dau. of Abiel and Rebecca (Chase) Richardson, b. at Waterford. Apr. 18, 1807. Six ch:—
927. BENJAMIN FRANKLIN, b. Mch. 12, 1835. 928. JOSEPH W^8.
929. ANNETTE R., b. Feb. 5, 1842. 930. ABIAL E., b. Apr. 19, 1845, d.
Sept. 2, 1846. 931. HERBERT B. M., b. June 22, 1848, d. Aug. 12, 1867.
932. ABIAL J., b. May 19, 1852.

(473) ORVILLE K., son of JOSHUA (221), b. at Royalston, Mass.,
Mch. 11, 1823. Resides in Westboro, Mass., where, Feb. 12, 1849, he
became connected with the State Reform School, as an assistant
teacher. He received the most of his education at Leicester Academy, and afterwards entered life as a teacher of youth. In Mch.,
1850, he was chosen assistant superintendent of the Reform School,
and Aug. 5, 1867, was promoted to superintendent, which office he
now holds, at a salary of $1,400. Md. June 26, 1861, Abbie A., dau.
of Otis and Adeline Brigham, b. at Westboro, Mch. 21, 1833; no
issue.

(474) OTIS K. A., son of JOSHUA (221), b. at Royalston, Mass.,
Feb. 14, 1828. Lived in Royalston, Newport, R. I., and rem'd thence,
in 1858, to Chicago, Ill., where he now lives in the practice of law;
also U. S. Commissioner, under the title of Hutchinson and Luff.

Md. Aug. 27, 1861, Katherine B., dau. of Hon. George and Elizabeth M. Engs. b. at Newport. R. I., Apr. 17, 1838. Four ch:—
933. JOHN MEIN, b. at Newport. Oct. 7, 1862, d. Aug. 27, 1863. 934. MARY ENGS, b. at Chicago, Oct. 10, 1863. 935. GEORGE ORVILLE, b. Jan. 7, 1865, d. Aug. 20, 1866. 936. KATHERINE E., b. Apr. 9, 1867, d. Apr. 21, 1867.

(481) JONATHAN A., son of DAVID (224), b. at Concord, Vt., Jan. 17, 1807; rem'd to Canaan, Vt., Jan. 19, 1854, where he now lives. Yeoman. Md. 1st, Dec. 9, 1835, Sarah D., dau. of John and Sally Williams, b. at Concord, Vt., Oct. 21, 1810, d. at Canaan, Dec. 30, 1856. Md. 2d, June 6, 1858, Melissa, dau. of Ezekiel and Gartrew Flanders, b. at Warner, N. H., Nov. 30, 1825. Four ch. by Sarah D:—
937. ALDEN, b. Aug. 28, 1838. 938. AROZINA, b. Feb. 8, 1841, d. 1861. 939. JOHN W., b. July 3, 1845, d. 1863. 940. CHARLES, b. Sept. 2, 1851.
Three ch. by Melissa:—
941. DAVID A., b. 1860. 942. ALBERT B., b. 1862. 943. SARAH A., b. 1864.

(482) TITUS, son of DAVID (224), b. at Concord, Vt., Feb. 11, 1809. Has lived in Concord, Vt., Littleton, N. H., and Waterford, Vt.; rem'd to St. Johnsbury, Mch. 20, 1854, where he now lives. Blacksmith. Md. Dec. 26, 1838, Susan, dau. of Sylvanus and Elizabeth Hemingway, b. at Waterford, Vt., Oct. 5, 1810. Two ch:—
944. SUSAN AMANDA, b. May 12, 1841. 945. JOHN, b. Dec. 20, 1845.

(486) HORATIO S., son of DAVID (224), b. at Concord, Vt., Dec. 17, 1820. Lives in St. Johnsbury, where he rem'd, Apr. 1, 1850. Blacksmith. Md. May 28, 1843, Sally, dau. of Sylvanus and Elizabeth Hemingway, b. at Waterford, Vt., Aug. 28, 1816. One ch:—
946. AN INFANT, b. and d. Feb. 29, 1848.

(487) GEORGE R., son of DAVID (224), b. at Concord, Vt., Aug. 19, 1823. Lives in St. Johnsbury, Vt. Yeoman. Md. Oct. 4, 1846, Hannah, dau. of Levi R. and Hannah Farr, b. at Waterford, Vt., Dec. 3, 1825. One ch:—
947. HANNAH ROSALTHA, b. July 20, 1847, d. Apr. 26, 1858.

(490) HIRAM, son of SAMUEL (225), b. at Concord, Vt., Jan. 29, 1802; rem'd Mch., 1814, to Charleston, Vt., where he now resides. Yeoman. Md. 1st, Oct. 7, 1830, Melinda, dau. of Benjamin Smith md. 2d, Mch., 1858, Clarinda Smith. Seven ch. by Melindia:—
948. EDWIN H., b. Nov. 3, 1831. 949. HARRISON E., b. Aug. 10,

1833, d. Nov. 10, 1845. 950. Alonzo E., b. June 8, 1835. 951. Irena
M., b. May 10, 1837. 952. Aurillia, b. July 23, 1839. 953. Mary M.,
b. July 15, 1846. 954. Silas L., b. July 1, 1848.

(498) STEPHEN, son of AMOS (227), b. at Concord, Vt., Oct. 3,
1818; rem'd to St. Johnsbury, Mch. 13, 1867, where he at present resides. Yeoman. Md. 1st, Aug. 12, 1849, Mary Jane, dau. of Joel and
Lucy Lewis, b. at Littleton, N. H., May 23, 1824, d. Oct. 3, 1855. Md.
2d, July 4, 1858, Adeline, dau. of John and Ruth McDonald, b. Mch.
20, 1834. Two ch. by Mary Jane : —
955. Edgar Stephen, b. Dec. 22, 1850, d. Dec. 29, 1866. 956. Solomon Elison, b. Dec. 22, 1850.

(502) HIRAM N., son of AMOS (227), b. at Concord, Vt., Aug. 30,
1829, where he now lives. Yeoman. Md. May 20, 1857, Ellen C.,
dau. of Dennis and Caroline May, b. at Waterford, Vt., Dec. 11, 1835.
Three ch : —
957. Aaron Freeman, b. Mch. 1, 1862. 958. Hannah Caroline, b.
Nov. 23, 1863. 959. Mary May, b. Apr. 24, 1867.

(503) STEPHEN, son of RICHARD (233), b. at Chebeague Isl.,
Me., July 23, 1794, d. June 9, 1837. Master mariner. Last part of his
life was pilot of Steamer Bangor. Md. Nov. 27, 1817, Susan, dau. of
Alexander and Patience Ross, b. at Gorham, Me., Oct. 29, 1792. Seven
ch : —
960. Lucinda, b. Sept. 10, 1818; md. Oct. 16, 1838, Joseph B., son
of Samuel and Jane Clark, b. at Lyman, Me., Jan. 11, 1813. Resides
at Cape Elizabeth Depot, Me. Keeper of a Livery Stable. Farmer
and Harness maker. Six ch : — Edward Rackleff, b. at Gray, Me.,
July 10, 1839; Susan Jane, b. Oct. 28, 1842, d. Feb. 30, 1843; Samuel,
b. at Portland, Mch. 16, 1845; Stephen H., b. Aug. 30, 1847, d. Sept.
17, 1847; Joseph B., b. Jan. 24, 1850, d. Dec. 29, 1857; Stephen H., b.
July 22, 1855.
961. William, b. Apr. 15, 1820, d. Apr. ——, 1820. 962. Susan, b.
June 15, 1822, d. Nov. 3, 1844. 963. Julia Ann, b. Apr. 10, 1826; md.
July 11, 1847, Alvin, son of Greenfield and Sarah Hall, b. at Cumber-
land, Me., Jan. 16, 1822. Ship-master. Lives in W. Weymouth, Me.;
no issue. 964. Frederick, b. ——, d. in infancy. 965. Charles, b.
Nov. 15, 1830, d. May 28, 1831. 966. FREDERICK AUGUSTUS⁸.

(504) SAMUEL, son of RICHARD (233), b. at Chebeague Isl., June
1, 1796; rem'd to Portland, Mch., 1848. Mariner. Md. Sept., 1817,
Jane, dau. of John and Anna Hamilton, b. at Chebeague, Mch. 23,
1797. Ten ch : —

967. ISAAC⁵. 968. WILLIAM⁸. 969. HENRY⁸, 970. JAMES⁸.
971. SAMUEL, b. Oct. 17, 1827, d. at Sea, Feb., 1845. 972. ADALINE, b.
Nov. 5, 1829. 973. ANDREW⁸. 974. STEPHEN, b. Sept. 27, 1834.
975. Two ch. d. in infancy.

(509) JOSEPH, Rev., son of Rev. DANIEL (237), b. at Hebron,
Me., Feb. 25, 1801. Lived in Hartford, Canton, Livermore, and Au-
burn, Me.; rem'd to Brunswick, Me., Nov., 1848, where he now lives.
Baptist clergyman. Md. May 10, 1821, Polly, dau. of Richard and
Betsy Dearborn, b. at Hartford, Me., Apr. 10, 1804. Ten ch: —
976. JOHN BUZZELL⁹. 977. BENJAMIN FRANKLIN⁸. 978.
MARY WILSON, b. at Hartford, Me., Feb. 5, 1825; md. May 27, 1853,
Thomas, son of Hector and Mary G. Foster, b. at Abington, Mass.,
June 9, 1833. Lives in Abington. Shoe manufacturer. One ch: —
Mary Jane, b. Dec. 26, 1853.
979. DANIEL⁹. 980. WILLIAM PENN⁸. 981. THURZA JANE, b.
at Hartford, Me., Dec. 28, 1833; md. Jan. 16, 1854, William, son of
Gideon and Elizabeth Owen, b. at Brunswick, Me., Mch. 22, 1832, d.
June 3, 1854. Lived in Abington, Mass. Ship joiner; no issue.
982. ALBION DEARBORN, b. Apr. 12, 1836. 983. EDWIN DARIUS, b.
Sept. 21, 1840. 984. ALZERNON ROSCOE, b. Feb. 21, 1843, d. Aug. 28,
1857. 985. CALVIN BRIGGS, b. Aug. 27, 1845.

(511) RICHARD, son of Rev. DANIEL (237), b. at Buckfield, Me.,
June 8, 1806. Resides in So. Hartford, Me. Yeoman. Md. 1st,
Mary, dau. of Edward and Sarah Blake, b. Oct. 31, 1809, d. at Hartford, Me., Feb. 8, 1855. Md. 2d, Jan. 23, 1856, Emma Cole, of N. Yar-
mouth, Me. Four ch. by Mary : —
986. SARAH H., b. Aug. 18, 1834, d. June 7, 1837. 987. MARY ELLEN,
b. Aug. 1, 1838; md. June 3, 1856, George F., son of William and
Joanna Stearns, b. at Paris, Me., Sept. 20, 1826. Resides in So. Paris.
Railroad contractor. One ch: — Mary Blake, b. at Paris, Feb. 11,
1857. 988. EDWARD BLAKE, b. at So. Hartford, Apr. 30, 1841. 989.
FRANCES A., b. June 26, 1845.

(512) JESSE D., son of Rev. DANIEL (237), b. at Hartford, Me.,
Dec. 29, 1807. Lived in Hartford, Me., Dorchester, Quincy, and rem'd
thence, Apr. 1, 1841, to No. Scituate, Mass., where he now resides.
Yeoman. Md. 1st, Mch. 20, 1834, Patience, dau. of Capt. Levi and
Patience Vinal, b. Feb. 21, 1812, d. July 22, 1841. Md. 2d, July 30,
1842, Sarah L. Vinal, dau. of the foregoing, b. Apr. 28, 1823, d. Dec. 27,
1856. Two ch. by Patience : —
990. MARY FRANCES, b. Mch. 17, 1837; md. Ephraim N. Gardner, of
Scituate Harbor. 991. ALBERT, b. Apr. 10, 1840.

Five ch. by Sarah L :

992. HARRIET LOUISA, b. May 9, 1843. 993. NELSON VINAL, b. Apr. 24, 1845. 994. JULIA AMANDA, b. Apr. 12, 1847. 995. JOSEPH DREW, b. Apr. 24, 1853. 996. SARAH L., b. Dec. 17, 1856.

(515) RODNEY, son of Rev. DANIEL (237), b. at Turner, Me., Jan. 7, 1813. Lives in Buckfield, Me. Yeoman. Md. Jan. 3, 1841, Olive B., dau. of Luther and Mary (Mason) Whitney, b. at Hartford, Me., May 16, 1822. Seven ch :—

997. NANCY A., b. Oct. 8, 1846. 998. CLIFFORD, b. Aug. 21, 1850. 999. CARROL B., b. Nov. 6, 1852. 1000. HERBERT L., b. Aug. 20, 1857. 1001. MARY A., b. Dec. 15, 1859. 1002. WILLIAM H., b. Dec. 18, 1862. 1003. BURTON A., b. July 8, 1867.

(518) JOSEPH, son of Rev. JOSEPH (239), b. at Hebron, Me., Apr. 19, 1807. Resides in Hebron. Farmer, School Teacher, and Insurance Agent. Md. 1st, Sept. 16, 1833, Lucy, dau. of William and Hannah Loring, b. at Turner, Me., Sept. 8, 1812, d. July 2, 1836. Md. 2d, Mrs. Celia A. Davis, and dau. of Hezekiah and Hannah Lovejoy, b. at Peru, Me., Aug. 1, 1812, d. at Hebron Me., May 26, 1845. Md. 3d, Laura, wid. of Lucius Cary, and dau. of Abel and Patty Kinsley, b. at Auburn, Me., Feb. 2, 1809. One ch. by Lucy : —

1004. LUCY ANN, b. Aug. 8, 1835; md. George Vernile, of California.

Two ch. by Celia :—

1005. MARY D., b. Apr. 10, 1840. 1006. ELLEN, b. July 4, 1842.

(526) BUZZELL, son of SAMUEL (240), b. at Gorham, Me., Aug. 15, 1809. Lives in Mechanic Falls, Me. Yeoman. Md. Harriet, dau. of George A. Bradman, b. at Minot, Me., Oct. 29, 1816. Six ch :—

1007. HARRIET ELLEN, b. Nov. 23, 1836. 1008. GEORGE WILLIAM, b. Apr. 4, 1839, d. Apr. 4, 1855. 1009. EBENEZER F., b. July 24, 1840. 1010. SOPHRONIA S., b. Jan. 18, 1844. 1011. FRANKLIN M., b. Sept. 4, 1846. 1012. WESLEY E., b. Nov. 25, 1851.

(527) JOSEPH, Rev., son of SAMUEL (240), b. at Gorham, Me., Apr. 5, 1811. Lives at Mechanic Falls, Me. Clergyman. Md. 1st, Oct. 4, 1835, Rhoda, dau. of William and Dolly (Chase) Tuttle, b. at Buckfield, Me., Mch. 16, 1810, d. June 4, 1843. Md. 2d, Oct. 25, 1843, Matilda, dau. of Levi and Louis Rawson, b. at Paris, Me., Aug. 6, 1812. Four ch. by Rhoda :—

1013. SAMUEL HIRAM[8]. 1014. JOSEPH HENRY[8]. 1015. ALMON HERBERT, b. Aug. 16, 1840. 1016. FRANCES ADELINE, b. July 29, 1842;

md. Jan. 15, 1861, Stephen D. Bailey. Shoe manufacturer. One ch :—
Willie, b. Mch. 31, 1862, d. Sept., 1866.

Three ch. by Matilda :—

1017. Louis Anna Alpha, b. Nov. 4, 1844, d. Dec. 10, 1861; md.
June 10, 1861, Elmer V. Walker. Lives in Minot, Me. Book-keeper.
One ch:—Alpha E., b. Sept. 24, 1861. 1018. William Alpheus, b.
July 7, 1847. 1019. Ada Eva, b. Apr. 17, 1852.

(529) EBENEZER, Rev., son of SAMUEL (240), b. at Gorham, Me.,
Mch. 5, 1817. Resides at Cape Elizabeth Depot, Me., whether he
rem'd, Apr., 1853. Clergyman. Md. June 30, 1842, Frances B., dau.
of Jonah and Elizabeth Dyer, b. at Cape Elizabeth, May 16, 1824.
Four ch :—

1020. Abby F., b. July 13, 1844, d. Aug. 11, 1844. 1021. Edwin F.,
b. Oct. 21, 1848. 1022. Willie H., b. July 5, 1853, d. May 16, 1854.
1023. Willie H., b. Feb. 3, 1857.

(532) ASA FOSTER, Rev., son of SAMUEL (240), b. Aug. 1. 1824;
settled in Sabatus, Me., where he rem'd, May 4. 1855. Freewill baptist clergyman. Md. Oct. 15, 1850, Elenor, dau. of Thomas and Lucy
Frank, b. at Portland, July 14, 1819. One ch :—

1024. Lucy Frank, b. at New Gloucester, Me., Oct. 24, 1854.

(533) STEPHEN D., son of STEPHEN (243), b. at Hebron, Me.,
Sept. 5, 1812. Lives in Paris, Me. For the period of eleven years
prior to 1858, was Register of Deeds for Oxford Co., Me.: at present
engaged in trade. Md. June 11, 1837, Mary, dau. of John and Lucy
(Chipman) Atkinson, b. at Minot, Me., Sept. 17, 1808. Five ch:—

1025. Mary Annette, b. July 29, 1838. 1026. John Randolph, b.
Apr. 11, 1840. 1027. Winfield Scott, b. May 27, 1845. 1028,
George Washington, b. Apr. 11, 1848. 1029. Katy Worth, b. July
27, 1851.

(534) CHANDLER. son of STEPHEN (243), b. at Buckfield. Me.,
Oct. 10, 1814, d. June 30, 1862. Lived in Buckfield, Augusta, and
Paris; rem'd to Norway, Me., May 10, 1854. Cabinet maker. Md,
Nov. 17, 1841, Clarissa A., dau. of Elisha and Caroline Buck, b. at
Buckfield, Me., Apr. 23, 1817, d. Aug. 25, 1862. Nine ch :—

1030. Albion L'Forest, b. Aug. 7, 1842. 1031. Henry Almerrin,
b. Apr. 20, 1844. 1032. Alice Adelaide, b. Mch. 19. 1846, d. June 18.
1865. 1033. Sarah Bannister. b. Sept. 17, 1847. 1034. Clark Bridgham. b. July 31, 1850. 1035. Lorena Isabel, and 1036. Carrol Leroy, b. July 27, 1853. 1037. Emma Lucretia, and 1038. Elmer Herbert, b. Dec. 25, 1854; both d. Apr. 24, 1855.

(535) HORACE, son of STEPHEN (243), b. at Buckfield, Me., Mch. 23, 1817; rem'd to Livermore, Me., where he now resides, Feb. 9, 1842. Yeoman. Md. Jan. 1, 1840, Gustava, dau. of Chandler and Thankful Alden. b. at Turner, Me.. Nov. 28, 1817, d. Dec. 11, 1863; md. 2d, Sept. 17, 1864, Mary S. Cheney. Two ch:—

 1039. BENJAMIN ALDEN, b. Dec. 25, 1840. 1040. HORACE AUBRY, b. Mch. 7, 1847.

(536) MARK, son of STEPHEN (243), b. at Buckfield, Me., Aug., 1819. Lives in E. Turner, where he rem'd, Mch., 1851. Yeoman. Md. Mch. 28, 1849, Eliza, dau. of Benjamin and Polly Alden, b. at Turner, Feb. 22, 1824. Two ch:—

 1041. WALTON, b. June 2, 1850. 1042. AUSTIN, b. Nov. 6, 1852.

(538) ALBION PARRIS, son of STEPHEN (243), b. at Buckfield, Aug. 29, 1825; rem'd Jan. 20, 1849, to Livermore, Me.; afterwards sold his farm and went to Canton, Me., where he purchased a grist mill. Md. Mch. 20, 1851, Emily Augusta, dau. of Tristram C. and Bethiah B. Norton, b. at Livermore, Me.. Nov. 1, 1829. Two ch:—

 1043. TRISTRAM NORTON, b. June 5, 1853. 1044. ASENATH E., b. 1860.

(543) HENRY H., son of HENRY H. (244), b. at Hebron, Me., June 30, 1814. Resides in Buckfield, Me. Yeoman. Md. Mch. 30, 1837, Ruth. dau. of Caleb and Polly Cushman, b. at Buckfield, Aug. 9, 1811. Three ch:—

 1045. CAROLINE, b. July 13, 1838; md. Nov. 20, 1856, William H., son of Levi and Polly Mitchell, b. at Turner, Me., June 2, 1821, where he now lives. Yeoman. Two ch:—Rose E., b. Feb. 8, 1859; Ruth A., b. July 29, 1862. 1046. SOPHRONIA, b. July 4, 1840; md. July 3, 1866, Edwin W., son of Henry and Olive W. Davis, b. at Lewiston, Me., Nov. 24, 1839; rem'd Nov. 29, 1863, to Lynn, Mass., where he now resides. Boot and shoe manufacturer. One ch:—Henry Albert, b. May 6, 1867. 1047. GEORGE D., b. Nov. 24, 1843.

(546) EDMUND, son of HENRY H. (244), b. at Buckfield, Oct. 19, 1819. Lived in Hartford, Buckfield, Winthrop, Stoughton and Hebron; rem'd thence to Minot, Me., Feb. 15. 1858. Boot and shoe manufacturer. Md. Feb. 29, 1840, Sarah, dau. of Isaac and Ann Young, b. at Hartford. Me., Oct. 18. 1815. Seven ch:—

 1048. FRANCIS, b. Sept. 27, 1840. 1049. BENJAMIN, b. July 17, 1842. 1050. MARTHA, b. Aug. 27, 1844. 1051. ELMER P., b. July 25, 1846, d. Mch. 24, 1849. 1052. ELMER P., b. Aug. 1, 1850. 1053. JULIA, b. Sept. 19, 1852. 1054. LEWELLER, b. Apr. 9, 1854, d. Sept. 13, 1857.

(549) JOHN COLBY, son of JOHN (248), b. at Hebron, Me., Dec. 30, 1824. Lives in E. Hebron. Md. Mch. 27, 1849, Martha B., dau. of Alvah and Nancy (Chase) Gilbert, b. at Buckfield, July 31, 1820. Two ch : —

1055. PERSIS MARIA, b. Sept. 5, 1852. 1056. CARRO ALMA. b. Dec. 25, 1855.

(555) JOHN, son of JAMES (250), b. at Wilton, Me., May 10, 1815; where he now resides. Yeoman. Md. 1st, Nov., 1838, Asenath Flint Chandler, b. Feb. 22, 1815, d. June 30, 1851; md. 2d, Feb. 17, 1852, Nancy Abby. dau. of Jacob and Sarah Rideout, b. July 17, 1823. Five ch. by Asenath : —

1057. JOHN ANSET, b. ———, d. in infancy. 1058. ASENATH ANN, b. Oct. 7, 1843, d. Jan. 19, 1851. 1059. JOHN STILES, b. Mch. 22, 1844. 1060. FRANCIS A., b. July 13, 1846, d. May 7, 1851. 1061. CHARLES A., b. Feb. 14, 1843, d. Oct. 20, 1851.

Two ch. by Nancy : —
1062. GEORGE ALVA, b. Sept. 16, 1855, d. Nov. 15, 1855. 1063. ANNA MALVINA, b. May 29, 1857.

(558) JEDSON MATTHEW, son of SEWELL (253), b. at Roxbury, Vt., Feb. 22, 1832. Lives in Nestoria, Wis. Md. Dec. 25, 1853, Diana M. Fuller.

1066. Three children, all of whom d. in infancy.

(566) EZRA BARTLETT, son of AMBROSE B. (255), b. at Roxbury, Vt., Nov. 27, 1831. Resides in Buffalo Co., Wis. Yeoman. Md. Mch. 20, 1856, Nancy Atilda, dau. of Amasa and Sally Blanchard. Two ch : —

1067. SARAH ROSETTA. 1068. AMASA BARTLETT.

EIGHTH GENERATION.

(578) NATHANIEL, son of ANDREW (257), b. at Milford, N. H., June 28, 1798, d. May 6, 1859. Lived in Milford. Yeoman. Md. June 2, 1822, Lucinda Pearson, b. Jan. 27, 1801. Two ch : —
1069. EVERETT, b. Sept. 17, 1825. 1070. ANN JANE, b. Nov. 2, 1827.

(584) STILLMAN, son of ANDREW (257), b. at Milford, July 19, 1812. Resides in Milford. Yeoman. Md. Apr. 5, 1834, Emeline, dau. of Moses and Rhoda Lull, b. Nov. 2, 1813. Four ch : —
1071. LUCRETIA A., b. Nov. 19, 1837; md. May 8, 1862, Edward A., son of Charles and Elizabeth Burns, b. at Milford, Nov. 4, 1836. Lives

in Charlestown, Mass. Milk dealer. One ch:—Harry Jewett, b. May 31, 1865. 1072. Sophronia A., b. Jan. 8, 1841, d. Feb. 24, 1866. 1073. Alvaro Oliver, b. July 5, 1846. 1074. Stillman Hubbard, b. Sept. 15, 1849.

(589) DAVID, son of JESSE (258), b. at Milford, Oct. 11, 1803. Resides in Milford. Yeoman. Md. Apr. 28, 1829, Betsy, dau. of Nehemiah and Rebecca S. Hayward (369), b. Mch. 19, 1807. Eight ch:— 1075. Georgianna, b. Jan. 23, 1830; md. Oct. 27, 1857, John N. Gatch, of Milford, Ohio. 1076. Hayward, b. Jan. 19, 1832. 1077. Jesse L., b. Feb. 5, 1834 rd. at Nashua, June 10, 1856. 1078. Elias S., b. Dec. 24, 1835. 1079. John W., b. Mch. 24, 1838. 1080. Virginia, b. June 16, 1840. 1081. Delia Florence, b. Aug. 4, 1845. 1082. Lucretia O., b. Aug. 12, 1848.

(590) NOAH B.. son of JESSE (258), b. at Milford, Jan. 26. 1805. Lives in Mt. Vernon, N. H., where he owns a valuable farm, which for many years he has tilled with great success. He md. Apr. 5, 1827, Mary. dau. of James and Azubah Hopkins, of Mt. Vernon, b. Jan. 9, 1806, d. May 16, 1866. Ten ch:— 1083. Frances Jane. b. May 21, 1828. d. Oct. 25, 1833. 1084. Andrew Buxton, b. July 9, 1830. Resides in Germantown, N. J. Carpenter. Md. Dec. 5, 1867, Ellen T.. dau. of Rev. David Kline, b. Mch. 29, 1845; no issue. 1085. Matthew Bartlett, b. Apr. 16, 1832. 1086. Aaron Bruce, b. Aug. 4, 1834. 1087. Ann Jane E., b. May 15, 1836; md. Nov. 16, 1864, Daniel, son of Daniel and Charlotte Sargent, b. at Goffstown, N. H., Aug., 1825. Lives in Mt. Vernon. N. H. Stone cutter. Two ch:—Willie, b. Sept. 5, 1865, d. Mch. 11, 1866; Eddie, b. Sept. 2, 1867. 1088. LUCIUS BOLLES⁹. 1089. David Judson. Merchant. Lives in N. Y. 1090. Mary Victoria. b. June 22, 1845. d. May 14. 1864, at So. Orange, N. J., while engaged in teaching school. 1091. Chestina Augusta, b. Oct. 5, 1847. 1092. Henry Appleton. b. Aug. 16, 1850.

(592) ANDREW B., son of JESSE (258), b. at Milford, N. H., Aug. 19, 1808. The earlier part of his life was spent on his father's farm, when he afterwards rem'd to Boston and engaged in mercantile pursuits, till his decease. Oct. 20, 1860. He possessed a fine musical talent, but never could persuade himself to quit his legitimate employment to engage, like his brethren, in a public profession of it. While they were maturing plans to enter upon their professional career as vocalists, his advice was sought in the matter; but he rather viewed it as a wild speculation, and urged them, in a spirit of caution, to

abandon the enterprise, but without avail. He md. June 22, 1834, Elizabeth Ann, dau. of Jacob and Catherine Todd, b. at Rowley, Mass., Dec. 27, 1813. Five ch : —

1093. JACOB TODD, b. July 10, 1836. 1094. ANDREW LEAVITT, b. June 11, 1838, d. 1867. 1095. MARCUS MORTON, b. Oct. 24, 1844. 1096. BENJAMIN PEIRCE. b. Apr. 14, 1848. 1097. KATIE, b. Nov. 15, 1850.

(593) ZEPHANIAH, son of JESSE (258). b. at Milford. Jan. 7, 1810; rem'd. 1832, to Greenville, Ill., where he d. Apr. 17, 1853. Yeoman. Md. 1st. Aug., 1836, Abby, dau. of Mark Perkins, b. at Mt. Vernon, N. H., Feb. 25, 1811, d. Apr. 20, 1848; md. 2d, Sept. 10, 1849, Elizabeth Nettleton, of Newport, N. H. Four ch. by Abby : —

1098. HARRIET, b. July, 1837. d. Apr. 17, 1842. 1099. HETTE, b. July 26, 1841. 1100. LEVI WOODBURY, b. Mch. 19, 1845. 1101. MARK PERKINS, b. Dec. 5. 1847, d. May 1, 1848.

One ch. by Elizabeth : —

1102. MARY FRANCES, b. Feb. 6, 1851.

(593) CALEB, son of JESSE (257), b. at Milford, Nov. 25. 1811, d. Jan. 16, 1854. Yeoman. Md. Feb. 18, 1835, Laura, dau. of Oliver and Susan (Smith) Wright, b. Nov. 22, 1816. Five ch : —

1103. LAURA ANN, b. Jan. 23, 1837. 1104. MARY JOSEPHINE, b. Nov. 26, 1839. 1105. SUSAN MARIA. b. July 24, 1842. 1106. CALEB GEORGE MASON, b. May 20, 1844. 1107. CAROLINE JENNETTE, b. Sept. 24, 1850.

(595) JOSHUA, son of JESSE (258), b. at Milford, Nov. 25. 1811. Yeoman and Vocalist. Md. June 3, 1835, Irene, dau. of Nathan and Sarah Fisher, of Francestown, N. H., b. Oct. 26, 1810. Three ch : —

1108. JUSTIN EDWARDS[9]. 1109. LOWELL MASON, b. Oct. 28, 1839, d. Aug. 7, 1843. 1110. JULIA ELLA, b. Aug. 23, 1847, d. Sept. 30, 1848.

[For further particulars concerning the history of Joshua, see Appendix B.]

(596) JESSE, son of JESSE (258), b. at Milford, Sept. 29, 1813, d. at Cincinnati, O., May 15, 1853; rem'd to Lynn, 1836, and built him a residence on that fine eminence called High Rock. His trade was that of a printer, and also possessed much mechanical skill. He was the inventor of an improvement on the air-tight stove, which was highly approved of, and was one of the original number in their attempt to penetrate the far-famed Pirate's Cave of Lynn, but without success. The songs composed by him are of a very distinctive and original character, among which are the "Old Granite State," "Good Old Days

of Yore," "Slave's Appeal," the "Congressional Song," and many others. He md. June 8. 1836, Susanna W. Hartshorn, b. at Amherst, Oct. 13, 1815, d. at Lynn, Sept. 10, 1851. Six ch :—

1111. JAMES GARRISON, b. July 3, 1838, d. Apr. 18, 1842. 1112. CHARLES FOLLEN, b. May 1, 1840, d. May 8, 1842. 1113. ANDREW EDWARD, b. Jan. 7, 1842, d. Apr. 27, 1842. 1114. JESSE HERBERT, b. Aug. 8, 1843, d. Apr. 23, 1844. 1115. JAMES, b. Jan., 1847, d. 1849. 1116. SUSAN MARY EMMA, b. Jan. 16, 1851, d. Sept. 21, 1851.

(598) JOSEPH JUDSON, son of JESSE (258), b. at Milford, Mch. 14, 1817, d. at Lynn, Jan. 11, 1859. As his history is identified with that of his musical brethren, John and Asa, a more extended notice of him will be given in Appendix B. He md. July, 1844, Jerusha Peabody (755), dau. of Abel and Betsy Hutchinson, b. at Milford, Apr. 20, 1825. Two ch :—

1117. KATE LOUISA, b. May 14, 1845. 1118. JENNIE LIND, b. Jan. 4, 1848, d. Mch. 15, 1863.

(600) JOHN WALLACE, son of JESSE (258), b. at Milford, Jan. 4, 1821. Resides in Lynn, on High Rock. He and his brother Jesse were two of the first settlers on that beautiful eminence, which commands a very extended view of the city and the ocean. For a further account of his history, see Appendix B. He md. Feb. 21, 1843, Fanny Burnham, dau. of David A. and Susanna (Parker) Patch, of Lowell, b. June 27, 1822. Three ch :—

1119. HENRY JOHN, b. Dec. 18, 1844. 1120. VIOLA GERTRUDE, b. Apr. 18, 1847; md. Apr. 15, 1868, Lewis A., son of Judge Campbell, of Cherry Valley, N. Y., b. Nov. 4, 1842. Lives in Toledo. Merchant.

(601) ASA BURNHAM, son of JESSE (258), b. at Milford, Mch. 14, 1823. Resides in Hutchinson, Minnesota. A detailed account of his history will be found in Appendix B. He md. Apr. 26, 1847, Elizabeth B., dau. of Frederick B. and Phebe B. Chase, of Nantucket, Mass., b. Mch. 14, 1828. Four ch :—

1121. ABBY, b. Mch. 14, 1849. 1122. FREDERICK CHASE, b. Feb. 4, 1851. 1123. OLIVER DENNETT, b. Jan. 15, 1856. 1124. ELLEN CHASE, b. May 22, 1861, d. at New York, Jan. 24, 1867.

(607) HIRAM, son of JOSEPH (260), b. at Middleton, Mass., Nov. 10, 1808. In 1853 he removed to France, where he became extensively engaged in the manufacture of India-rubber goods. He established two large factories there, and one at Manheim, Grand Duchy of Baden. These were the first factories of the kind of any importance introduced in Europe, and gave employment to nearly one thou-

sand people. He md. July 5, 1831, Mary Ann, dau. of Abraham and Elizabeth Lufberry, b. at Burlington, N. J., Mch. 13, 1815. Eight ch :—

1125. ALCANDER[9]. 1126. ABRAHAM LUFBERRY, b. at New Orleans, Nov. 24, 1834, d. July 10, 1835, on passage from N. O. 1127. SARAH ELIZABETH, b. at N. Brunswick, N. J., June 19, 1836; md. Dec. 8, 1864, Right Rev. Horatio Southgate, for a number of years Bishop of Constantinople.

1128. MARY FRANCES, b. Dec. 1, 1837; md. 1st, Nov. 11, 1862, Capt. W. L. Gwin, of the U. S. N., who was killed Jan. 3, 1863, while bombarding the fortifications of Haine's Bluff, near Vicksburg, Miss., with the Iron Clad " Benton ;" md. 2d, Aug. 15, 1864, to Henry P. Moorhouse, Esq.

1129. JOHN GARDNER, b. Oct. 5, 1839, d. Nov. 3, 1845. 1130. CHARLOTTE CARTER, b. June 24, 1841, d. Sept. 16, 1841. 1131. HIRAM, b. Aug. 25, 1843. 1132. CHARLES LOUIS RICHARD, b. at Paris, France, Oct. 1, 1859.

(610) ELISHA PUTNAM, son of JOSEPH (261), b. at Danvers Aug. 9, 1813. Lived in S. Danvers (now Peabody), where he carried on the shoe and grocery business ; rem'd thence to Lynn and engaged in the wholesale trade of shoes, under the firm of Richardson and Hutchinson. He afterwards went to Beaufort, S. C., where he lived till the decease of his wife, when he returned to New York. Md. Mch. 14, 1837, Ruth Louisa Richardson, of Middleton, b. Dec. 12, 1817, d. July 30, 1868. Nine ch :—

1133. JOSEPH CURTIS, b. July 27, 1837. 1134. WALTER DERBY, b. Feb. 2, 1840. 1135. EZRA ALMON, b. May 22, 1842. 1136. ANN AMELIA, b. June 6, 1844. 1137. JULIA LOUISA, b. Sept. 4, 1846, d. Sept. 15, 1849. 1138. ELLA PUTNAM, b. Aug. 31, 1848. 1139. ELISHA MORTON, b. Dec. 14, 1850. 1140. SUSAN WHITE, b. Mch. 30, 1853. 1141. CHARLES SUMNER, b. Apr. 24, 1856.

(614) GEORGE PUTNAM, son of LEVI (263), b. at Danvers, Oct. 25, 1812. Resides in Danvers. Yeoman. Md. June 24, 1841, Mary (609), dau. of Joseph and Sally Hutchinson, b. Feb. 14, 1812. Four ch :—

1142. GEORGE HENRY, b. May 23, 1842. 1143. MYRAN RUSSELL, b. Apr. 14, 1844. 1144. MARY ELIZABETH, b. Apr. 3, 1846. 1145. HIRAM LUFBERRY, b. Apr. 15, 1849.

(615) SAMUEL, son of LEVI (263), b. at Danvers, Nov. 28, 1814. Lives in So. Danvers. Yeoman. Md. May 9, 1847, Rebecca H., dau. of Amos and Rebecca (264) King, b. at So. Danvers, July 3, 1820. Two ch :—

1146. George Thomas, b. May 1, 1840. 1147. Albert, b. Apr. 7, 1849.

(618) LEVI RUSSELL, son of LEVI (263), b. at Danvers, Dec. 9, 1820; rem'd to Lynnfield Centre, where he at present resides. He md. ——, Harriet Smith, dau. of William and Lois Parker, b. Dec. 27, 1816. Three ch: —
1148. Elizabeth, b. Sept. 28, 1845, d. Mch. 10, 1846. 1149. Francis, b. Mch. 3, 1846. 1050. Wilbour, b. Apr. 28, 1851.

(620) CLEAVES KING, son of BENJAMIN (266), b. at So. Danvers, Oct. 21, 1827; rem'd to Conklinville, N. Y., July, 1864. Tanner. Md. Oct. 12, 1865, Caddie, dau. of Henry and Mary Poor, b. at So. Danvers, Sept. 28, 1839. One ch: —
1151. Henry Poor, b. at Hadley, N. Y., Apr. 13, 1867.

(625) WILLIAM H., son of BENJAMIN (266), b. at Lowell, Mass., Mch. 7, 1838. Lives in Gallipolis, O. Dealer in hardware, cutlery, etc. Md. Nov. 15, 1866, Sarah T., dau. of Dr. Augustus and Alice O. Peirce, b. at Tyngsboro, Mass. One ch: —
1152. Alice Olivia, b. at Gallipolis, Nov. 19, 1867.

(629) AUGUSTUS RICHARDSON, son of DAVID (268), b. Feb. 22, 1821. Lives in Wenham. Yeoman. Md. Feb. 26, 1846, Hannah Goldsmith, dau. of Jacob and Rebecca Dodge, b. at Wenham, July 21, 1819. Three ch: —
1153. Levi Curtis, b. May 30, 1846. 1154. Lucy Goldwait, b. May 28, 1848. 1155. William Augustus, b. Feb. 11, 1857.

(635) AUGUSTUS LUCAS, son of IRA (271), b. Dec. 11. 1825. Lives in Milwaukie, Wis. Formerly a shoe manufacturer. At present engaged in the grain trade. Md. Sept. 23, 1851, Susannah R., dau. of Zaddock and Lucinda Lawrence, b. at Groton, Mass., July 20, 1827. Two ch: —
1156. Mary Susan, b. July 19, 1853. 1157. George Augustus, b. Oct. 9, 1857.

(637) BENJAMIN PETERS, son of IRA (271), b. July 24, 1829; rem'd, 1856, to Milwaukie, where he engaged in the shoe trade; afterwards went (1858) to Chicago, where he has amassed a fortune in the grain and packing business. Md. Aug. 24, 1853, Sarah M., dau. of William and Lydia Ingalls, of Lynn, b. Feb. 18, 1833. Five ch: —
1158. Charles Lawrence, b. Mch. 7, 1854. 1159. Helen Maria, b. Sept. 3, 1855. 1160. Katie, b. Nov. 24, 1858. 1161. Hattie S., b. Aug. 16, 1863. 1162. Annie L., b. Sept. 6, 1866, d. Feb. 24, 1868.

(645) WILLIAM HENRY, son of WILLIAM (279), b. at Danvers, Dec. 3, 1828, where he now lives. Shoe manufacturer. Md. July 18, 1852, Caroline A., dau. of Jereiniah and Mary Peabody, b. June 7, 1831. Two ch : —

1163. ALVAN AUGUSTUS, b. Oct. 11, 1852. 1164. HENRY WILLIS, b. Dec. 25, 1855.

(646) JAMES AUGUSTUS, son of WILLIAM (279), b. at Danvers, Oct. 14, 1830. Lives in Danvers. Shoe manufacturer. Md. May 7, 1851, Nancy Ingalls, dau. of Joseph B. and Patty Perkins, b. Nov. 7, 1831. One ch : —

1165. EMMA INGALLS, b. Mch. 23, 1853.

(662) HORATIO D., son of JOSEPH (317), b. at Winthrop, Me., Mch. 7, 1829 ; rem'd, 1853, to Boston, where he engaged in the practise of law. Commenced the study of law, in 1850, under Hon. Seth May, of Winthrop, Me., Judge of Supreme Court. Grad. at Dane Law School, Cambridge, July, 1853. Md. Dec. 31, 1854. Harriet Sophronia, dau. of Sheldon and Sarah Stone, b. at Newbury, N. Y., Feb. 22, 1833. Two ch : —

1166. HARRIET ELEANOR, b. Sept. 8, 1855. 1167. HORATIO, b. July 17, 1858.

(670) JEREMY, son of PERLEY (338), b. at Danville, Vt., Dec. 31, 1817. Lives in California, where he rem'd, Nov. 2, 1852. Yeoman. Md. Dec. 6, 1842, Martha, dau. of Noah and Mary (Cram) Lane, b. ———, d. Aug. 18, 1851. One ch : —

1168. ALDEN PERLEY, b. Aug. 26, 1848.

(672) EDWARD, son of ELIJAH (341), b. at Danvers, Sept. 14, 1833. Residence at Danvers. Engaged in the shoe business in Boston, under the name of E. and A. Mudge & Co., 39 Pearl st. Md. Feb. 23, 1858, Almira, dau. of William and Serena Preston. b. at Danvers, Sept. 13, 1833. One ch : —

1169. CLARA, b. May 29, 1866.

(681) WILLIAM AUGUSTUS, son of ELISHA (357), b. Nov. 10, 1825. Resides in Plaistow, N. H. Shoe manufacturer. Md. Feb. 7, 1856, Mary Esther, dau. of John and Mehitable Emery, b. at W. Newbury, Aug. 23, 1834. Three ch : —

1170. WILLIAM ELISHA, b. Apr. 5, 1858, d. Apr., 1861. 1171. FRANK EMERY, b. Nov. 8, 1862. 1172. HOMER SCOTT, b. Feb. 22, 1864.

(691) FREEMAN, son of SAMUEL (359), b. at Milford, N. H., Oct.

24, 1805. Lives in Wilton, N. H. Yeoman. Md. Feb. 19, 1828, Louisa, dau. of Joshua and Beulah Moore, b. at Milford, Aug. 31, 1806. Nine ch : —

1173. MARIAH LOUISA, b. July 29, 1828; md. Mch. 18, 1844. Joseph A. Brown, b. Jan. 5, 1824. Lives in Nashua. Four ch : — Martha Jennette, b. June 21, 1850; Rebecca Ann, b. Jan. 31, 1853; Ella Maria, b. Apr. 26, 1855; William Henry, b. June 9, 1857.

1174. MARTHA JANE, b. Feb. 11, 1830, d. Oct. 13, 1846. 1175. MATTHEW FREEMAN, b. Feb. 11, 1830, d. July 6, 1847. 1176. FRANCIS CLIFTON[9]. 1177. DORINDA BEULAH b. Mch. 7, 1834. 1178. CHARLES LEROY, b. Feb. 18, 1837. 1179. JAMES WILSON, b. Dec. 24, 1839. 1180. TIMOTHY NEWELL, b. July 21, 1842. 1181. ISAAC NEWTON, b. May 15, 1844.

(700) HARVEY, son of JOTHAM (362), b. at Wilton, Aug. 6, 1816. Lives in Wilton. Yeoman. Md. Apr. 9, 1846, Hannah, dau. of Isaac and Eunice Jewett, b. at Nelson, N. H., June 6, 1824. Two ch : —

1182. MARIETT, b. Nov. 28, 1851. 1183. HANNAH JANE, b. Oct. 6, 1856.

(702) CHARLES, son of FREDERICK (363), b. at Wilton, Jan. 5, 1812; rem'd, 1836, to Pepperell, Mass. Shoe manufacturer. Md. Nov. 30, 1842, Thirza, dau. of David and Betsy Shattuck, and wid. of Charles B. Shattuck, of Pepperell, b. Feb. 13, 1804; no issue.

(705) ABEL FISK, son of FREDERICK (363), b. at Wilton, June 27, 1818; rem'd to Mechanicsburg, O. Merchant. Md. June 18, 1839, Mary Mowry. Two ch : —

1184. MARY ELIZABETH. 1185. WILTON.

(708) FREDERICK LYMAN, son of FREDERICK (363), b. at Wilton, Sept. 13, 1827. Lives in Wilton. Shoemaker. Md. May 15, 1852, Joanna Sophronia (1213), dau. of Robert and Eliza Ann Hutchinson, b. at Milford, Aug. 6, 1836; no issue.

(714) SARDIS MILLER, son of ABIEL (365), b. at E. Wilton, May 11, 1830; rem'd with his father to Nashua, where he d. Jan. 10, 1857. Md. Sept. 24, 1853, Charlotte Leonard, of Nashua. Two ch : —

1186. A child, b. ———, d. ———, aged 2 years. 1187. A child, b. Feb., 1857.

(715) STEPHEN BARNARD, son of ABIEL (365), b. at E. Wilton, Oct. 4, 1831. Lives in Springfield, Mass. Md. Feb. 5, 1853, Susan H. Merrill, of Nashua. One ch : —

1188. A child, b. ———, 1857.

(716) ANDREW JACKSON, son of ABIEL (365), b. at E. Wilton, Nov. 30, 1833. Lived in Nashua; rem'd to So. Reading, July, 1859. Iron moulder. Md. July 11, 1855, Eliza A., dau. of Lewis and Mary Green, of Granby, Canada East, b. Feb. 23, 1834. One ch :—
1189. WILLIE ANDREW, b. July 24, 1856.

(722) ROBERT, son of SOLOMON (366), b. at E. Wilton, Sept. 16, 1814. Lived in Nashua, Milford, and Boston; rem'd July 17, 1839, to Iowa City, Iowa, where he now resides. Mechanic. Md. Oct. 19, 1843, Julia M., dau. of Zelah and Elizabeth Whetstone, b. at Cincinnati, Jan. 8, 1842. Ten ch :—
1190. JULIA C., b. Sept. 23, 1844. 1191. ZELAH W., b. Feb. 6, 1846. 1192. LAURA C., b. Dec. 1, 1847. 1193. CHARLES J., b. Oct. 21, 1849. 1194. FRANK P., b. July 15, 1853. 1195. WILLIE V., b. June 6, 1856, d. Sept. 13, 1857. 1196. SOPHIA W., b. July 6, 1858. 1197. HANNAH J., b. Apr. 5, 1860. 1198. CARRIE W., b. Apr. 4, 1862. 1199. SARAH A., b. Mch. 23, 1864.

(723) JACOB F., son of SOLOMON (366), b. at E. Wilton, Aug. 14, 1816; rem'd from Nashua to Salt Lake City, where he d. May 7, 1867. Trader. Md. Constantia E. C. Langdon, who d. at Salt Lake City, Dec. 1, 1865. Seven ch :—
1200. NATHANIEL, b. ——, 1837. 1201. CATHERINE, b. ——, 1843. 1202. GEORGE, b. ——, 1844. 1203. JACOB, b. ——, 1846. 1204. ELLAR, b. ——, 1850. 1205. DAVID, b. ——, 1853. 1206. RUTH, b. ——, 1858.

(724) GEORGE W., son of SOLOMON (366), b. at E. Wilton, July 18, 1818. Lived in Nashua; rem'd, 1831, to Boston; 1850 to Indiana; 1856 to Iowa City; thence to Kansas, and one year after to the Rocky mountains, where he lived five years, and thence to Osawkie, Kansas, where he now lives. For several years a hotel keeper; at present a painter. Md. Sept. 7, 1840, Mary, dau. of John F. and Margaret Blankenburgh, b. at Portland, Me., Mch. 29, 1817. One ch :—
1207. GEORGIANNA, b. June 15, 1842, d. Feb. 10, 1843.

(727) HENRY O., son of SOLOMON (366), b. at E. Wilton, July 17, 1826; rem'd, 1856, to Iowa City. Lived in Nashua, Boston, and other places. Painter. Md. ——, 1849, Judith, dau. of Thomas and Anna Hamlett, b. at Nashua, Nov. 11, 1832. Two ch :—
1208. NELLIE V. A., b. July 27, 1850. 1209. HENRIETTA, b. Oct. 5, 1853.

(732) ERASTUS, son of NATHAN (368), b. Mch. 16, 1810. Resides

in Cambridge, Mass. Md. Sept. 13, 1835, Sarah Beers, of Lynn. Two ch : —

1210. HENRY ERASTUS, b. July 4, 1839. 1211. KATE OLIVIA, b. Sept. 10, 1846.

(736) ROBERT, son of REUBEN (370), b. at Milford, Jan. 15, 1809, d. Jan. 8, 1852. Lived in Milford. Yeoman. Md. July 4, 1833, Eliza, Ann, dau. of Nathan Holt, b. at Temple, N. H., Jan. 3, 1815. Seven ch : —

1212. ELIZA AUGUSTA, b. Sept. 8, 1834, d. Oct. 30, 1837. 1213. JOANNA SOPHRONA, b. Aug. 6, 1836; md. Frederick L. Hutchinson (708). 1214. CHARLES MASON, b. Oct. 25, 1838; md. Hannah Eaton, of Wilton. 1215. JANE AUGUSTA, b. Jan. 30, 1842; md. Geo. French, of Nashua. 1216. ROBERT BRUCE, b. Jan. 16, 1845, d. Oct. 18, 1846. 1217. CLARA JENNETTE, b. Aug. 23, 1847; md. Oct. 8, 1866, William, son of Patrick and Hannah Dillon, b. at Lowell, June 2, 1844. Lives in Wilton. Overseer and wool carder. One ch : ——, b. Jan. 30, 1867. 1218. ELLA SYRENA, b. July 20, 1850.

(739) REUBEN, son of REUBEN (370), b. at Milford, Sept. 9, 1814. Resides in Milford. Yeoman. Md. Jan. 15, 1840, Judith, dau. of William and Abigail Daws, b. June 12, 1816. Two ch : —

1219. JAMES HARRISON, b. Aug. 27, 1840. 1220. MARY ELIZABETH, b. Feb. 6, 1846.

(741) EDMUND P., son of REUBEN (370), b. at Milford, Nov. 1, 1818. Lives in Milford. Yeoman. Md. Apr. 6, 1845, Mariah L., dau. of Jonas and Sarah T. Center, b. at Greenfield, N. H., Aug. 11, 1821. Four ch : —

1221. FRANK EDMUND, b. at Wilton, July 31, 1848. 1222. SARAH FRANCILLA, b. at Millford, Nov. 4, 1853, d. Sept. 16, 1854. 1223. FRANCILLA MARIAH, b. Sept. 8, 1856. 1224. GEORGE B., b. Apr. 15, 1858, d. Mch. 17, 1861.

(753) ABEL FORDYCE, son of ABEL (374), b. at Milford, Mch. 20, 1820; rem'd, 1856, to Madison, Wis., thence back to Milford, where he now resides. Merchant. Md. Apr. 11, 1848, Deborah, dau. of Levi and Rhoda (Griffin) Hawkes, b. Jan. 22, 1822. Four ch : —

1225. GEORGE EDWARD, b. Mch. 14, 1849, d. Apr. 28, 1851. 1226. ELLA MARY, b. June 12, 1851. 1227. FREDERICK SAWYER, b. Feb. 14, 1854. 1228. GRACE DARLING, b. Nov. 10, 1864.

(754) GEORGE CANNIN, son of ABEL (374), b. at Milford, Dec. 7, 1822, d. Nov. 11, 1863. Lived in Milford. Keeper of a livery stable.

Md. Jan. 1, 1850, Margaret, dau. of Andrew and Hannah Fuller, b. June, 1823, d. Feb. 17, 1855. One ch:—
1229. CHARLES GEORGE, b. Jan. 31, 1855.

(756) ANDREW JACKSON, son of ABEL (374), b. at Milford, May 19, 1827; rem'd to Hutchinson, Min., where he lived a few years and returned to Milford, where he d. Jan. 5, 1864. Md. Mch. 19, 1857, Harriet, dau. of Hiram A. and Syrena (Emerson) Daniels, b. Aug. 8, 1833. One ch:—
1230. ANDREW JUDSON, b. Apr. 30, 1859.

(757) ISAAC BARTLETT, son of ABEL (374), b. at Milford, June 27, 1829. Lives in Milford. Yeoman. Md. Oct. 20, 1859, Lizzie A., dau. of James and Almira (Goodale) Morrill, b. at Milford, Oct. 26, 1840. One ch:—
1231. NELLIE E., b. Oct. 1, 1860.

(759) NATHAN, son of ABEL (374), b. at Milford, Mch. 26, 1835. Keeper of a livery stable at Milford. Md. Dec. 25, 1862, Louisa M., dau. of Gilbert and Nancy (Stiles) Tapley, b. at Wilton, June 3, 1833. One ch:—
1232. LEWIS J. H., b. Dec. 21, 1864.

(765) BENJAMIN F., son of BENJAMIN (375), b. at Milford, June 10, 1814. Lives in Milford. Yeoman. Md. Dec. 25, 1839, Eliza, dau. of William and Lydia (Putnam) Richardson, b. Nov. 14, 1816. Two ch:—
1233. MARY ELIZABETH, b. Jan. 31, 1846. 1234. EMRI ORLANDO, b. July 50, 1849.

(768) EVELYN MILTON, son of LUTHER (378), b. at Milford, Aug. 17, 1815. Lives in Waltham, Mass. Painter. Md. Nov. 1, 1840, Esther P., dau. of Ebenezer O. and Cynthia Hawes, b. at Boston, Nov. 12, 1819. Three ch:—
1235. ESTHER, b. Oct. 7, 1841, d. Oct. 18, 1841. 1236. ANGELINE, b. June 18, 1843. 1237. GEORGE MILTON, b. May 17, 1846.

(769) ELBRIDGE, son of LUTHER (378), b. at Milford, Dec. 9, 1817. Lives in Milford. Yeoman. Md. Nov. 3, 1844, Cynthia Knight. One ch:—
1238. JOSEPHINE ANNABELLA, b. Aug. 7, 1850.

(770) GERRY, son of LUTHER (378), b. at Milford, Mch. 21, 1820; rem'd to Waltham, thence to Worcester, where he now lives. Painter.

Md. Jan. 22, 1848, Elizabeth R., dau. of John and Lydia Robbins, b. at
Wilton, Me., Sept. 23, 1822. Two ch:—

1239. ELLA ROSABELLA, b. at Waltham, Nov. 2, 1851, d. May 4, 1857.
1240. ELBRIDGE GERRY, b. at Worcester, Mch. 5, 1856, d. May 7, 1856.

(775) EBENEZER, son of EBENEZER (381), b. at Weld, Me., May
8, 1806, where he now resides. Yeoman. Md. Mch. 10, 1829, Mary,
dau. of Phillip and Hannah Judkins, b. Jan. 21, 1809. Nine ch:—

1241. NATHAN[9]. 1242. CHARITY, b. Mch. 12, 1831; md. Oct., 1855,
Bradley Wait, of Dixfield. Lives in Mexico, Me.; no issue. 1243.
LUTHER[9]. 1244. CHARLES, b. Nov. 20, 1835. 1245. PHEBE, b. Oct.
15, 1837. 1246. HANNAH, b. Jan. 10, 1841. 1247. PERMELIA, b. Sept.
23, 1843. 1248. EMERY, b. Feb. 11, 1847. 1249. TYLER, b. June 10,
1849.

(778) JOHN, son of EBENEZER (381), b. Apr. 16, 1810. Resides
in Weld, Me. Yeoman. Md. 1st, Nov. 27, 1834, Hannah, dau. of
Philip and Hannah Judkins, b. Mch. 4, 1813, d. Oct. 26, 1853. Md.
2d, Apr. 8, 1854, Martha, dau. of Seth and Sally Phinney, of Weld, b.
Aug. 2, 1834. Five ch. by Hannah:—

1250. LUCINDA, b. Mch. 4, 1838; md. Dec., 1857, Low, son of Loren
and Drucilla P. Phinney, b. Apr. 19, 1838. Lives in Weld. Yeoman.
Four ch:—William Lee, b. July 13, 1858; Elizabeth J., b. June 15,
1861: Sarah, b. May, 1864; Mary E., b. June, 1867.

1251. HIRAM H., b. June 11, 1842, d. Mch. 28, 1865. 1252. GORHAM
MURCH, b. Mch. 11, 1844. 1253. ISAIAH WHITE, b. Oct. 29, 1846. 1254.
JAMES HANNIBLE, b. Mch. 24, 1852.

Four ch. by Martha:—

1255. STILLMAN WYMAN, b. Apr. 2, 1857. 1256. RHODA M., b. Apr.
27, 1859. 1257. JOHN E., b. June 5, 1862. 1258. MARTHA A., b. Nov.
7, 1864.

(780) REUBEN, son of EBENEZER (381), b. at Weld, May 30, 1814.
Lives in Weld. Yeoman. Md. May 19, 1841, Isabel C. Pratt, of
Weld, b. May 19, 1820. Six ch:—

1259. REUBEN C., b. Sept. 29, 1841. 1260. JULIA ANN, b. Apr. 5,
1844, d. May 29, 1847. 1261. GRACE OLIVE, b. Apr. 6, 1846. 1262.
JULIA ANN, b. Jan. 22, 1848, d. Aug. 28, 1857. 1263. ELISHA TURNER,
b. Nov. 22, 1850. 1264. MARY JANE, b. Jan. 3, 1856.

(782) LUTHER, son of EBENERER (381), b. at Weld, Mch. 14,
1819, d. June 16, 1844. Yeoman. Md. ——, Lucy Baker. Three ch:—
1265. ALMEDA, b. ——, d. June 13, 1856. 1266. LIVONIA. 1267.
BETSY.

(790) HEZEKIAH ALVIN, son of HEZEKIAH (384), b. at Bedford, Mass., Apr. 10, 1809; rem'd, 1833, to Westford, Mass., where he now lives. House carpenter. Md. Apr. 11, 1833, Abigail, dau. of Lemuel and Abigail Bicknell, b. at Westford, Dec. 20, 1813. Seven ch : —
1268. MARTHA ALMIRA, b. July 23, 1833. 1269. WILLIAM, b. Dec. 4, 1834. 1270. ELIZA ANN, b. Mch. 20, 1836; md. Jan. 30, 1855, George, son of John and Lois Hutchins, b. at Westford, July 28, 1828, where he now lives. Yeoman. Two ch : — Elizabeth Ann, b. Jan. 21, 1856; Georgianna, b. Dec. 27, 1857.
1271. GEORGE, b. Oct. 16, 1839. 1272. EMILY, b. Nov. 1, 1841. 1273. FRANCIS, b. Mch. 4, 1843. 1274. ELLEN, b. Mch. 2, 1845, d. Aug. 21, 1867.

(791) BENJAMIN, son of HEZEKIAH (384), b. at Bedford, Mass., June 23, 1812. Lived in Lowell, Alexandria, N. H., and Billerica, Mass. Resides at present in Manchester, N. H. Md. Mch. 22, 1835, Mary L., dau. of John T. and Mary Symonds, b. at Alexandria, N. H., Oct. 21, 1814. Nine ch : —
1275. MARY L., b. Apr. 18, 1836. 1276. B. FRANKLIN, b. Oct. 17, 1837. 1277. ELIZA A., b. Aug. 19, 1839. 1278. GUSTAVUS B., b. Nov. 10, 1840. 1279. JOHN G., b. July 7, 1843. 1280. CAROLINE R., b. Jan. 14, 1846. 1281. LYDIA J., b. Sept. 3, 1848. 1282. AUGUSTA E., b. June 2, 1852. 1283. WILLIE H., b. Apr. 15, 1855, d. Sept. 9, 1855.

(796) JOHN GOULD, son of HEZEKIAH (384), b. at Bedford, July 21, 1822; rem'd Apr. 1, 1851, to Reading, Mass., where he now lives. Yeoman. Md. May 15, 1851, Martha Emeline, dau. of Wm. S. and Susan M. Bryer, b. at Boothbay, Me., Dec. 17, 1821. One ch : —
1284. CHARLES HOLMES, b. Apr. 3, 1854.

(799) ISAIAH, son of SYLVESTER (385), b. at Wilton, Jan. 26, 1819. Lives in Milford. Yeoman. Md. Nov. 11, 1847, Calista A., dau. of Erastus and Anna Brown, b. Feb. 6, 1829. Two ch : —
1285. LUELLA CALISTA, b. Aug. 5, 1848. 1286. ANNA FRANCILLA, b. Oct. 28, 1851.

(800) FERDINAND, son of SYLVESTER (385), b. at Wilton, N. H., Mch. 16, 1821, where he now lives. Shoe manufacturer. Md. May 28, 1846, Lucy Jane, dau. of Oliver and Lucy K. Barrett, b. at Wilton, Oct. 27, 1825. One ch : —
1287. OLIVER B., b. June 16, 1849.

(801) EDWARD B., son of SYLVESTER (385), b. at Wilton, June

12, 1823. Lives in Wilton. Md. Aug. 26, 1846, Caroline E. Jones, b. Sept. 16, 1820. Four ch:—

1288. ALONZO E., b. May 10, 1847, d. Apr. 19, 1850. 1289. EMILY A., b. Jan. 3. 1849. 1290. CHARLES E., b. Aug. 28, 1850, d. Mch., 1857. 1291. CAROLINE E., b. July 14, 1852, d. Sept. following.

(802) ISAAC B., son of SYLVESTER (385), b. at Wilton, Sept. 4, 1826. Lives in Wilton. Operative. Md. Nov. 8, 1849, Sarah O., dau. of Eli and Sarah Hinds, b. at Eden, Vt., Mch. 14, 1828. Two ch:—

1292. IZETTA, b. Aug. 1, 1852. 1293. CLARA, b. June 6, 1857.

(803) APPLETON, son of SYLVESTER (385), b. at Wilton, Apr. 17, 1829, where he now resides. Laborer. Md. Aug. 7, 1853, Mary A., dau. of William and Rebecca Currier, b. at Wilton, Nov., 1835. Two ch:—

1294. FRANK A., b. Nov. 26, 1855. 1295. WILLIS M., b. Mch. 29, 1857.

(805) SYLVANUS, son of SYLVANUS (386), b. at Wilton, Oct. 12, 1831. Lives in Wilton. Mechanic. Md. Sept. 29, 1853, Clarinda, dau. of Mark D. and Lucy (Whipple) Langdell, b. at Lowell, ——, 1832; no issue.

(823) RODNEY K., son of ALFRED (393), b. at Milford, Aug. 7, 1812. Lives in Milford. Carpenter. Md. 1st, Nov. 12, 1840, Susan E. R., dau. of John and Susannah Hartshorn, b. at Hancock, Vt., Dec. 9, 1818, d. Aug. 17, 1853. Md. 2d, Oct. 6, 1855, Sirepta J. Hartshorn, sister to his first wife, b. at Lyndeboro, June 21, 1826. Five ch. by Susan:—

1296. ALFRED ALONZO, b. Jan. 7, 1842. 1297. RODNEY LORENZO, b. Feb. 4, 1844, d. Aug. 27, 1847. 1298. MARY OLIVIA, b. Oct. 3, 1846. 1299. SUSAN LOUELLA, b. Oct. 6, 1849, d. July 27, 1856. 1300. VILETTA JANE, b. Mch. 2, 1853, d. July 17, 1856.

Four ch. by Sirepta:

1301. SUSAN VILETTA, b. Nov., 1857. 1302. JOHN C., b. Dec. 22, 1859. 1303. WILLIE E., b. Dec. 21, 1861. 1304. GRACE B., b. June 7, 1866.

(824) JONATHAN D., son of ALFRED (393), b. at Milford, Mch. 3, 1814. Lived in Amherst; resides at present in Nashua. House carpenter. Md. Apr. 11, 1837, Nancy J., dau. of Hugh and Nancy McConikee, b. at Bedford, N. H., Apr. 11, 1819. Two ch:—

1305. CHARLES ALONZO, b. May 1, 1838. 1306. MARTHA JANE, b. Dec. 25, 1840.

(826) FRANCIS P., son of ALFRED (893), b. at Milford, July 28, 1817. Lives in Manchester, N. H. Carriage maker and blacksmith. Md. Apr. 23, 1839, Lorinda Goodwin. Two ch :—
1307. ASENATH, b. Aug. 14, 1839. 1308. ADELINE, b. Nov. 14, 1841.

(830) NATHAN C., son of ALFRED (893), b. at Milford, Nov. 14, 1828. Lives in Milford. Carpenter. Md. Apr. 8, 1852. Sarah, dau. of David and Sarah Willoughby, b. at Milford, June 14, 1827. Four ch :—
1309. ALICE D., b. Aug. 31, 1858. 1310. FRED. ALBERT, b. Jan. 4, 1862. 1311. MYRTA BELL, b. Nov. 11, 1864. 1312. EVA DRUCILLA, b. June 25, 1867.

(843) SYLVANDER, son of NATHANIEL (403), b. at Braintree, Vt., July 14, 1815. He commenced teaching school in his native town, in the fall of 1834, and after an experience of two winters, he engaged in a school in Randolph, Mass.; afterwards in Wilton, Northboro, Hingham, and the last twelve years, till June, 1864, in N. Bedford, where he now resides. At present engaged in the sale of books and stationary. Md. Aug. 6, 1855, Elizabeth Horton, dau. of Capt. Thomas and Elizabeth Horton Howland, b. at So. Dartmouth, Mass., May 20, 1833. Four ch :—
1313. ELIZABETH HOWLAND, b. Dec. 7, 1856. 1314. HENRY SYL-VANDER, b. Oct. 9, 1860. 1315. FRANK THOMAS, b. Sept. 3, 1863, d. June 21, 1864. 1316. HARRIET ELIZA, b. Mch. 1, 1866.

(844) JOHN, son of NATHANIEL (404), b. at Braintree. Aug. 30, 1819; rem'd to Keytesville, Mo., where he arrived Nov. 16, 1852, and was keeper of a hotel in that place till his removal, Apr. 15, 1860, to Salisbury, Mo., where he is at present engaged in the sale of stoves and tin-ware. Md. 1st, July 1, 1841, Elizabeth Lucy, dau. of Uriel and Elizabeth (Prescott) Stone, b. at Hartland, Vt., June 23, 1819, d. at Keytesville, Aug. 25, 1853, without issue. Md. 2d, Sarah Ann Stone, sister to his first wife, b. at Hartland, Vt., Aug. 19, 1821. Two ch. by Sarah :—
1317. HERBERT, b. July 2, 1855. 1318. LIBBEY NANCY, b. Jan. 26, 1859.

(847) JOHN B., son of RUFUS (408), b. at Braintree, Vt., Oct. 8, 1819, d. at W. Randolph, Vt., Mch. 26, 1867, of Consumption. He grad. at the University of Vt., Aug., 1843; rec'd degree of A. M., Aug., 1848; admitted to the Bar, in Orange Co., June 1, 1845, and commenced the practice of law at W. Randolph, in 1848, where he continued till his decease. Elected Judge of Probate, from the District of Randolph, and held the office from Dec. 1, 1853, to Dec. 1, 1856.

Elected in Mch., 1855, a member of Council of Censors (a body of thirteen members chosen every seventh year), for the revision of the State Constitution. He represented the town of Randolph in the Legislature in 1856, and was chosen Senator from Orange Co., 1857. He was universally respected for his moral and intellectual worth, and died lamented by all who knew him. He md. Oct. 24, 1849, Lucretia M., youngest dau. of Hon. N. P. Gregory, of Plattsburgh, N. Y.; no issue.

(848) CHARLES, son of RUFUS (408), b. at Braintree, July 31, 1820; rem'd June 12, 1854, to River Falls, Peirce Co., Wis., where he now resides. Yeoman. Md. May 20, 1845, Jane Velina, dau. of Calvin and Deborah Randall, of Braintree, b. Dec. 5, 1828. Three ch : —
1319. MANORA JANE, b. Sept. 16, 1849. 1320. LUCY EUGENIA, b. Mch. 12, 1854. 1321. CHARLES ARTHUR, b. June 12, 1860.

(849) RUFUS, son of RUFUS (408), b. at Braintree, Dec. 31, 1823. Lives in Braintree. Yeoman. Md. 1st, June 2, 1850, Sarah, dau. of David and Polly Partridge, b. at Braintree, May 29, 1821, d. Jan. 17, 1854. Md. 2d, Oct. 4, 1854, Minora, dau. of Daniel and Arvilla Loomis, b. at Braintree, July 2, 1834. One ch. by Sarah : —
1322. CHARLEY R., b. Dec. 29, 1853.
One ch. by Minora : —
1323. JOHN H., b. Jan. 16, 1865.

(852) GEORGE, son of RUFUS (408), b. at Braintree, Mch. 6, 1833. Lives in Braintree. Yeoman. Md. Dec. 19, 1853, Rosina Mary, dau. of Jesse H. and Polly Cram, b. at Braintree, Apr. 30, 1856. Two ch :—
1324. MARY INEZ, b. Apr. 30, 1854. 1325. ANNA MARIA, b. Oct. 7, 1855.

(854) WILLIAM, son of JAMES (410), b. at Randolph, Vt., Jan. 24, 1823; rem'd Mch., 1856, to Lawrence, Kansas, where for a while he engaged in mercantile affairs, and afterwards, in 1861, went to Washington, where he is at present engaged as Examiner in the Pension Bureau. At an early age he betrayed a marked intellectual ability, and soon after his marriage he became editor and publisher of the *Green Mountain Herald*, printed at W. Randolph, which was conducted with more than ordinary skill. He was always considered a radical reformer, a strong anti-slavery man, and an ardent supporter of the temperance cause. Since his removal to Kansas, and under its Territorial government, he was prominently engaged in most of its public affairs; was a member of both branches of the Free State, or Topeka Legislature, and was a member of the Wyandot Constitutional Con-

vention, where he was Chairman of the Committee on Bill of Rights. He has been a member of both Generals Lane and Robinson's staff, and was actively engaged in the local war for two years. Has been both Secretary and Treasurer of the State Central Committee during the time that most of the eastern aid was received by them. He also was a prominent candidate with the Free State party on different occasions, for both a delegate to Congress, and Secretary of State, under a state organization; and throughout has acted with what has been known as the radical wing of the Free State party. In addition to this he has been correspondent of the *N. Y. Times* for three years, under the nom-de-plume of *Randolph;* and also for the *Chicago Tribune, Washington Republic, Boston Traveller,* and *St. Louis Democrat.* Also during this period was a member of the Senate and House of Representatives under the Topeka Constitution.

He md. Mch. 3, 1847, Helen M., dau. of Lewin and Anna (Burch) Fisk, of Randolph, b. Oct. 8, 1827. Six ch : —

1326. ERWIN VERONE, b. May 23, 1848, d. Sept. 26, 1849. 1327. ALMA VALORA, b. Mch. 22, 1851, d. Jan. 6, 1857. 1328. HELEN MARIA, b. June 19, 1854. 1329. WILLIAM JAMES, b. Oct. 5, 1857. 1330. ANNIE, b. Apr. 28, 1864, d. Sept. 22, 1864. 1331. ALICE R., b. Mch. 22, 1866.

(855) JAMES, son of JAMES (410) b. at W. Randolph, Vt., Jan. 1, 1826. Resides in Randolph. Yeoman. He was elected in Nov., 1856, a delegate from Orange Co., Vt., to the State Constitutional Convention. In Sept., 1864, was elected Associate Judge of the Co. Ct., and again in Sept., 1865, was elected to the same office, and Sept. 1, 1868 was elected State Senator. He md. Nov. 2, 1847, Abby B., dau. of Elijah and Patience (Neff) Flint, b. at Braintree, Oct. 1, 1828. She is a descendant of the seventh generation from Thomas Flint, who emigrated from Wales, Eng., and settled in So. Danvers, now known as Peabody; no issue.

(856) HENRY, son of JAMES (410), b. at W. Randolph, Oct. 27, 1827. Lives in Randolph, Wis., where he rem'd Mch., 1864. Yeoman. Md. Oct. 3, 1852, Laura, dau. of Nathan A. and Abigail B. Parish, b. at Braintree, June 22, 1833. Four ch : —

1332. CHARLES PARISH, b. Feb. 19, 1855, d. Mch. 27, 1858. 1333. MARY, b. Oct. 24, 1858. 1334. CARLETON, b. Oct. 16, 1861. 1335. JAMES, b. Mch. 31, 1866.

(857) JOHN, son of JAMES (410), b. at W. Randolph, Vt., Mch. 27, 1830. Lawyer. Grad. Dart. Coll., July, 1853. He was one of the first who emigrated to Kansas, and settled, Oct., 1854, in Lawrence. He became a member of the first Territorial Legislature, and was also

elected to the first State Legislature, and at its second session was chosen Speaker of the House. In April, 1861, he was appointed by President Lincoln, Secretary of Dakotah Terr., and held the office till April, 1865, when he was appointed Consul at Leghorn, Italy. He md. Oct. 1, 1857, Lydia A. Fowler, of Yates Co., N. Y. Two ch: —
1336. ESTELLA, b. at Minneapolis, Min., Jan., 1861. 1337. FLORENCE, b. at Leghorn, Dec. 22, 1866.

(860) LYMAN, son of JAMES (410), b. at W. Randolph, Aug. 12, 1837. Md. Nov. 22, 1859, at De Ramsey, Canada East, Paulina M., dau. of James and Lucy (Horton) Read. Three ch: —
1338. WILLIS HORTON, b. Aug. 21, 1860, d. Apr. 26, 1864. 1339. EDWIN, b. Feb. 1, 1865. 1340. CARRIE, b. July 6, 1866.

(869) ALMON, son of LEWIS (424), b. at Norway, Me., June 10, 1820, d. Mch. 17, 1856. Lived in Milan, N. H. Yeoman. Md. July 4, 1842, Martha M., dau. of Obadiah and Elizabeth (Hanson) Witham, b. at Milton Mills, N. H., Nov. 19, 1824. Five ch: —
1341. CHARLES A., b. Sept. 1, 1843. 1342. MARTHA ROSETTA, b. June 8, 1845. 1343. ELLEN MAHALAH, b. Nov. 16, 1847, d. July 14, 1853. 1344. EMMA ABBY, b. Aug. 11, 1850. 1345. FRANK WILLIAM, b. Jan. 11, 1854.

(871) FREELAND, son of LEWIS (424), b. at Norway, Me., Aug. 14, 1831. Lives in Milan. Yeoman. Md. Feb. 14, 1857, Adrianna, dau. of J. L. and A. (Emery) Blake, b. at Milan, Jan. 2, 1838. One ch:—
1346. THEODOCIA, b. Mch. 21, 1858.

(874) SULLIVAN, son of GALEN (424), b. at Milan, June 10, 1826. Lives in Contoocookville, N. H. Md. Jan. 2, 1850, Elzina Eastman, b. at Whitefield, N. H., Nov. 4, 1831. Two ch:—
1347. AURIN, b. Feb. 13, 1851. 1348. OLIVE, b. Feb. 24, 1853.

(877) LYMAN, son of M. RAWSON (427), b. at Albany, Me., Jan. 4, 1828; rem'd to Madison, Wis., 1851, where he now lives. House joiner. Md. 1855, Martha Stone, of Prairie Du Sac; no issue.

(878) CHARLES, son of M. RAWSON (427), b. at Albany, Me., May 2, 1831; rem'd Nov., 1862, to Gray, Me., where he now lives, in the practice of medicine. Grad. Med. Coll., at Albany, June, 1858, and commenced practice at Cape Elizabeth, in the same year. Md. Jan. 4, 1865, Mrs. M. J. Hatch, dau. of Dr. Solomon P. and Harriet (Whitney) Cushman. b. at Brunswick, Me., 1831. Two ch:—
1349. LAURA CUSHMAN, b. Oct. 18, 1865. 1350. CHARLES LYMAN, b. Feb. 17, 1868.

(882) HORACE, son of HAVEN (430), b. at Albany, Me., July 22, 1837. Lives in Waterford, Me. Yeoman. Md. Dec. 3, 1863, Hattie, dau. of John and Lucinda Procter, b. at Waterford, Feb. 16, 1835. Two ch:—

1351. IRVIN, b. Sept. 28, 1864. 1352. LAURA F., b. May 4, 1867.

(905) LOT PERRY, son of DANIEL P., (450), b. at Darien, N. Y., Sept. 9, 1823; rem'd Jan. 29, 1852, to Milwaukie, where he still resides. Milk dealer. Md. Jan. 23, 1849, Aurelia, dau. of Jabez and Asenath Backus, b. at Hebron, Conn., Aug. 24, 1823. Five ch:—

1353. JULIA LOUISA, b. Sept. 7, 1850. 1354. EMMA JANE, b. May 8, 1853. 1355. FREDERICK PERRY, b. June 10, 1857, d. Dec. 18, 1859. 1356. NELLIE ANDALUSSIA, b. June 7, 1861. 1357. MAY FRANCES, b. June 4, 1865.

(912) DELOSS, son of CHESTER FLINT (451), b. at Darien, N. Y., Sept. 5, 1828. Lived in Johnstown and Waupaca, Wis.; rem'd thence in 1850, to Farmington, Wis., where he d. May 2, 1857. The circumstances attending his death are as follows:—He was returning from his father's in Waupaca, to his home in Farmington, about eight miles distant, when he overtook George Severance at the road side, who was awaiting his return. On being asked to ride, he got into the wagon and took his position behind Mr. Hutchinson. They had proceeded but a short distance when Severance, alluding to difficulties that had existed between them, struck him on the head with a walking stick, knocking him out of the wagon, and repeating the blows till he was dead. Severance then took the body and threw it into a stream near by, where it was found the following evening. He was afterwards arrested, confessed his guilt, and placed in confinement in a jail in Portage Co., from which he soon after made his escape. He was subsequently re-arrested, but through the corruption of the officers having him in charge, was permitted to escape, and has not since been heard of.

He md. 1st, Mch. 14, 1850, Sarah, dau. of Henry Cope, b. at Ohio, 1829, d. July 20, 1851; md. 2d, May 30, 1852, Adaline, dau. of George and Laura Smith, b. at Vermont, 1831. One ch. by Sarah:—

1358. HENRY CHESTER, b. July 20, 1851.

Three ch. by Adaline.

1359. DEELBERT, and 1360. DEELTON, b. Sept. 20, 1853. GARDNER G., b. May 30, 1855.

(913) GEORGE, son of CHESTER FLINT (451), b. at Darien, N. Y., Mch. 15, 1833; rem'd Apr. 2, 1855, to Waupaca, Wis., where he still lives. Yeoman. Md. 1st, Mch. 25, 1855, Susan, dau. of John and

Susan Severance, b. 1839, d. July 27, 1856; md. 2d, Dec. 5, 1859, Catherine, dau. of Michael and Mary Clinton, b. Feb. 17, 1843. Two ch. by Catherine : —
1361. Julia, b. Feb. 11, 1860. 1362. Mary, b. Mch. 22, 1864.

(923) MILO, son of FARWELL J. (469), b. at Waterford, Vt., Nov. 20, 1825. Lives in Concord, Vt. Yeoman. Md. July, 1858, Lucy A., dau. of Dominicus and Lucy Jordon, b. at Chelmsford, Mass., June 30, 1828. Two ch : —
1363. Ward B., b. Feb. 7, 1857, d. July 14, 1859. 1364. Harry D., b. May 12, 1866.

(928) JOSEPH W., son of BENJAMIN (470), b. at Waterford, Vt., July 23, 1838, d. in the battle at Cold Harbor, June 10, 1864. Md. Mch., 1861, Mary Stacy. Two ch : —
1365. Irvin. 1366. Estella.

(966) FREDERICK AUGUSTUS, son of STEPHEN (503), b. at Portland, Me., Mch. 15, 1833. Lives in Portland. Steamboat engineer. Md. June 22, 1854, Elizabeth Lilly of Gray, Me. One ch : —
1367. Lizzie, b. Oct. 13, 1856.

(967) ISAAC, son of SAMUEL (504), b. at Chebeague Isl., Me., Dec. 1, 1818. Resides in Portland. Shipmaster. Md. Oct. 23, 1836, Jane A., dau. of Jonathan and Elizabeth Hamilton, b. at Chebeague, Nov. 25, 1809. Three ch : —
1368. Irene Pratt, b. Feb. 14, 1838; md. Dec. 18, 1855, Daniel O. Holmes. One ch : — Charles Fremont, b. Aug. 24, 1856. 1369. Levi, b. Nov. 8, 1840, d. May 20, 1851. 1370. Isaac James, b. Sept. 3, 1844.

(968) WILLIAM, son of SAMUEL (504), b. at Chebeague Isl., Mch. 11, 1820. Lives in Portland. Shipmaster. Md. 1st, Aug. 31, 1840, Hannah, dau. of Simeon and Thankful Webber, b. at Chebeague, Sept. 21, 1819, d. Feb. 10, 1842; md. 2d, Caroline M., dau. of Elijah and Fanny Baker, of Falmouth, Me. One ch. by Hannah : —
1371. Mary, b. Jan. 19, 1842.
One ch. by Caroline : —
1372. William Henry, b. Oct. 27, 1851.

(969) HENRY, son of SAMUEL (504), b. at Chebeague Isl., Nov. 4, 1823, d. at sea Feb., 1845. Mariner. Md. Feb. 4, 1845, Harriet, dau. of Elijah and Fanny Baker, b. May 14, 1821. One ch : —
1373. Harriet Abby, b. Nov. 18, 1845.

(970) JAMES, son of SAMUEL (504), b. at Chebeague Isl., Nov. 5,

1825. Lives in Portland. Shipmaster. Md. Dec. 9, 1845, Jane A. S. York, dau. of Reuben and Elizabeth (Pearson) Gage, b. at Portland, Dec. 12, 1824. Two ch : —
1374. ELIZABETH JANE, b. Jan. 4, 1847. 1375. CHARLES HOWARD, b. Mch. 8, 1856.

(973) ANDREW, son of SAMUEL (504), b. at Chebeague Isl., June 27, 1832; rem'd Nov. 1, 1855, to Henry, Ill., where he now lives. Painter. Md. Feb. 8, 1857, Rebecca, dau. of Margaret and Abel Snyder, b. at Lancaster Co., Pa., Nov. 20, 1835. One ch : —
1376. EDWARD STEPHEN, b. Feb. 12, 1858.

(976) JOHN BUZZELL, son of Rev. JOSEPH (509), b. at Hartland, Me., Nov. 13, 1821. Lived in Hartford, Me., Bridgewater, Mass., and rem'd to Abington, Mass., Mch. 1, 1842. Shoe-cutter. Md. Oct. 31, 1842, Susanna P., dau. of Eliab and Mary Noyes, b. at Abington, Nov. 11, 1824. Five ch : —
1377. SUSAN FRANCES, b. Jan. 11, 1845. 1378. JOSEPH WILSON, b. Oct. 11, 1848. 1379. CHARLES AUSTIN, b. Feb. 3, 1851. 1380. SAMUEL SOULE, b. Nov. 30, 1854. 1381. ROSCO ALGERNON, b. Aug. 23, 1857.

(977) BENJAMIN FRANKLIN, son of Rev. JOSEPH (509), b. at Canton, Me., Oct. 20, 1823. Has lived in Livermore; rem'd Nov., 1844, to Abington, Mass., where he now resides. Housewright. Md. Mch. 12, 1848, Mary W., dau. of Hector and Mary G. Foster, b. at Abington, Oct. 25, 1829. Four ch : —
1382. ELIZABETH WILLIAMS, b. Apr. 24, 1849. 1383. HERBERT FRANKLIN, b. May 12, 1851. 1384. GEORGE BREWER, b. Feb. 6, 1853, d. May 28, 1858. 1385. ROBEMER NANCY, b. Oct. 10, 1857.

(979) DANIEL, son of Rev. JOSEPH (509), b. at Hartford, Me., Apr. 20, 1828. Lived in Harpswell, Me., and N. Bridgewater, Mass. Lives at present in Brunswick, Me. Ship carpenter. Md. Apr. 25, 1850, Harriet C., dau. of Houghton and Margaret Rideout, b. at Brunswick, Nov. 3, 1830. Four ch : —
1386. WILLIAM EDWIN, b. Feb. 1, 1851. 1387. GEORGE ALBERT, Apr. 19, 1852. 1388. WENDELL PHILLIPS, b. May 22, 1854. 1389. MAHALA DEARBORN, b. Oct. 25, 1856.

(980) WILLIAM PENN, son of Rev. JOSEPH (509), b. at Hartford, Me., Mch. 8, 1831. Resides in Brunswick, Me. Shipsmith. Md. Feb. 4, 1857, Mary, dau. of David S. and Jane S. Perkins, b. at Brunswick, Aug. 28, 1837.
1390. A child (nameless), b. Jan. 23, 1858, d. same day.

(1013) SAMUEL HIRAM, son of Rev. JOSEPH (527), b. at Peru, Me., Aug. 28, 1836. Lives in Mechanic Falls, Me. Md. Feb. 16, 1858, Laura, dau. of Benjamin and Eveline Hodgdon, b. at Turner, Me., Jan. 28, 1841. One ch : —

1391. ARTHUR L., b. Jan. 1, 1860.

(1014) JOSEPH HENRY, son of Rev. JOSEPH (527), b. at Minot, Swan's Island, Me., from whence he rem'd Nov. 20, 1862, to Rockland, Me. Housewright. Md. Apr. 24, 1860, Sarah, dau. of James and Jane Joyce, b. at Swan's Island, May 12, 1841. Two ch : —

1392. NELLIE J., b. Jan. 31, 1861. 1393. AURESSA, b. Sept. 15, 1867.

(1088) LUCIUS BOLLES, son, of Noah B. (590), b. at Mt. Vernon, N. H., Jan. 6, 1839. Lives in N. Y. City. Commission broker. Md. Jan. 6, 1864, Alice M., dau. of Boynton and Alice Rollins, b. at Hopkinton, N. H., July 6, 1841. One ch : —

1394. ALICE, b. June 22, 1867.

(1108) JUSTIN EDWARDS, son of JOSHUA (595), b. at Milford, Dec. 21, 1837. Lives in Amherst, N. H. Yeoman. Md. July 11, 1864, Mary, dau. of Thomas and Catherine Lewis, b. at Kingston, Ireland, Mch. 17, 1847. Two ch : —

1395. LUDLOW MASON, b. July 23, 1865. 1396. THOMAS JOSHUA, b. Aug. 22, 1867.

NINTH GENERATION.

(1121) ALCANDER, son of HIRAM (607), b. at New Brunswick, N. J., Dec. 31, 1832. He accompanied his father to France in 1853, and md. at Chatillon-sur-Loing (Loiret) France, Jan. 19, 1858, Henrietta-Emma-Aimés Torrens, eldest dau. of Henri-Louis. Count de Loyante, and niece of Duke and Duchesse de Montmorency de Luxemborg. "His wife's grandfather, the Count Anne-Phillippe de Loyanté was one of those French officers who came to America and helped us to gain our Independence. He was Lieut. Col. of Artillery and Inspector General of the Fortifications of Virginia, and member of the order of Cincinnatus, and remained in America from 1778, till the close of the war. He left his order of Cincinnatus to his son, who has transmitted it, in default of male issue, to his son-in-law, Alcander Hutchinson." Since his marriage he has resided in India, and was U. S. Consul at Singapore, from 1860 till 1862. Lives at present at Langlie, *pres Montarges Loiret*, and is extensively engaged in the rubber business. Four ch : —

1397. RENÉE CAROLINE, b. Feb. 14, 1859. 1398. MARIANNE GRIZELLE,

b. May 2, 1860. 1399. BARNARD-ALCANDER-RICHARD DE LOYANTÉ, b. Sept. 24, 1862. 1400. HIRAM-EMMANUEL-HENRI-DIEUDONNE DE LOYANTE, b. July 24, 1866.

(1176) FRANCIS CLIFTON, son of FREEMAN (691), b. at Milford, N. H., Mch. 17, 1832. Md. Jan. 17, 1853, Susan Adelia Blake, b. Sept. 4, 1832. Two ch : —
1401. WILLIS ORRIN, b. Dec. 12, 1853. 1402. FRANCIS FREEMAN, b. Aug. 3, 1856.

(1241) NATHAN, son of EBENEZER (775), b. at Weld, Me., Sept. 6, 1829. Md. Dec., 1855, Mary Elizabeth Newhall. One ch : —
1403. CHARLES.

(1243) LUTHER, son of EBENEZER (775), b. at Weld, Feb. 11, 1833. Md. May 13, 1855, Juliett, dau. of William and Anna (Hutchinson, 776) Winter, b. Mch. 3, 1840. Two ch : —
1404. ELLAH, b. Oct., 1855. 1405. WALLIS EVERETT, b. May 3, 1857.

13

APPENDIX.

A.

The following is a copy of the WILL of RICHARD HUTCHIN-SON, as found recorded in the Probate Office, in Salem, Mass.

28 : 9mo. 1682.

In the name of God Amen, I Richard Hutchinson, of the towne of Salem bein of pfect (perfect) memorye, & vnderstanding & Thought weake in body by Reason of age, doe make this my last will & testament.

1. First I doe bequeath my soule into the hands of the Lord whoe gave it when it shall please him to call for it, and my body to be decently buried by my executor with assured hopes of a resurection.

2. In respect of that outward estate, which it hath pleased the Lord to bestow vpon me & is now at my dispose my will is as followeth.

1. In relation to my deare & loueing wife, my will is that shee shall be & remaine at my son Joseph Hutchinson house during her natural life if shee see cause there to be prouided for with convenient house roome meat drink & lodging & all other things whatsoeuer that may be comfortable & suitable for one of her age, during her life, and ten shillings yearly to be at her dispose to be paid by him in money or butter, or if shee see cause to remoue from thence & to live in any other place Then shee shall haue all that estate, which was in her hands, when I marryed her excepting that pcell (parcel) of land which Samuel Leach of Manchester had, which was for the palment of her debt, the sd estate to be at her dispose to whome soeeuer shee pleaseth, But if shee remaine at my son Hutchensons house during her life, then the said estate shalbe in the hands of my executor & be fully at his dispose only her wearing apparrell shalbe at her liberty to dispose of at her decease.

2ly. In respect of my lands my will is

1. That my sonn in law Anthony Ashby & my daughter Abigaile his wife, shall have twenty Acres of land lying by the hill, called Hathorne's Hill & lying the whole length of my land, this land being free to them theire heirs & assignes.

2. I giue to my sonn in law Daniell Bordman & my daughter Hanah his wife theire heirs or assignes, twenty acres of land, lying by and adjoyning to the land aboue expressed & lying the whole length of my land.

3. I giue to my Grand children Bethiah Hutchenson & Sarah Hadlock & each of them ten acres free to them & their assignes, lying by & adjoining to the land, aboue expressed & lying the whole length of the land.

4. I giue vnto black Peter my seruant, four acres of land lying by & adjoyning to the land aboue expressed to him & his heires, or if he

haue noe heires then it shall returne to my executor his heires & assignes.

5. I give unto my son in law nathaniell Putnam & my son in law Thomas Hale & my son in law James Hadlock, each of them forty shillings to be paide by my executor within two years after my decease.

6. Alsoe I give to my son in law Daniell Bordman & Anthony Ashby each of them forty shillings, to be pd. by my executor within two years after my decease, all ye sd. aboue written sums to be pd. in comon pay at price currant.

7. Lastly I make my son Joseph Hutchenson sole executor to this my last will & testament enjoyning him his heirs & assignes to pay all my debts and leagacies & I doe freely give vnto him his heirs or assignes peeter my seruant & all the rest of my estate both moueable & Imoueable. This is my last will & testament made by me this 19 January in ye yeare of our Lord one thousand six hundred seaventy nine.

This clause (twenty acres of land betweene the 28 & 29 line) interlined before the signing thereof.

Witness
James Baily
Joseph mazury.

His
Richard H Hutchenson [seal]
mark

B.

The following account of the Hutchinson vocalists, is condensed from a book published by them called the "Book of Words of the Hutchinson Family;" and as their history is inseparable, and of common interest, it was thought best to include a biographical sketch of each, viz:—Judson, John, Joshua and Asa, under one head. At an early age they evinced a passionate fondness for music; self tutored, and graduated from beneath the paternal roof, a company of singing brothers, such as the world has seldom had the good fortune to patronize and enjoy. Their career has been fertile with incident, both humorous and productive of much good. Temperance and Freedom were the themes on which they paved their way to notoriety and ultimate success. They were bold, outspoken, and fearless of results; even in that portion of our country once infested with the scourge of Slavery, they were tolerated even more than any one else would have hoped for. As they progressed in their home instruction some of their number ventured to foreshadow thoughts of future fame and distinction, to illuminate their pathway through life. Their progress was marked first, by Judson's procuring at the age of fifteen, a violin, which he obtained on credit, for the paltry sum of four dollars, the result of some extra labor done upon the farm. Next, Asa equaly ambitious and persevering, procured of his brother Andrew, then a merchant in Boston, a bass-viol, which had been played on for over thirty years in the Old South Church, in Boston. It was the first Yankee bass-viol ever constructed, and was made with a simple jack-knife, by an ingenious American. Contemporary with this event occurred the production of another violin, which John procured by raising vegetables. Armed and equipped, the lads prepared themselves for a long and thorough course of self tuition; but owing to their father's conscientious scruples concerning the *profanity* of such exercises, they were obliged to resort to some portion of a retired and unfrequented field, where their drill was conducted for at least twelve months in a primitive style. So persevering were they in their secret practice that at the end of two years they astonished their friends and neighbors generally, and their father especially, in the sudden production of a programme consisting of a few select pieces, such as "Washington's March," "Hail Columbia," "Yankee Doodle," "Wrecker's Daughter," and others of like merit, which so completely allayed the former prejudices of the Senior Hutchinson, that he after this allowed them the free use of the mansion in which to complete their musical education. During this period their vocal powers were not by any means neglected, and often the combined effect of their voices with the instruments sent a thrill of perfect delight throughout the household. As time sped on attempts were made at concertizing beneath the paternal roof on Thanksgiving and Fast days; and even the old minister of the village church became so elated as to invite them to give their first PUBLIC CONCERT in the Baptist meeting house, which offer they at once accepted. On the appointed evening Squire Livermore addressed the people on music, after which "Old Hundred" was sang by all present, followed by various other pieces, aided by their two sisters Abby and Rhoda. When Asa and John had arrived at their majority their father intimated to them the propriety of self-maintenance; and taking the hint, they proceeded at once with horse and sleigh to Boston, where they met their brother Andrew, and were soon joined by Judson and Joshua with whom they consulted as to the practicability of entering life as public singers. The plan was acceded to by all but Joshua, who pleaded more pressing duties at home, he then being engaged as teacher of a singing school. Although the plan was not entirely dropped they did not enter at once upon their project, and being in want of the necessary means to advance their first stage of action, they went to work with their hands in Lynn. While in Boston, in 1840, they attended a temperance lecture delivered by Mr. John Hawkins, at the Marlboro chapel, at the conclusion of which they signed the pledge, and have ever since publicly advocated that cause through the medium of their songs. Labor by day and rehearsals by night, after a number of months, eventually put them in a proper condition to realize the beginning of their aspirations, by their first professional appearance in the town of Wilton, adjoining Milford, in the Baptist Church, under the name and style of "Æolian Vocalists," which was heralded through printed *posters*, 3x2½ inches in size. This concert was attended by upwards of fifty persons, at twelve and a half cents each, which, deducting expenses, left them a clear profit of exactly six and a quarter cents. Not at all disparaged at such a meagre beginning as this, they took a tour for a week through several other small towns, and so persevering were their efforts, that in the end they declared a dividend of thirty-seven and a half cents each, which so discouraged their brother Judson, "that if they did not meet with better success next week he would quit." On the following week another trial was made, travelling through the northern part of the county, which resulted in a much larger profit of four dollars each, and better hopes of the future. They visited Nashua, where they gave three concerts, and afterwards went to Lynn, where they were still more successful in their financial affairs. At these Lynn concerts they were joined by their sister Abby, then in her twelfth year, where she became a great favorite. From Lynn their next move was a journey "down East," visiting Salem, Newburyport, Portsmouth, and Kennebunk. Jesse for the first time accompanied them. Arriving in Kennebunk they discovered that through some mismanagement not a bill had been posted. It was five o'clock and something must soon be done, when suddenly a happy thought striking the mind of Jesse he seized the huge dinner bell, rushed into the street, and cried the programme for the evening. Taking all things into consideration this journey proved rather unprofitable, and with a spirit of despondency they returned to Lynn, where they gave a few concerts without very great pecuniary results. While here they received a letter from their father entreating them to return home and settle down to farm work. Jesse resumed his labors in Lynn, while the rest heeded the invitation of their father, and Abby went to school. But this state of things could not last forever; they were in a continual state of unrest, which lasted for a number of months, when happily the spell was broken by the appearance of a gentleman in their midst, who, having heard their performances, infused new zeal into their hearts by his approbation and recommendations to a farther public trial of their musical skill. A span of horses was procured, and they drove to Nashua, where they gave a 4th of July concert with good success, in connection with Mr. Lyman Heath. At Concord they gave a series of concerts and were handsomely received. Hanover was next visited, where they received a liberal share of patronage from the faculty and students of Dartmouth College. Their attention was then turned to the Green Mountain State, heralding their way as they entered each town, by some heart stirring air from the vehicle. Crossing Vt., they entered Whitehall, and thence to Saratoga Springs, where they were well received, but left the place with more commendations of praise than pennies. Schenectady was next visited with like success, having given a free concert in consequence of the presence of the Rainer Family, and taking up a contribution to defray expenses. When they came to Albany they assumed the name of the "ÆOLIAN VOCALISTS, OR THE HUTCHINSON FAMILY." Here they gave a series of concerts, and when the bills were settled they found to their dismay that they had but a sixpence left. Horror stricken at such dire results they naturally bethought themselves of the old homestead, and like prodigals in a far off land, were nearly on the point of returning again to their home, when their thoughts were directed into another channel by the interference of a Scotch gentlemen, Mr. Luke F. Newland, who, becoming acquainted with their ill success and penurious condition proposed to give them a benefit, requesting them to wait a week. During this interim they repaired to a Dutch settlement, where lived a known friend and became his guests. In that place a concert was given, realizing a clear profit of $15, with which they returned to Albany, and found that Mr. Newland had nearly completed the arrangements for the benefit. The whole preparation was gratuitous, and when the night of the concert arrived, the hall was filled, and success was stamped on every feature of the enterprize, besides realizing the comparatively mammoth sum of $110.

Inspired by this sudden turn of affairs, they boldly set off for Boston, where they announced a concert at the Melodeon, at fifty cents per ticket, with tolerable results, and securing many valuable musical friends. Leaving Boston they visited several of the eastern towns, after which they returned home for a short visit, preparatory to a southern tour. But in this they were doomed to disappointment, for at Nashua, where they gave their first concert on this new route, they were surprised on the following morning at the sudden appearance of their father on horseback, who had come to take Abby back to her home. As Abby was a great help to them, a consultation ensued, which ended in a longer lease of her services, and signing a written obligation to return her at the end of three weeks time. They next visited Boston and Lowell, after which they concluded as their project had proved a failure, to return home once more. During this interval their sympathies were fully enlisted into the Anti-Slavery cause by means of a convention held in Milford, conducted by Wm. Lloyd Garrison, N. P. Rogers and others, which called forth the production of new songs, and were afterwards sung with a varied degree of success in different sections of the country. These songs, in connection with their temperance melodies, brought them into great repute, and during a subsequent visit to N. Y., they complied with an invitation to be present at the Anniversary of the American Anti-Slavery Society, and afterwards at the Anniversary of the American Temperance Union, where they were greeted with the utmost enthusiasm. At N. Y., Gen. Geo. P. Morris presented them four of his best songs, "My Mother's Bible," "The origin of Yankee Doodle," "We're with you once again," "Westward Ho!" which were, within a space of ten days set to their own music. After a considerable stay they went to Philadelphia, where they sang in the Philharmonic Society and the Musical Fund Hall, and were encored in all their pieces, afterwards receiving the congratulations of the city. Washington was also visited with like cheering results, receiving the particular favor of the President, and other prominent officials. An amusing scene, not included in the programme, took place one evening during their stay. Judson was to sing the song of "The Humbugged Husband," which commences thus : —

> "She's not what fancy painted her;
> I'm sadly taken in," &c.

Now it so happened that the temporary platform upon which he stood was so peculiarly arranged that he had no sooner declared himself to be "Sadly taken in" metaphorically, than he was "taken in" in the most matter-of-fact manner possible, the boards giving way, precipitating the rather humbugged vocalist in a most summary way, to the depths below. Notwithstanding this temporary disarrangement of affairs on his part he soon recovered his equanimity and good standing, the audience apparently applauding the affair as a bona-fide transaction. After this they visited Mt. Vernon, and returned home, where, after a short vacation they ventured once more for the northern part of N. H., making another eastern tour, and subsequently while at Lynn, they imbibed the idea of making a trip to England, which became the great act of their lives. Within a fortnight they were landed in Liverpool, where they made their first debut in three successful concerts. Their visits to London, Manchester, Dublin, and other places was a complete ovation — making the acquaintance of many notable gentleman, among whom were Dickens, Macready and the Howitts. Their European tour ended where it began, at Liverpool, where they gave their farewell concert, and took their departure for America, leaving behind many pleasant reminiscences and a host of friends. The basis of their fortune was now firmly constructed; and their subsequent success in America is well known to all admirers of good music. But the time at last came when an unavoidable change took place in the family circle by the marriage of Abby, which for a season proved an obstacle to any farther effort in that direction. But John determined to persevere, and selling his farm, ventured into the world alone, leaving Asa and Judson upon the farm, where they remained for about a year when they clubbed together with John, and travelled harmoniously together till 1855, when they, in company with nine others, removed to Wisconsin, and settled a new township on Hassan river, which they afterwards named Hutchinson, in honor of themselves. In 1862, the town was attacked by a band of three hundred Sioux Indians, who burned their sawmill, the Academy, and most of the dwelling houses, scattering the inhabitants and leaving sad havoc in their train. The first tree cut in these regions, was cut by the hands of John, and was used in the construction of their log cabin. From this time onward their time has been divided in cultivating their extensive farm, and giving occasional concerts. In the beginning of the war, John, with his family, Henry and Viola, made their appearance on the Potomac, and sung their songs to the soldiers in camp. They had formed themselves into a distinct organization and made it their peculiar vocation in singing, during the war, for the Soldier's Aid Societies, and other institutions of like character. The Hutchinsons have sung for the cause of "Emancipation, the Union, Temperance, for the advancement of Humanity and Freedom everywhere," and on many occasions have lent their aid gratuitously, being warmly welcomed and enthusiastically received wherever they made their appearance. They are noted for their untiring zeal and industry in the promulgation of radical reforms, one of which the overthrow of slavery, some of them have lived to see accomplished, and are happy in the idea that their labor has not been in vain.

ADDENDA.

In the compilation of this book the following account of marriages, with the date of the same, were not received in season for insertion in their proper places.

On page 76, JESSE L., son of DAVID (589), md. June 10, 1856, Sarah Beard, of Mt. Vernon, N. H. Two ch.: — Frederic and Helen Virginia. Reside at Baltimore, Md.

On page 76, ELIAS S., son of DAVID, md. May 20, 1858, Lizzie Wilder of New Boston, N. H. Five ch.: — Alice E.; Lena H., d. 1862, at Baltimore; Harris H., Howard E., and Emma Burr.

On page 76, JOHN W., son of DAVID, md. Sept. 1, 1863, Victoria Neville. Lives at Milford. Two ch.: — Ernest N., and John W.

On page 76, VIRGINIA, dau. of DAVID, md. Mch. 15, 1864, Frederic Kendall. He was an officer in the U. S. Infantry during the rebellion. One ch.: — Nathan Gould.

On page 78, add to the family of John Wallace: — JUDSON WHITTIER, son of JOHN W. (600), and FANNY B., b. Feb. 17, 1862.

INDEX

OF

HEADS OF FAMILIES.

14